What the critics are saying:

Action, political intrigue, and a strong love story make this book come alive...A great addition to a super strong series! Highly Recommended - *Sara Sawyer, The Romance Studio*

Mari Byrne`s dynamic imaginative world of passionate twins and the courageous strong-willed women who love them is back. - *Cynthia, A Romance Review*

...I thought this was an excellent book and a great read, and I went right out and bought the first one--and that's the highest praise I can give a book! - *Jean, Fallen Angel Reviews*

Queens' Warriors is delicious and I highly recommend it... - *Rogue Storm Erotic Paranormal Romance*

For an outstanding romance filled with adventure, love and very steamy sex scenes pick up Queens' Warriors by Mari Byrne today...I highly recommend both Queens Warriors and the first in the series, Stephanie's Ménage. - *Lisa Lambrecht, In The Library Reviews*

QUEENS' WARRIORS

An Ellora's Cave Publication, October 2004

Ellora's Cave Publishing, Inc.
PO Box 787
Hudson, OH 44236-0787

ISBN #1-4199-5016-9

ISBN MS Reader (LIT) ISBN #1-84360-856-1
Other available formats (no ISBNs are assigned):
Adobe (PDF), Rocketbook (RB), Mobipocket (PRC) & HTML

Edited by *Mary Moran*
Cover art by *Syneca*

QUEENS' WARRIORS

Mari Byrne

Prologue

"*Frech!*" The large, dark-haired Warrior sitting opposite his identical twin exclaimed as he rubbed his hands together in a bid to gain warmth in the absurdly cold hovel. "I'm getting damned tired of sitting watch, waiting for an attack that's never going to come." Shan Lin muttered to his twin brother Vincent as both men crouched in the barren shack in the middle of the Aranakian mountain range. What few items lay scattered here and there in the dilapidated building belonged to the brothers, who had carried everything needed to survive on their backs up the mountainside.

"And they say we're envied in the Queen's Guard for our prestigious postings given personally from the Queen." Vincent pointed out, in a sarcasm-laced voice.

A snort of disbelief sounded next to him, but Vincent continued to toss things about the shack as he listened to his brother.

"Oh, please. Let them come and have this fantastic location where all that ever happens is an *averon* comes scratching at the door every other week. I swear I see more action from Winters, than from anything going on out here." Shan Lin smiled at the image of their butler/majordomo/surrogate father/friend getting any "action" and nearly laughed out loud.

"Well, we won't be here all that much longer. Might as well finish setting up the scene here and get some rest before more of the Horrd figures out we're really still here. Shouldn't take long. All we have to convince them of is that we're drifters passing through." Vincent suggested as he tossed the pack he had been pulling items out of into a corner.

"We need to be at our full strength when the rest of that small army reaches us." Shan Lin agreed.

Vincent heard a deep sigh before he heard his brother reach out for the second pack they brought with them.

"Yeah. I've been missing my beauty sleep lately." Vincent quipped back. "My face still hasn't launched any ships out of the galaxy, but those triplets I fucked last night sure thought I looked adorable with the lights on or off."

"As long as they were worth the loss of sleep." Shan Lin replied, a smile in his voice.

"Just shut up and sleep. You're getting old, and need all the rest you can get." Vincent shot back as he unrolled his sleep blankets and crawled between them before closing his own eyes and relaxing. This time it was he who nearly laughed out loud at his brother's response.

"Sure thing, old man. Though I'll never be as old as you are big brother. After all, you shot out first, and that makes you the oldest. Damned, ancient wise-ass that you are."

* * * * *

Vincent sat up, wide-awake from an unknown and as yet unidentifiable noise. He reached down next to his body and groped along the floor for the short sword he slept with every night. Searching inside his mind for his brother, he found Shan Lin lying a few feet away, still asleep.

Shan Lin! Wake! He pathed, through the brothers' mind-link.

Shan Lin came awake instantly, crouching in a defensive position.

Have the Horrd returned for another round? Shan Lin asked, all sleep instantaneously cleared from his mind.

Vincent nearly laughed out loud.

No. I think they've left one of their victims instead. Possibly trying to set a trap.

The brothers both listened to a tapping sound against the door.

Well, no reason to disappoint them brother mine. Let's see what they've thrown at our feet.

Getting up, Shan Lin walked cautiously to the shack's door, Vincent trailing behind him silently.

Ready whenever you are. Vincent heard his brother's soft words in his mind. Vincent reached his hand out to the latch even as he continued to watch through the slit. As quick as he could, he jerked on the latch and the door slammed open into the room's wall. A body fell through the opening onto the floor and emitted a torturous groan of pain.

He knelt by the body and felt Shan Lin brush by him on his way out the door. He knew his brother would locate any enemies lurking in the shadows.

Vincent ran his hands lightly over the figure on the floor, checking for traps. All he could find was blood and bits of flesh clinging to the person lying before him.

Vincent started to stand, wiping the gore on his own clothing, when he heard a whisper.

"What?" He bent closer, ready in case the blood, which covered the body, didn't belong to the person lying on the floor.

"Try again. I can barely hear you." Bending closer, he cocked his ear toward the figure in an attempt to hear better.

"Vin...Queen...kill Mit...Kri...get Warriorsssss..." The words trailed off into a hiss, then stopped altogether as the man sank into unconsciousness.

Vincent looked down at the mess in front of him, recognition coming into his eyes, and swore softly.

Shan Lin came back in just as Vincent gently picked the body up and placed it on a scarred table at the far side of the room.

"What's up with... What the *freching* Hellious is that?" Shan Lin gestured to the figure Vincent draped on the table.

"Help me clean him up. I think I know who he is, and whatever he was babbling about has to do with the Queen, Mitch, Kristain, and death." Even as he spoke, Vincent ran over to their supplies to dig for the emergency kit.

"And if what I think has happened, we're going to need all the information he can give us."

Chapter One

Shan Lin and Vincent Carrucci-Rayan crouched over the battered body of their fourth cousin on their father, Thaddeus', side and listened to an incredulous tale of brutal torture and murder. The man telling it, Dorian Goeron, was showing every indication of being racked with an excruciating pain neither of the brothers thought he would survive.

"The Old Crone...*Riad*. Queen Sara...she...dead." Dorian's voice broke as he stifled a moan. "Sara slit the old woman's..." Dorian's voice trailed away as he paused to swallow with difficulty, "throat as she climaxed."

Shan Lin watched a look of sheer terror spread across the young man's face before Dorian squeezed his eyes closed and shuddered. A sudden groan of pain escaped from the wounded man's mouth as Dorian tried to sit up. Failing utterly in his attempt, he began to weep softly.

"You knew the Queen had been driven over the edge when it was announced Mitch and Kristain had found and married their bride. What possessed you to crawl into the woman's bed?" Vincent asked while getting out the rations the brothers had packed in preparation for a siege.

"I imagine it was his other personality guiding him, Vincent. I'm sure you remember what it was to be in your twenties and wanting to fuck anything and everything that moved." Shan Lin reached out to staunch the flow of blood from a deep gash in Dorian's temple.

"And fucking some *things* that stood stationary," Vincent quipped dead-pan.

Shan Lin watched a pained smile slip across Dorian's face before the inevitable whimper escaped.

"Don't." The word hissed out of Dorian's mouth as Shan Lin continued his limited first aid.

"Try to relax." Shan Lin spoke absently as he poured liquid "gut out" over the numerous wounds covering his cousin's body.

"Tell us exactly what happened." Vincent spoke from behind his brother's back before speaking into Shan Lin's mind.

It will distract him from the pain you're going to have to inflict.

"She nicknamed me Lovely. Like I was...a...*Riad...p*et." Dorian sucked in a hissed breath as Shan Lin poured more "gut out" over a deep wound in the man's thigh. Panting heavily, he breathed out the words more than he spoke.

"She...she...called me into...her room and...demand...ed...I lie on the...bed. As a subject to the Queen, I never...questioned her. As her lover, I...became excited. It wasn't anything she hadn't asked...of me before."

Shan Lin nearly growled out his anger as he worked over Dorian's body. The destruction was extensive, and would have been fatal had Dorian not been able to reach someone with knowledge of medicines. His aunt was going to have much to answer for. But this... This was insane.

Easy, Shani. Patch him up.

The story continued to pour out of Dorian. As he spoke, his voice flowed more smoothly with the telling and there were fewer interruptions due to the pain. Vincent had been correct. The telling of his horrific time with the Queen was cathartic, even as terrifying as the story was.

"She was screaming words at me I neither understood nor wanted to listen to. I couldn't understand but one in maybe fifteen things she said, but the feeling I got when I heard her shrieking them..." He paused in the telling as a fine tremor began in his injured body.

The silence went on unbroken for so long, Vincent finally spoke up.

"Dorian," Vincent called in an authoritative voice, but Dorian didn't seem to hear him.

"Dorian." Vincent tried again with little success.

"Dorian!" Vincent shouted, startling Dorian out of his own personal hell.

The man looked toward his cousin with a mixed look of loathing and horror before blanking his face and answering.

"Yes?"

"Continue." Vincent commanded.

His body continuing to shake with tremors, Dorian did so.

"When she had nearly finished whatever she was rambling, her climax nearly upon her, she leaned over and picked up what looked like a ceremonial dagger." He stopped here in his recitation and a blush seeped into his cheeks.

"Whatever it is, you're among family," Shan Lin said softly, never pausing in his first aid.

An unhappy groan sounded before Dorian mumble out a reply.

"It's because you're family I'm embarrassed. But still..." Taking a deep breath before continuing, Dorian's face turned slightly redder.

"The knife didn't bother me so much... That is to say, a little pain with my sex... Erm...well, pain can be a good aphrodisiac if done correctly."

Dorian looked up at the brothers who both gave a short nod.

"Well, anyway... She held the knife up, and I just kept slamming away at her and the next thing I know, she's screaming in ecstasy as blood begins to flow all over me." He paused, a far—away look coming into his eyes. "Whatever she had done had apparently felt good as I came at nearly the same time. If it hurt, or if I was injured anywhere, I can tell you I'd have died a happy man at that moment."

Dorian's eyes stayed glassy as he seemed to be calming down significantly. When his words came now, they began to slur as if he was on the verge of sleep.

"But it wasn't my blood. Queen Sara had killed the old woman. The Crone... Her beloved companion of...the next thing I knew, I was being hauled out of the room and... She said I had done it. They took me to a torture chamber and..." Again a shudder racked his body.

"Then the woman...came in and I hurt so bad. Pain was a constant companion...she dragged me out of that room, my chains... I think she pulled a spear and rod out of my back... She started talking about bones sticking out... Then I passed out. The next thing I...remember, I was here."

His words trailed away and his eyes closed heavily, the glassy-eyed look having taken over completely.

"Dorian!" Vincent nearly shouted the name.

Groggily, Dorian opened his eyes, mumbling a response.

"What was the woman's name?" Shan Lin asked gently.

"Woman? What woman?" Dorian asked, his voice a thread of sound.

"The woman who helped you escape?" Vincent asked.

"Candice," Dorian whispered before finally losing consciousness.

* * * * *

"Looks like we need to take a trip, brother mine," Vincent murmured as Shan Lin finished sewing up the fifth slash wound on his cousin's upper thighs.

"Agreed. If what he says is true..." Shan Lin said.

"Yes. If what he says *is* true, the *freching* bitch has finally slipped the bonds of reality and entered the realm of *Try Nee Sinj*."

"I would believe *Try Nee Sinj* if she had actually loved her husbands, but we saw her throughout her marriage and beyond. Now, over twenty years after her husbands' deaths, she is just finally entering into a state of mourning over the loss of them?"

Shan Lin shook his head.

"I can't believe it. I would more readily believe she is only reacting to the reality of losing the throne."

Vincent agreed.

"Either way, we must find our Princes and warn them."

Vincent sighed heavily.

"Yes, we must."

* * * * *

It had taken quite a bit of talking to convince Queen Sara their time spent in the shack had been for naught, but finally their aunt had listened. An almost unheard of event when the news the messengers imparted was not to the Queen's liking.

Their orders for the mission they just returned from had been to observe the inhabitants of a little village called Driknan located on the outskirts of the Aranakian Mountains and report back any incidents of treason against the Queen. While the brothers had indeed encountered a few of the Horrdian soldiers who managed to slip over the Aranakian border, they could honestly tell their ruler no Aranakians were committing treason.

Before Driknan, they had been sent to a remote camp on the outskirts of Aranak to settle some minor dispute happening on one of the Queen's holdings, only to find the villagers surrounding the camp in an uproar over the Queen's actions. Their grievances were valid. The Queen had been gathering their lands illegally over a long period of time and forcing out those villagers who wouldn't comply with her edicts to hand over their land.

Shan Lin and Vincent were left little choice but to follow the Queen's orders and imprison the rowdy few who had incited the violence. That taken care of, the villagers dispersed, angry still, but finding they had little choice.

After reporting to the Queen things were quiet in Driknan, Shan Lin and Vincent had asked if they could be allowed a bit of personal time. Queen Sara had actually given in and allowed them both to do as they pleased for a bit. Her exact words had been crude and left the men sickened.

"Why don't you take your leisure time here? Go and find your cousin Theresa, I'll lend you the housekeeper, and you can show both of them a good time while I watch. It'll be a study of youth versus experience I'll enjoy, and you'll get laid."

She had roared incessantly after her suggestion, and the idea had so appalled both men, they quickly took their leave.

Knowing the term "a bit" could mean anywhere from an hour to a month, both men hurriedly made preparations for their journey to the Realm of Earth.

"We haven't any choice, Shan Lin. We've got to tell Mitch and Kristain what was done to Dorian and pray Theresa never finds out."

Shan Lin nodded his head. He knew Theresa, their cousin who also stood by their sides in the Queen's Guard as a high-ranking Captain, would use her considerable skills to see Queen Sara dead for what she had done to Dorian.

"I can't believe the boy thought he'd move up in the court if he slept with that vindictive bitch! What the hell did he think she was going to do, give him a title and send him on his merry way?" Vincent raged as he sent his fist swinging into a nearby tree trunk.

"You know what it's like to come into money and be recognized by the Queen. The only way we escaped notice was because it suited her to send us as far from her as she could get us. We earned our cynicism the hard way." Shan Lin spoke as he waited before the portal opening.

"Besides, the information Dorian had to impart was priceless. It's true, it isn't quite the way I'd have gone about finding out what was going on in the Queen's mind, but you have to admit it's helped us put the final pieces together."

Vincent's grunting answer made Shan Lin smile.

"We're going to take down the Queen and we have to do it before she destroys our home. We have to find the Princes and this is the only way it can be done secretly. Our cover story of going to find a bride is perfect. So much the better if we actually bring a woman home with us."

"Find a bride. Mustn't forget to find a bride I don't want," Vincent snorted. "Look, I know we're going to have to follow our Princes and tell them their mother is the scourge of our realm, but I don't have to like it. I still think we could find a *Tractow* sorceress to impart the message to Mitch and Kristain." Vincent grumbled as the brothers prepared to open the portal to Earth. "You know I hate it when this damn thing lands us so far from our intended destination! The last time it took us *four* days to cross a damn mountain only to find out later we could have gone *through it* in hours instead!"

Shan Lin laid a consoling hand on his brother's shoulder. "It's all in the way you look at it, brother mine. The last time we were dropped in the middle of an unfamiliar area, we spent the night catering to one of the horniest women I have ever had the pleasure to meet in my life! The walk through the desert was worth damn near every scratch and bite she left on my body." With a smile of reminiscence, Shan Lin gave his brother a friendly pat on the back before stepping toward the ever-widening misty portal. "Besides, we need to find out if it's true."

"If what's true?" Vincent asked.

"Queen Sara's throne will soon be usurped and the new Queen is truly willing to relocate to Aranak."

With a malicious grin riding his mouth, Vincent walked into the chasm, a gleeful note in his voice, "One can only hope and pray it's true, brother. Hope and pray."

* * * * *

"What the *hell* is wrong with you Candice?!? Did I not make myself clear?" Pacing back and forth in front of the sobbing woman hanging against the wall, Sara took great pleasure in swinging her favorite toy. Every time the toy, a round, blunt-studded "ball" hanging from a steel rod, skimmed the terrified woman's exposed backside, a cry of terror escaped.

It pleased Sara immensely to both hear and see the woman's terror. But to feel her terror... Ah, that was simply exquisite. Sara wondered just how much the woman could take before death overcame her.

"Not to worry, I'll soon find out." The whispered words were spoken into the ear of the terrified subject. The shiver Sara felt go through the female caused her own body to perk up in preparation for the sexual play, which would indeed follow soon.

"Now, if I remember correctly, my little Flower, I gave you an order. I seem to recall myself saying something along the lines of...what was it?" Sara remembered all too well what she had demanded of her "Flower", and the penalty the woman's petals were going to pay would indeed be an enjoyable game!

Pretending to think for a moment, Sara reached out with the steel end of the rod and ran it between the woman's legs. Enjoying the shrieking woman's pain and the sight of the wriggling body before her, Sara smiled, pretending her memory had found the exact words to the woman.

"Ah yes! It's coming back to me now. What I said was: 'Lovely is to die in the morning. Insure he is sent to the Queen's Guard immediately after I have finished with him'."

Even if it wasn't what she had said, it was what Sara had meant and her subjects should know better.

Casually raising the rod upward, Sara began to rub it back and forth gently along the inner thigh of her prisoner.

"It really is a shame you don't know how to follow orders."

Sara sighed heavily but all too quickly brightened.

"I am ready to pronounce your punishment now."

Sara removed the rod and heard the gratifying sound of a moan. Pleased, she turned the rod around in her hands and spoke in the tone of voice she used for making proclamations.

"Let it be said I am a generous Queen. Your sentence shall be given with this instrument only, and when I am satisfied you are repentant, you will be freed."

Extending the rod once more toward the woman, Sara ran it from the woman's belly to the woman's groin and back again. Even as she hoped the torture would last for days, she thought to herself, *This woman won't last more than two hours.*

Smiling, the punishment began.

* * * * *

I'm going to die, Candice thought as Queen Sara began her torture once again. Dorian had been right. It was going to cost her everything she had. Gritting her teeth to stifle a scream as the hot rod came within inches of her skin, Candice tried to settle on the image of just why she was going to die. Dorian's life had better be worth her death. If someone didn't stop the Queen, all this would be for nothing.

* * * * *

Sara squirmed sensually on the bed as the four men left her chambers. The quick romp had left the bed wrecked, but her temporarily sated. Her anger at Candice's failure to carry out orders Sara had given inflamed her.

"As if the bitch didn't know exactly what her defiance would cost her. As if defying me wouldn't matter in the slightest. Why she practically asked for the punishment she received. After all, I am Queen here."

Lovely thoughts floated through her head of the time she'd spent on the throne of the Queendom of Aranak, and she smiled wickedly. Everything had fallen into place when her sons' fathers, Dain and Larik, had died before the twins were born. She had been widowed, and glad of it.

Being Queen had given her the status she had craved all her life, and the power to do as she pleased. Which was a good thing, as pleasing herself was all she cared about.

Wallowing in memories of the men and women she'd gone through made her cunt ache and caused her mood to swing once again. All those lovely bodies she'd had at her disposal. The peasants, royalty... The royals were by far the best of them. Not for any reason most people would assume, though. It had nothing to do with men and women of royal birth being trained better in the arts of sexual pleasure. No. It was that royal born members of Azaya nearly always thought they were above such things as sex. Their screams of denial at the things Sara did to them gave her more pleasure because the same upstarts never thought she would actually hurt them. Sara smiled wickedly. Oh yes. The snobs nearly always ended up coming back begging for more. Thinking of the last man she had put under the heating rod and Sara's hands began to caress her own body at the memory.

"Yes..." Her fingers made a foray into her pussy and she quickly decided to call back the four men who had just departed, reminding herself of how good it was to be Queen, until a stray thought leaked into her mind.

But you are not the Queen of Aranak. That upstart, Stephanie, is now Queen.

Sara's eyes flew open as a scream of rage flew from her mouth, her fingers drawing her own blood as she let go of herself roughly.

Sara threw herself out of bed and, with a strength few knew she possessed, proceeded to demolish her royal chambers. An antique chair, older than her dead grandmother, went flying ten feet across the room and smashed into the couch farther into the room. Art flew off the wall as the Queen randomly proceeded to demolish whatever was within arm's reach.

"The upstart whore! The *frechie* slut! Who does she think she is?!? Just because my sons' wife is to hold the throne of Aranak doesn't mean I am going to give up my place. It will be a cold day in the seven rings of Hellios before she gets any of my power!"

The screeching went on for what must have been hours.

By the time Sara had worn herself out, she was tired, but still horny. The only thoughts running through her mind were for herself as Sara got up from the chair she'd collapsed into and ran to the chamber door. Yanking it open and slamming it against the wall so it nearly bounced back into her, she began to yell.

"I want seven men, I don't care who they are. I want them here now! Their cocks had better be at the ready and able to serve me for hours. And then I want that *freching* slut, Candice, brought to the black chamber and stripped. Hang her in chains and have her raped. By no less than three people. Man, woman, I don't care. Get it done!!!"

The three guards standing outside her door snapped to attention.

Sara went back into her chamber and slammed the door shut behind her. Her breathing coming in heaving pants and her eyes nearly glowing with rage, she made a scan of the ruined chamber.

Growling once again in frustration, she went back to the door and yanked it open once again.

"And get somebody in here to clean up this *freching* mess!"

Feeling marginally better, Sara went back into her room and started to calm her breathing.

This Stephanie would die before Sara ever let her take the throne of Aranak.

Chapter Two

"Oh where, oh where has my little doggie gone? Oh where, oh where can he be?" The homeless woman sang loudly and off-key, as her cart bumped along the broken concrete, the fifth of liquor she'd had blunting her vision. The tiny dog hidden in the folds of many blankets struggled to extricate itself from the load of wool smothering him as he yipped and whined for release.

In front of her, the wind had begun to swirl in fast arcing circles, sending leaves, twigs, and dirt blowing in a tiny tempest through the park. The sound of the fabric of the universe ripping barely made a dent in the surroundings as the rip between worlds widened. The rip grew wider, wide enough for a body to step through if you were two and a half feet tall.

The sudden flash and ear-popping pressure came up suddenly as a hole appeared in the middle of the view directly in front of the woman.

"Clyde! Clyde! They're a comin' for me! Hep' me Lawd! Hep' me!" Her cries were suddenly drowned out as a figure came barreling out of the opening in a roaring scream.

A head full of silky brown hair showed in the opening, similar to a mother birthing a child. The wide, brawny shoulders squeezed out followed by a barreled chest, lean hips, and bulging muscled thighs. Suddenly, a warrior dressed in the ancient uniform of another era sprang forward, then rolled to a stop and immediately leapt to his feet in front of the inebriated woman's cart.

Slightly out of breath, Vincent straightened to his impressive height of six-foot, five-inches, shaking himself to rid his essence of the otherworldly feeling he felt running through his body. The five-foot sword, which hung at his side, immediately cleared the scabbard in a motion made smooth by many years of practice.

No sooner had the woman taken another breath to scream for the police when she saw the beginnings of a second figure of equal proportions start to come through the opening.

A hand pushing at his back caused Vincent to step forward a few yards. Stopping, he turned and waited. He watched the fabric once more part into a diamond-shaped slit as his brother, Shan Lin, went through the same grunts and growls as he pushed his own way into and through the *Tear*.

When the pop of pressure sounded, Shan Lin straightened from his tumble, somehow never affected in the least by the travel between worlds.

The drunken woman gaped, frozen in a soundless scream as the second man's equally long sword cleared its holder.

For one brief moment the woman's lips quivered as if to speak before her eyes rolled toward the top of her head and her body fell in a heap nearly taking the shopping cart and still yipping dog with it.

Turning back to their audience of one, Vincent spoke.

"Well, hell, Shan Lin! If they all drop at our feet like this, it shouldn't be too damn hard to find willing women to bed." Chuckling heartily at his own brand of wit, Vincent sheathed his weapon and went to lift the woman into his arms.

"Funny, brother. But the last time we landed in a city, one of the locals tried to behead us on sight. Better to keep one's head and panic the natives than to lose one's head."

"So? What are we going to do with this one?" Vincent asked as he cradled the fragile woman in his arms. Barely hearing his own question, all Vincent could think of was the misery radiating off the old woman, even in her present state of drunkenness. The memories he was seeing from the contact with her sent a stab of anger mixed with grief through him.

The woman hadn't deserved to lose her children in a flood two days after being given the news of her husband's death in a car accident. Vincent wanted to mend the woman's heart and take the grief and aloneness as his own, but knew there wasn't a magic gift in any realm to cure the pain of losing ones you loved.

"Brother." Vincent looked up at Shan Lin's soft rebuke and nodded his head.

"I know. We can't help them all, but this one I can. And I don't need you laying hands on her to see if it's in her future. I'll help her regardless." The grief he was experiencing leaked into his voice making his reply sound harsh.

Clearing his throat of the woman's agony threatening to choke him, Vincent sat down on a nearby crate and continued to cradle the woman.

Shan Lin watched his normally gruff brother use his not-so-inconsiderable powers to ease the grief of a total stranger. This side of Vincent wasn't widely known about in the Realm of Azaya as both he and Vincent were considered two of the most blood-thirsty Warriors to inhabit the Queen's Guard in over three hundred years.

While it was an accomplishment Shan Lin was damned proud of, it wasn't all the brothers were. They'd come to Earth to warn their Princes and meet their True Queen, if the rumors were to be believed, along with informing them of the machinations of their pretender Queen. They had also come to Earth to bid for clemency and put a stop to the slaughter of the Aranak landscape and more importantly, its people. Something Queen Sara had recently begun.

Their only hope of success lay in convincing Prince Mitch and Prince Kristain the truth of their words. They also prayed for compassion in their new Queen, if indeed there truly was a new ruler.

"Vincent, we have to go." The majority of the Guards who knew Shan Lin would never have recognized him from the gentleness in his voice.

"I know. One more minute and she'll be fine."

* * * * *

The brothers left the aged woman with the knowledge she would soon awaken, take stock of her current lifestyle for the first time in a long while, and finally find the courage to move forward out of her drunken grief. It wouldn't be a perfect life, but the woman would soon find comfort in her drive to help others through times as rough as her own.

They made their way through what seemed to be an alley between new and old buildings. The ambiance of the surroundings was quaint, but not quite what they were looking for.

If Shan Lin remembered correctly, their Queen and Princes now lived on the outskirts of a city called Pinion Hills. They needed to get their bearings and find a way to locate the twins soon.

"Well. Once more have I risked my mind and body to go along with you, brother mine." Vincent spoke as he scanned his surroundings, a slight touch of sarcasm threading his voice. "And just where in *Riad's* name are we?"

Shan Lin looked around as well, gathering himself. Brushing at his clothing, he straightened to his full impressive height of six-foot five-inches.

"Well, we're at least somewhere we haven't been before." The answer, quibbling at best, was given in an equally sarcastic tone. "I realize you don't look fondly on Realm travel, but you must admit, some of the very best adventures we've had were when Queen Sara ordered us through the *Tears*."

Vincent looked to his brother, "It's not the new Realms I have problems enjoying,; it's the way in which we travel to arrive in those Realms." Moving forward, Vincent continued to speak while his brother fell into step behind him.

"I must admit, the Realms have produced some of the happiest times in my life, but I'd still rather not have to 'walk' through the rips between them."

Chuckling, Shan Lin asked, "Does this imply you fear what you don't understand, brother mine? Is the 'Queen's Most Vicious Warrior' afraid of a tiny jolt of electrical juice flowing into and through his veins?" Shan Lin gave a tsking sound. "What would your admirers say if they knew the big, bad, scourge of Aranak trembled at Realm travel?"

Vincent winced at his brother's reminder of the title some woman bestowed on him when the story of his escapade with four Horrdian border raiders came to light.

"It wasn't really a huge deal. So I went a bit overboard when I shouted such a ridiculous line."

He nearly winced at the memory.

Die for my Queen, for you'll never live again for your family!

He did wince as his brother spoke in his mind. It had been a stupid spur of the moment, adrenaline-pumping battle cry, which he would never hear the end of if his brother had any say in the matter.

Which is convenient, because I do have a say in it. You'll be hearing me rag on you about it until we die.

His brother was laughing at him. Before Shan Lin could take it further, Vincent drowned out Shan Lin's laughter.

"My admirers would no doubt beat you around the head for even thinking I would be afraid of anything." Vincent gave his own chuckle as he remembered the woman who had flung herself into his arms directly after the battle had ended and proclaimed him "Queen's Most Vicious Warrior". The thanks she had given him more than made up for any ribbing he had taken from his fellow Warriors.

"Just as Lyssa would more than likely lop off your head if she heard you call me by such a moniker. You know how she feels about her brothers' nicknames coming to light. We're her pride and joy. We wouldn't harm any who didn't try to harm us first."

The last was said with a touch of disbelief. They were part of Queen Sara's Elite Guard. What the Hellios their sister thought they did in a military campaign was beyond Vincent. But he would tear apart anyone who tried to disabuse his gentle, loving sister of the idea her brothers were only deadly weapons their Queen dispatched with practiced ease when the situation suited her.

Shan Lin gave a snort of exasperation. "If Lyssa had her way, we'd be known as the kindest, most gentle Warriors to ever walk the Realm of Azaya. You'd think she wasn't familiar with our Aunt Sara's reputation. She must know just what the *frechie* whore is capable of!"

Anger settled heavily in Shan Lin's gut as he thought about the last official assignment the Queen had sent them on. It was a trumped-up mission that went *fubar* almost immediately after they arrived at the village. They had found their cousin, Captain Theresa Lawsai, there in full command of the situation. What had transpired had been nothing short of a disaster. Whatever had set the Horrd off had been instigated by someone in Aranak and carried out by those very close to the Queen.

It still made Shan Lin sick to think on it.

Easy, brother mine, it is done. Captain Lawsai will take care of it, and we will finally have the documented proof we need to give to our Princes. The Princes will believe what we tell them about Dorian and Queen Sara's determination to kill him. But it will all be as before. We have no concrete proof. There is little we can do until we verify there is truly a new Queen. Dwelling on it now will only bring back more grief.

Shan Lin took a few deep breaths of the air surrounding him and did his best to bring his anger under control. The knot in his belly softened when he felt the soothing calm his brother eased into his being.

Even as they continued on their journey, Shan Lin felt the comfort his brother pathed into his mind. The corner of Shan Lin's mouth lifted as he conveyed his thanks through the mind-link they shared.

My pleasure, brother mine.

Shan Lin knew there had been times that the telepathy the twins shared had been the only thing keeping him from going mad when his mind turned in on itself and the visions he saw jerked him into their world. Vincent never thought twice about having to pull Shan Lin's consciousness back to itself. His brother had commented on it only once when they were but eight years old.

"I am your other self. I am but half of a whole, which will not be complete until we are *juniane'*. Where you go I will always follow. You belong to me as much as I belong to you. Until we are *juniane'* and belong to our mate, I will pull you from the ending brink of your journey just as you will drag me kicking and screaming from my fear of losing you to that horrifying end."

As complex at it had seemed to both the young boys, they had understood Vincent would continue to travel through Shan Lin's mind when the visions came to find his brother. At one point, Shan Lin had voiced the unfairness of the situation to his brother, and Vincent had shrugged it off.

"For you, brother mine, there is no other thing I can do."

The words had humbled Shan Lin. No other, including their father, believed what Shan Lin saw. Even through the mind-link, Vincent couldn't see what Shan Lin saw, but never questioned Shan Lin when he spoke.

The only thing Shan Lin could give in return to his brother was his love and protection against any and all that would deem it necessary to harm Vincent.

The two of them had become known for the way they fought. One would always protect the other's back when vulnerable, and they nearly always fought side by side. It was how they had climbed so far in the ranks of the Queen's Guards.

Which was how they had come to be in this place at this time.

"As if you would harm a hair on the spoiled child's head." Vincent spoke aloud at Shan Lin's thoughts. *Thank you, brother mine.*

"No. Neither of us would want the slightest thing to mar her pleasure in life."

Both men did their level best to insure their younger sister's life was a string of one wonderful event after another. The death of their mother when Lyssa was so young drove her two brothers to shower her with more affection than they would have had their mother still been alive.

The two men being so far apart in age from their little sister played a heavy role in their feelings toward their younger sibling. There was a seventeen-year difference between them, and their mother's death had come almost directly after Lyssa's second birthday.

"She's been spoiled beyond any other man or men to imagine," Shan Lin pointed out reasonably.

"True," Vincent replied grudgingly.

Both Shan Lin and Vincent had vowed their sister would know all memories the two brothers could offer her of their gentle-loving mother.

The belief their mother, Evelyn, would still be alive if Shan Lin and Vincent's father, Thaddeus, hadn't sent Evelyn to stay with Aunt Gwen and Uncle Darias, while he trained the boys, played a heavy factor also. Lyssa had been left behind because Thaddeus hadn't wanted to part with his beloved daughter.

In Shan Lin and Vincent's eyes, Thaddeus had sent Evelyn to her death. All four had paid the price for Thaddeus' beliefs. Vincent came to an abrupt halt, Shan Lin stopping beside him as the two looked around them once more. They had come upon a sprawling lawn at the end of which stood what looked to be a stately home.

"What is it, Vincent?" Shan Lin asked as they came to a halt. He looked at the home, then scanned the surrounding area for some danger he had not picked up himself.

They had been walking for no more than twenty minutes, leaving the buildings of the city behind as they made their way through what had to be the back alleys of the city. It was early morning now, the sun had barely risen over the horizon and the soft glow of the morning was quickly turning into the beginning heat of the day. Both men quickly realized they had directed themselves toward this specific home. They had already passed a few other dwellings, but had unconsciously ignored them.

"I suppose she's in there." Shan Lin made the statement in a gruff voice. A feeling stirred through his mind that someone had guided them to where they now found themselves.

To finally be within reach of their new Queen brought an excitement brewing in both men. If there was a new Queen...

They let the thought trail away.

"You sure?" Vincent asked.

"Don't know," Shan Lin answered, beginning his forward progress once again, even though he could be wrong, "but I'm not going to stand here and wait to find out."

Vincent watched his brother walk forward toward what most likely was their new Queen and quickly took off at a loping gait to catch up with him.

"Then let's go find out for sure."

Chapter Three

Shan Lin and Vincent knocked on the door to the lavish house that stood before them.

"*Riad*," Vincent muttered. "Queen Sara's got to be ticked."

"Why do you say that, brother?" Shan Lin asked as the two waited for the door to be answered.

"You know her. She's got to be going into tantrums left and right if it's true there's a new Queen. She thought her sons would never marry and she'd rule Aranak forever. Never mind that she's never had her throne challenged, she now has to give it all up. Power, treasures, everything. To a woman who isn't even Aranakian. How exactly do you think she's feeling?"

Shan Lin paused for a moment before speaking.

"I imagine the woman is ticked. If it's true. If this is the True Queen as we've been hearing…"

Before he could finish his thought, the door was finally opened, a servant of some kind stood before them with an inquiring gaze.

"We're looking for one of the Aranak Princes. Are they here?" Vincent used his best soldier face, the one that made lower-ranking soldiers, and some high-ranking officials, do his bidding.

The servant opened the door wider and gestured them in to a small hallway.

Shan Lin looked around and stepped further into the next room after the servant had asked them to wait here and then left. He went even further into the room when an item caught his eye. It reminded him so much of home he couldn't help himself. He walked over to the artifact that lay in a prominent place in the room and picked it up. After he had turned it a few times in his hand and it wouldn't work, he turned to Vincent and showed him.

"Recognize this?" Shan Lin asked as he held it out to Vincent.

Vincent took the sculpture in his hands and turned it in the same way Shan Lin had. He waited for it to come to life and when it didn't, he hastily put it down with exaggerated care.

He looked at Shan Lin and raised his eyebrows. "So. It's true then."

When Shan Lin looked at the statue again, he nodded his head and turned to stand fully in front of Vincent.

"Look. Let's wait to see. After all, just because it no longer answers to us doesn't mean it no longer answers to Mitch and Kristain." Shan Lin waited for Vincent to agree, and when he didn't immediately reply, Shan Lin looked at him questioningly.

"What? You don't agree it might not have happened?"

Vincent looked back at the statue and shook his head, "No, I don't agree with you." He continued to stare at the statue as he spoke. "Every time I've touched that statue, throughout my entire life, mind you, it has responded to me as one who could be in line to the throne." He took a deep breath while he pondered the situation a moment, then looked directly at Shan Lin and continued. "It has *never* not responded. And since it no longer responds, I know I am no longer in the fight for my Queendom's crown." Staring deeply into Shan Lin's eyes, he made the obvious statement.

"And neither, dear brother mine, are you. It has come to pass, and we will accept it."

Shan Lin knew in his heart it was true, but he didn't have to like it. "Fine. You believe it. But until Mitch and Kristain say different, I'll hold onto what I have been raised to be." He paused as if his brother didn't already know what the answer was. "A mate to a Queen."

He walked back over to pick up the statue.

Vincent turned to watch while Shan Lin picked it up once again and ran it around in his hands.

When he finally set the statue back in its place, Shan Lin looked up at Vincent with near desolation, then went to him and embraced his brother.

Vincent knew what his brother was thinking. He knew Shan Lin didn't mind losing the throne. Though his brother would mind all the time, wasted, training for a throne they would never gain.

If they had believed Shan Lin when he had told their mother that the brothers would never marry a Queen, they would have realized all of Shan Lin's prophecies would come true. There would have been more time spent as a family instead of their father continually sending their mother away so he could concentrate on properly training them in the ways of a Queen's Consorts.

Let it go, Shani.

Shan Lin looked to his brother. "Thank you for believing in me when nobody else would. I realize it's the one thing we won't ever share until we're matched, but it is always better with the knowledge of your belief in me."

Vincent sent soothing thoughts to him.

"It hurts just to know our mother could have been with us instead of Aunt Gwen when the Horrds came to take their village. She would still have been alive if Father had believed me." Shan Lin took a deep breath and waited for his emotions to come under control. When he had them mastered, he looked around for a place to sit and came face to face with a goddess.

He smiled a moment before he realized just who she was.

He looked back to his brother and found Vincent prostrate on his knees with his forehead bowed to the floor. Shan Lin whipped his head back around to look at the woman, then immediately took the same position as his brother.

She had the deepest midnight blue eyes he'd ever seen. If you looked at them long enough, he knew you could drown in them. Her hair swept her shoulders and was the color of the fierce, dark plains he had glimpsed in Aranak. On her, it was the loveliest color he'd ever seen. She truly was a goddess in her own right, and most definitely their Queen.

Stephanie looked down in exasperation at the two men with their heads bowed on the floor. She stepped closer to the one directly next to her and touched his head. "Oh, not again. Everyone who comes does that," she said under her breath. Louder, she said, "Get up, please."

In turns, it continued to amaze and irritate her when a man or woman from Aranak came through their door. People took one look at her then dropped to their knees with their foreheads on the floor.

Mitch and Kristain had explained it had been their mother's wish. This was how Queen Sara required she be greeted, and any royalty who visited her of a lower rank also had to adopt this position.

For herself, Stephanie would have been more than happy to have everyone stop bowing before her, but since she hadn't wanted to offend Mitch and Kristain about their Realm's customs, she hadn't said anything. She vowed she would though, and soon!

She went to the other man and touched his head while she asked him to get up. When this one came to his feet, he blanched when he saw her.

"What is it?" Stephanie sounded almost alarmed.

Shan Lin couldn't speak. The ability to form any kind of sound left his mind and took most of his ability to stand. He swayed toward the beautiful woman and would have fallen over if she hadn't caught him.

"Are you all right? Do you need to sit down?" When Shan Lin still couldn't get a word to come out, she guided him to a nearby chair and sat him down. Gesturing for the same servant who had answered the door, she asked the man to go and get her a glass of water.

By the time the servant had taken a couple of steps, Shan Lin found his voice. "Wait." It came out croaking and squeaky, but it still came out.

"Better?" Stephanie asked while she stroked his sleeve. She had looked through his mind when he had first come up and seen her. Even though she herself thought it was an intrusion, Mitch and Kristain repeatedly informed her they wouldn't ever leave her side if she didn't start scanning every mind she came in contact with. They informed her there were enemies out there who would dearly love to get their hands on the True Queen, and since it was her, they weren't going to take chances.

The man before her didn't want to hurt her; he was just feeling overwhelmed at the moment.

When he nodded, she looked to the other man she had immediately read. He was staring at her intently.

"He'll be fine," Stephanie murmured. "I understand you're looking for my husbands." Stephanie almost snickered at the phrase. *My husbands.* No matter how long they were together, she suspected the "husbands" part would always give her a tickle of pleasure. Saying it just made her laugh, but living it had made her deliriously happy.

Vincent watched the woman stroking his brother's arm and nodded his head absently. There was a poetry of motion in the way she moved. It wasn't anything which would be seen as overt, but a natural gesture. She wanted very much to soothe the man before her. Put him at ease as he was having difficulty managing it himself.

The gesture, more than her being their Queen, endeared her to him forever. This woman was exactly what their world needed.

Stephanie smiled laughingly at him. "I'm glad you think so. I've often worried about it myself, but my husbands assure me I'll do just fine. I now find it's not as difficult as I once thought it would be."

Stephanie patted the sitting man's arm once more while he seemed to come out of his shock.

She then fully turned toward the other man. "I could always pick it out of your minds, and I might just still, but would you mind introducing yourselves?"

Vincent made a face to let Stephanie know he realized he had made a faux pas, then bowed to her. "My name is Vincent Carrucci-Rayan, and this is Shan Lin, my brother. We are cousins to Mitch and Kristain and have come to see if the rumors are true." He looked over at his brother then back to Stephanie. "I see they are."

Stephanie nodded to him. "Yes. I get the honor of being both Wife and Queen. Took me by surprise, both roles I now have." She chuckled as she remembered how Mitch and Kristain had told her she was now their wife.

She had been innocently going to get the Sunday paper. She had opened her door with Kristain behind her, bent over, grabbed the paper and had seen a man in the hall. He had tipped his hat politely, and she had nodded then backed into the apartment.

Kristain had almost gone berserk. When he had finally gotten himself under control, both he and Mitch had spilled the beans. Talk about a shock!

Shan Lin and Vincent watched their Queen's face softened into a look of reminiscent joy. It made both of the men smile in return.

Stephanie looked from Shan Lin to Vincent and remembered where she had heard their names before.

"I know who you two are!" She gestured to them both, "Follow me, there are a few things I need to discuss with my top advisors. And from what I understand, you two are them." She turned and started down a hall toward the living room.

Shan Lin and Vincent watched as she walked away mumbling and giggling about having advisors.

* * * * *

Stephanie looked toward her husbands who both sat in stunned disbelief. She could feel their shock and anger at the information both Shan Lin and Vincent had just imparted. The astonishment of being informed their mother had truly crossed a line neither man ever dreamed she would, tore her husbands' last vestiges of love for their mother away. As hard as they had tried to believe there was love somewhere in Sara, the news Shan Lin and Vincent shared ripped away any chance of believing in Sara's goodness.

Stephanie "listened" as well as "watched" in amazement as the memories of her husbands scrolled through her mind. It was all she could do not to cringe away from actually living with the cruelty Sara had inflicted on the men over the years. That the two men had held onto any love for Sara this long was a miracle.

Imagine! A mother turning on her own offspring. The woman who should have cherished and nurtured them, fostered their dreams, insured both men got a chance at happiness, even if she couldn't. Instead, hurting them both physically and mentally, trying to ruin their future—the concept was beyond Stephanie.

On the other hand, Stephanie's parents had done nothing but! In everything, both her mom and dad had encouraged, supported, and praised their children. Stephanie couldn't imagine a life in which her parents ruled her before loving her.

My hearts. Stephanie reached out with her mind to soothe and comfort her husbands, even as she wrapped her arms around them both, turning her face back and forth, showering physical and mental love on them equally.

Both men clung for a brief moment before each asked simultaneously. "Why?"

Stephanie's heart broke as the two most important people in her life bled from their souls.

Slowly easing their grasps on their wife, both men's faces remained stoic as they turned toward their cousins.

"If what you say is true, then there is much to be done." Mitch and Kristain stood, turning in opposite directions to walk around and stand in back of the sofa where Stephanie still sat. Each stood slightly to the side of her, both resting a hand on each of her shoulders.

Kristain spoke, "You know you'll have to go back. Stephanie is the True Queen of Aranak, but until the Bell of Coronation is rung, she is cut off from hearing Moth...Sara's thoughts." He didn't want to think of the woman, who was Queen, as any relation to himself at this moment.

If what Shan Lin and Vincent said was true, Mitch and Kristain's mother had indeed tried to murder her own children and the mother of her future grandchildren.

"You will learn all you can and report back here. No one else must know, and you will make damn sure Dorian doesn't breathe a word of this to anyone!" Mitch, never one to remain passive when a call to arms should be sounded, clenched his teeth, seething as the import of just what the *Bitch* had set into motion meant.

Their mother was planning to eradicate the royal family.

To have suspected a family member of past betrayal was one thing. To now know it was the truth was beyond devastating.

"*Damn the woman!*" The roar sounded through the spacious house in a terrifying echo as Mitch turned and slammed a fist through the wall behind him. Plaster, wood, and fibers rained down from the sizable hole in the wall as he growled his fury out and pounded his other fist against the wall.

Stephanie cringed at the fury she felt coming from her husbands, all directed toward their mother. Kristain also stood with his back toward her, Shan Lin, and Vincent. She knew there was little she could do right now to ease the hurt and anger they felt toward their mother, but she had to try.

Even feeling both Kristain's and Mitch's anger, Stephanie didn't hesitate as she got up, going around the sofa and walking directly to both men who stood closely together. Kristain had refrained from the physical outburst Mitch had reveled in, but it was a close thing. Stephanie could feel the struggle he had to keep himself from reacting just as his twin had.

Knowing neither of her husbands would ever think to harm her, and in fact had done nothing since she met them but shower her with love, Stephanie put herself in front of them both, her back to the wall.

Gently, she extracted Mitch's fist from the wall brushing away the bits and pieces covering his fist. He had cut the skin and blood trickled slowly onto the floor as Stephanie brought his hand to her lips, kissing the hurt. Reaching out blindly, she waited for Kristain to take her hand, and when he did, she grasped them both once again to her.

When their emotions had leveled a bit, Stephanie remembered their audience.

"Shan Lin. Vincent." Looking at them both, she opened her mind and found both men hurting for their cousins. Finding out the cruelty Queen Sara had heaped on her sons was a long-standing contention with the people of Aranak, reassured her in some way. It would only be one of the many things she would be held accountable for.

Maintaining her composure as best she could, Stephanie let out a tiny breath, then gave her first official order.

"While you have enough proof with the tale of Dorian's escape to convince my husbands, I doubt you have enough proof to convince the people of Aranak. Or more importantly, its equivalent of a court of law. At this point, it's still our word against Sara's. Queen Sara is to be brought down at all cost. Watch, listen, and wait. I don't care how long it takes. The people of Aranak have suffered enough. It doesn't matter how I got this position, it only matters the position is now mine." Taking a deep breath, feeling pride threaded through the anger coming from her husbands, Stephanie continued.

"From what I understand, what I'm about to ask of you can only be asked by a Queen's successor?" Stephanie made it a question.

Shan Lin nodded.

"Then let it be known I, Queen Stephanie, successor to Queen Sara, am demanding it of you."

"Yes, my Queen. Ask and it shall be done." Shan Lin knew in that moment he would do all in his power to accomplish what his new Queen asked of him. He also knew that if he touched her again he would see a determination to protect her mates at all cost.

From the love and affection the Queen had shown her mates, Shan Lin knew he was finally seeing how a true ruler should act. Even if his visions hadn't foretold the coming of the True Queen, he would have known who she was the moment he had glimpsed her. As it was, her touch had been the catalyst for the vision, which had brought him to a halt upon first seeing her. In his mind, he had seen her coronation, had seen both Mitch and Kristain in all their regal finery, resplendent in the colors of their Queendom, at her side.

Shan Lin and Vincent had watched for no more then a few moments as the Queen and Princes enveloped one another in comfort and grief before he and his brother had left the room to give them privacy.

The "servant" who had answered the door approached them as soon as they exited the room.

"Is there something I can do for either of you, Warrior Vincent? Warrior Shan Lin?"

The brothers exchanged knowing looks.

"What's your name?" Vincent asked gently as the man took a step back at Shan Lin's expression.

"Brock, Sirs." The man stood his ground finally.

"My name is Vincent, and he's Shan Lin. There's no need for formal address to either of us, unless you plan on doing something you'll need to be arrested for." Vincent smiled as he spoke.

The man gave a tentative smile in return and seemed to relax some.

"Warri...Vincent. I have no desire to do anything that will mar the reputation of Queen Stephanie. She is..." A soft smile and a far-away look came over the man's face as he continued to speak.

"...wonderful. I haven't known so much contentment in..." The smile remained even as the distant look left, "...well too many years to count."

"So she treats her servants well?" Shan Lin asked.

Brock turned to Shan Lin, a look of confusion now on his face.

"Servants?" He made it a question, then shook his head in the negative.

"Queen Stephanie has no servants...Shan Lin."

"What?!?" the brothers nearly roared in unison.

Both speaking at once, their questions stumbling over one another's words, they grilled Brock.

"What do you..." Vincent shouted.

"Why the Hellios..." Shan Lin interrupted.

"...mean the Queen hasn't any..."

"...isn't there a shit load..."

"...servants to attend her! Good *Riad*! Why it's an..."

"...of retainers here to wait on that..."

"...outrage! This is Queen Sara's doing, isn't it! She's so damn wrapped up in..."

"...goddess of a woman in there? Queen Sara had them damn well..."

"...ruining Aranak she can't even greet her successor properly. Damn the..."

"...tripping over each other to see to her needs. *Riad* be da..."

Brock had begun to back away at the anger coming off the two Warriors and understood in that moment why the men had earned their nicknames. He continued to back further away as quietly as possible until he finally began to realize the two men had misunderstood him.

Brock tried to set them straight by breaking into the tirade of inventive suggestions both were now hurling at Queen Sara.

"Wait! Listen to me!" It took a minute to get the two men to stop, but when they did, it was all Brock could do to look the two in the eyes because of the expressions they now wore.

"You m-mis...misunderstood me." He swallowed unobtrusively, or tried to, but watched as both men noticed the action.

"Queen Stephanie has all the servants she could want. Queen Sara, via couriers, offered her as many as she could handle, but Queen Stephanie refused. She told Queen Sara she was fine and didn't have any need for servants. To which Queen Sara smiled wickedly and all but purred at Queen Stephanie, 'A true ruler always needs servants, and what was the problem?'"

Taking a breath, Brock spoke once again, a note of pride in his voice.

"I am proud to say, the Princes had summoned me as soon as they found their Queen, but I was delayed in getting to them. I wasn't here for the very beginning, but I was the first to arrive from Aranak behind the Princes."

When he didn't speak again immediately, Vincent took a step toward him with the intention of shaking the rest of the story from the man, but was held back by Shan Lin when the man's eyes widened alarmingly.

Easy, brother mine. Give him his moment.

Shan Lin looked at the man expectantly.

After another quick look toward Vincent to reassure himself of his safety, Brock resumed his explanation.

"Yes... Well. At any rate, Queen Stephanie told Queen Sara, anyone who wished to join their Princes was welcome, but there would be no servants in her home. They would be paid for their time, and given a place to stay if they wanted to work here. No one was to be coerced to serve. After all, Queen Stephanie lived in what would be to them a foreign land, and no person should ever be ordered from their homes on the whim of another. So if Queen Sara knew of anyone who wouldn't mind, Queen Stephanie would welcome them, but they weren't to be forced."

A smile once more graced Brock's face, "It was a sight, Sirs. I can't tell you how much of a privilege it was for me to be at this exchange. It did my old heart good to see..."

Vincent cut the man off.

"Okay. Tell me this then. If Queen Stephanie doesn't have servants, why are you here? Is she doing everything in this place by herself?"

Shan Lin looked around him noticing the cleanliness and order of the home, then remembered the sheer size of the place from the view outside.

"She mentioned when we arrived others have... She said there had been others who visited. Where are they, and what are they doing to justify being here?"

There was still a note of anger in Shan Lin's voice as he asked. Were the visitors freeloading from the new Queen and taking advantage of her?

"They all have been assigned duties if that's what you're asking." Brock said, a note of censure in his voice.

"We did not accept the invitation offered by our Queen without giving our loyalty to her whether she wanted it or not." There was also a note of possessiveness toward the Queen, which told both brothers immediately Brock was the best choice Mitch and Kristain could have made for their wife. Vincent was just going to make sure their choice was the best.

"And which Queen would that be?" Vincent questioned as his eyes narrowed.

"I give my loyalty to only one Queen. The *True Queen*, Queen Stephanie. Every person who comes through her door gives Her Majesty their loyalty, or they are denied entrance."

Brock's reply, given immediately, held a bite of steel.

Satisfied, Vincent nodded his approval, and clapped the stiff man on the back, then spoke.

"Well, that's all settled. Where's the grub?"

Shaking his head at his brother's shift in attitude, Shan Lin knew Brock would soon become part of their very small, and equally new, family.

* * * * *

In the time they waited to be summoned once more by their Queen, the brothers had explored the house and had even come across a few people from Aranak they knew.

After questioning the household staff, the brothers were assured the people, who resided there, would indeed stand beside Queen Stephanie, defending her life and right to rule Aranak. It was more than they had hoped for, and less than they wanted for a woman, who they prayed, would be able to seize Queen Sara's hold on their beloved home.

It was Stephanie herself who found them in the kitchen about an hour later. Both Shan Lin and Vincent had put a sizable dent in the stock of Aranak delicacies Lairn, the chef, had cooked for the brothers.

Vincent, who spotted Stephanie as she stood watching the two brothers eat, quickly stood, and started to go to his knees before a word from Stephanie stopped him.

"No. If you feel you must, you can bow or tip your head, but no going to your knees or forehead. It's both ridiculous and damn uncomfortable."

Shan Lin, who had stood with his brother and stopped when Queen Stephanie spoke, bowed deeply from the waist.

"As you like, Your Majesty," both brothers replied simultaneously.

"And you can call me Stephanie. We're family after all." The smile returned as she spoke, and made the brothers feel truly welcome for the first time since their mother had passed on.

"As you wish…Stephanie."

It felt strange to call a Queen by her given name, even in an informal surrounding. Vincent would never have imagined his new ruler offering the use of her given name. But he would abide by it when they were as a family.

"But I might add, when we're in front of others, you'll always be Your Majesty. It is the way of our world, and until the law is changed and accepted more widely, I would make the suggestion we leave it that way." Shan Lin nodded in agreement with his brother.

"As you say, we are family. It will still take a bit of getting used to."

Stephanie sighed, "So Brock continues to tell me. And I keep assuring him I'm not trying to be disloyal, or even change customs, which have been in practice long before I ever became a part of it; I'm just trying to fit in."

She looked from one brother to the next, and gave a decisive nod.

"Perhaps all three of you are right. Brock included."

A surprised sound came from behind Stephanie and she turned to look. Brock stood with his mouth open, staring at Stephanie.

"You all right, Brock? Has the grilling been too harsh?" Stephanie asked, laughter in her voice. Guessing what the look was about, Stephanie's smile turned into a grin.

"Yes, you, dear man. You were right."

Brock blinked, then turned all shades of red while a proud-as-you-please grin shown on his face.

Turning back to Shan Lin and Vincent, Stephanie lost her smile as she switched topics and spoke to the brothers.

"I need to…" Stephanie began and watched from the corner of her eyes as three faces latched onto her every word. She wanted to shake her head at these people and tell them her every thought wasn't always the things heads of state normally thought of; most of her thoughts were merely mundane normal things. Except she knew these people were placing their lives into her hands, and she didn't want to do anything to disappoint them.

"…talk to you about Queen Sara. I want you…"

Vincent and Shan Lin both held up their hands, one nearly mimicking the other, movement for movement, as they looked left and right. They didn't need to speak. The rest of the staff in the kitchen stopped what they were doing, and left.

Even Brock, who could have stayed, Stephanie told him as much, left.

Stephanie waited. She knew what they were doing, and knew they wouldn't yet believe no other member of her household would betray her. She would dispel their worries eventually, but for now, the dethroning of Sara was uppermost in her mind.

"Go ahead." Shan Lin spoke.

I think she knows. Vincent drawled.

"As a matter of fact I do. We'll deal with the rest later. For now, let's talk about Sara and how we're going to bring her down."

Stephanie paused taking a deep breath.

"I want you both to become my spies." She watched for any sign from either man that would indicate a problem with her request. She gave a small nod of approval when neither man reacted negatively, before continuing.

"I still have things I need to learn about the ways of your people and what will soon be my new home before I can take any kind of leadership role in Aranak. I currently can't be there myself due to my residual commitments here on Earth, and I need all the proof I can get to take this woman down without outright killing her myself."

The last was said with enough bitter venom to fill a nation. Whatever Mitch and Kristain had told Stephanie about their mother, added to what Shan Lin and Vincent had imparted when they arrived, had put the final nail in Sara's coffin as far as Stephanie was concerned.

Chapter Four

Shari had done it. Finally, she had freed herself from the bump and grind of nine to five. No more setting the alarm for o'dark thirty to primp and prepare herself for a day of closed-in office space. No more conferences, meetings, lunches, or drop-in surprises for this lady. No sirree, Phil! She was free to pursue her dreams of...

Shari paused on her trek down the hall to Karen's apartment and grimaced in pain, both mentally and physically. Her body ached in all the wrong places and her mind vacillated between thoughts on what exactly she would do now and focusing on the minor accident she had just been in.

Sighing silently, she made her way down to Karen's door. All she wanted to do was get inside and crash on the nearest flat surface. Walking as fast as her sore body would allow, forcing one foot in front of the other, she made her way down the hall.

Lord, my head hurts.

The scrape down the side of her hip had left her body aching and throbbing, and she would be lucky if she lived long enough to reach the apartment's door.

Stop it. You're exaggerating because you're doing your best not to freak out about handing in your two-week notice.

Smiling wryly, Shari White pushed thoughts of worrying about not having enough money in her savings account, having to tuck her tail between her legs and go back to a "real" job, and now the pain her body was signaling to her. The tiny aches and pains from the accident were becoming more and more intolerable by the moment. Shari supposed walking home after the accident hadn't been the smartest thing she could have done.

Finally, she thought as she reached her friend's door, *I can go in and crash!* Fumbling her key out of the pocket of her ruined pants, she unlocked the door and stepped inside. Shari dropped her purse and the equally ruined briefcase where she stood and turned to push the door closed, allowing it to shut behind her.

Immediately the doubts began to creep in once again. Would she be able to find something she truly enjoyed doing before her "Freedom" money ran out. Shari had given herself what should be a year's "cushion" of money to pay necessities, minor frivolities and, if needed, emergency spending money.

But can I?

Her muscles interrupted her second thoughts, screaming viciously in protest as she walked forward. She was determined to land on a soft spot this time, and not settle for curling into a little ball of pain in front of the door.

"That's all I need. Karen would come in and smack me on the other side of my aching skull to make a complete job of it."

Even talking quietly out loud hurt her head too much, so she concentrated on making it to the couch and thinking thoughts softly.

The car coming out from the underground garage probably hadn't been going more than five m.p.h. The poor rattled driver had been coming up the blind ramp faster than he had thought and, *Bam!* Knocked her clean off her feet. But when the car had rammed into her, Shari felt as if it had been going at light speed.

She had been dazed, but other than probably needing an aspirin, she was pretty sure her injuries did not need a doctor. She flat refused to have an ambulance called. She hadn't lost consciousness, and most of the abrasions only needed bandages and cleaning. She would be fine once she got home.

"Not too smart, was it, Shari 'you're a twit' White?" Shari mumbled, wishing someone was there to whine to.

As pain continued to lance its way through her head, she remembered her comment not to talk out loud. Maybe if she just whispered. Besides, she did not have time to spend seven hours sitting in an emergency room somewhere in the city waiting to be told she was fine, go home. She knew her body well enough to know she would probably be fine in a few days.

Turning slowly, she spotted the couch and stumbled to it. She was on the verge of simply falling on it carefully, and sleeping for a week, when a hammering noise sounded against the front door.

No! She gripped her head as the noise reverberated against the inside of her head. It would just top her *Day from Hell* if it ended up being a damn salesman intent on getting someone to buy the five thousand dollar set of encyclopedias, which would become obsolete the minute the next *coup d'état* in Peru erupted.

Wasn't there somebody trying to take over Peru at the moment?

Shari's head throbbed as her thoughts scrambled around in her head. Inconsequential things popped up and chased after one another until the pounding at the door started once again.

I could just ignore it, pretend there's no one here.

She grimaced at the thought. She had never been able to ignore answering a knock at the door or a ringing phone.

The pounding thundered again.

Muttering low in her throat and immediately wincing at the renewed pain, Shari forced her body toward the door. Standing slowly, she started to rise. It took her longer than she would have thought as her head began to whirl. Raising her arms with difficulty, she held her head between her hands long enough for it to stop doing merry-go-round imitations, then started for the door.

Shit! The heartfelt, whispered word ran through her.

Not bothering to check through the view hole in the door, she braced herself with a hand on the doorknob and wrenched the door open, leaning heavily against it for support.

Truly, she had every intention of stripping skin off whoever stood on the other side. Until, that is, she came face to face with the pair of sex gods. Her words died a flaming death. The pain, which had so recently radiated through her body, fled.

There stood two of the most gorgeous men she would ever lay eyes on. In front of her were two six-foot-five, muscle-bound, sable-haired, chisel-jawed, Chippendale dancers. Animal magnetism rolled off the pair in waves, making her pussy weep. Taking shallow breaths, Shari saw black spots appear before her eyes.

"Please…"

She drew in the last of a shallow breath and let out a moan so close to a howl she almost scared herself. Her vision went gray at the pleasure streaking through her body and she fell to her knees, the pain in her body forgotten. Her head would have hit the floor as she bowled over if not for a skin-roughened hand slipping between her forehead and the floor.

Shari felt herself grind her hips on an erection she was sure was between her legs. She ground down as if riding a man, then gave a final shuddering scream as an orgasm rolled over and through her body in mind-numbing bliss.

It took a few moments to gather her scattered thoughts. Panting in the aftermath, Shari felt muscled arms surround and cradle her body as if it was a delicate piece of porcelain. Turning her head slowly, she looked up into a pair of eyes the color of a sunset and had to blink, thinking she was imagining things.

The eyes she gazed into were glowing.

Squeezing her eyes closed in hopes she was seeing things, she blinked several times, then looked once again.

Nope. Not glowing at all.

She stared into two different colored eyes. One a golden bronze, the other the color of crisp, green, summer leaves. She closed her eyes once more and shook her head slightly for good measure, vaguely remembering her headache. When she opened her eyes again, she still saw the same set of eyes, both different colors.

A voice, low and resonating sensations against her stimulated body seemed to be making soothing sounds to her.

Tilting her head back a little more Shari took in the whole picture. She seemed to be in the arms of one of the men who had stood on the other side of Karen's door.

"Er…should I thank you and be offering a cigarette about now?"

* * * * *

Vincent stopped rumbling nonsensical noises and looked away from the woman in his embrace. Biting his lip at the woman's cheeky mouth, he locked eyes with Shan Lin. His nod telling his brother the woman was all right, he gave his attention once more to the woman he held.

"We have come to insure your safety. We saw what transpired and know you for a strong woman. It is our wish to have you for a wife. I have already given you a glimpse of what is to come. You seem very susceptible to it. You also seemed to enjoy it. But since you almost blacked out from it, I will have to hold back until you are more used to our ways."

Vincent, finishing the only explanation he intended to give, propped the woman up so Shan Lin could see the woman was better. He didn't know if he was pleased she could climax so easily, or disappointed he would have to be so gentle with her. As he looked her over, a sense of familiarity came over him, and he wondered just where he had seen the woman previously.

Not to worry, he thought, *I'll remember soon enough.*

* * * * *

Shari looked at the hunk-of-the-month still holding her firmly enough she might have trouble getting out of his grip, and gave him her 'you've gotta be kidding' look.

Carefully shaking her head at him, Shari tried to free herself unobtrusively from his powerful grasp. This barbarian was in for a huge surprise. Give her pleasure beyond her imagination, indeed!

Cripes! First the stupid man in the car who didn't know how to watch for pedestrian traffic, now a couple of horny men at her door giving her orgasms…

She snorted to herself, then paused.

Okay. Maybe the orgasms sounded pretty good, but…

"Look, Hunk-o-Rama. I appreciate a fantastic orgasm just as much as the next woman, but I think you have me confused with someone else." Again she tried to free herself from Vincent's grip. This time he let her go as a pondering look crossed his face.

Shari braced herself so her legs would actually hold her and climbed off his lap. Stumbling immediately, she tried to move and put space between the man who had recently held her and herself. All too quickly, she realized she would have fallen on her face if another pair of arms hadn't reached out and caught her.

"Thanks." Shari mumbled, feeling the dizziness begin to abate. Turning slowly Shari looked into another pair of dual eyes. Slowly rotating her head in disbelief, she looked across the room, doing a double take.

Well Hell! There were *two of them. Identical twins, right down to their different colored eyes!* She thought perhaps that her vision had gone double. But no, here they both stood, male studs for the taking. Gorgeous didn't even begin to cover it, and there were *two* of them!

Shari's mind reeled. There was something one of them had...

"Did you say...wife?"

"Yes." The word rumbled out huskily in unison.

"I thought you...yes..."

It was too much. First, the bastard of a client who had tried to paw her to death, then the being hit by a car thing. The orgasm... Before she could finish her thought, blackness swallowed her whole.

✱ ✱ ✱ ✱ ✱

"At least we won't need to go into the explanation of trying to convince her we need her to participate in a sham." Shan Lin drawled sarcastically as the two men made their way to the back door of the apartments.

"True." Vincent answered shifting Shari a bit higher and tighter toward his chest. Reaching a hand under her very female body to shift the heavy erection bulging beneath his pants, he grimaced at the sexual hunger thrumming through his cock.

"We also won't have to explain the plan we came up with." Shan Lin pointed out.

"Excellent. It makes things much easier. This way, if she stays out long enough, we can just tell her we're married and be done with it."

Shan Lin scoffed. "You don't think she'll buy it, do you?"

Vincent thought about it for a moment.

"Sure. Why not? It makes perfect sense. She hit her head and won't realize she's forgotten. We can use the old amnesia ploy and tell her she must have forgotten a...we'll make it a week of her life. Trust me, things will go easier for us."

Shan Lin remained silent for a moment before replying.

"Or we could tell her a version of the truth." Shan Lin said.

Vincent grunted an affirmative as he walked down the stairs thinking about their first encounter with Shari. He knew her name was

Shari because the brothers had skimmed the surface of her mind when she'd opened the door.

The climax Shari had experienced upon opening the door had been a thing of magnificence. Even as practiced as he and Shan Lin were, there were few women they had both shared who brought his shaft so quickly to attention as this woman had.

In his mind, he listened to Shan Lin agree, then grumbled about the sexual tension both men still carried. There was an added bonus to it though. With this much hunger riding both Warriors, anyone foolish enough to engage them in battle would surely pay with their lives.

Reaching the bottom of the stairs, both brothers turned to each other with grinning smiles.

If only we could be so lucky. The battle would indeed be legendary, if short for our adversaries.

Chuckling at Shan Lin's assessment of the brothers' predicament, Vincent moved forward.

The woman in his arms stirred and mumbled something incomprehensible and Vincent shushed her soothingly. Keeping his voice to a low rumble, he stopped to work out a plan for getting an unconscious woman outside with no one seeing them.

"We need to get to a *Tear* near this building. Do you remember any?" Vincent asked as his brother reached the ground floor behind him.

Shan Lin looked toward Shari nestled in his brother's arms and suddenly had an overwhelming urge to grasp onto the woman and take her away from Vincent. When she was safely away from his brother, Shan Lin could violently beat Vincent bloody.

Where the Hellios did that come from? Shan Lin heard Vincent path in his mind.

Shaking his head and trying valiantly to dislodge the vision from his mind, Shan Lin looked into the astonished eyes of Vincent.

Extending his arms out from his sides, his hands palms up, Shan Lin shrugged in a helpless gesture, shaking his head. He was clueless. But what was worse, he had *never* felt this kind of killing anger directed at his brother.

"I'm...Vincent...?" Struggling helplessly to put into words his true sorrow at the stray thought, his complete bafflement, Shan Lin looked to his brother with all the love in his heart.

He heard Vincent sigh, then listened as his brother gave him an out.

"It's probably just having been in contact with our True Queen, and the sexual tension determined to ride both our cocks like a *griptou* lashing our bodies until we explode."

Breathing out the pent-up breath he held, Shan Lin grasped at the explanation. It didn't feel like the truth, but it was damned close, and good enough for him.

He saw Vincent look at him, then felt his brother give a mental shrug.

"At the moment, it doesn't matter," Vincent was saying. "We need to get to the *Tear*. Can you remember where it is around here?"

Shan Lin looked out the clear glass of the back door to the building directly in front of him and scanned the surrounding area. He knew there was one close by and almost missed it with the clutter the alley held.

He spotted the alley and could see the park, which he and Vincent had been heading for when they had spotted the woman Shari. They had both seen the determination the woman had when walking down the street. She had given off waves of anger that took little enough of either brother's telepathy to read.

She had been thinking of scenarios ranging from a particular man's emasculation and how she would love to be brave enough to do the emasculating herself. Or perhaps, hanging him by various body parts from hooks and chains and having him harassed by droves of women cackling about his sexual prowess.

Shan Lin had to laugh as the woman mentally shook the images away and began to prepare a wicked legal brief she would then send to the man who was starring in her thoughts, and another who looked to be in a position of authority. This was a woman whom he could get to like in a hurry. One who could indeed be an ally in any battle he needed to engage.

Vincent broke into his thoughts while he scanned the area for the *Tear* opening.

She has a truly amazing mind. I nearly had a heart attack when the car came out of the structure and hit her.

Shan Lin nodded absently as he remembered seeing the accident.

The woman had been in deep thought and hadn't heard the quiet vehicle coming toward her. The driver must have thought the woman had seen him because he had plowed ahead as if there were no one walking in the path of his car.

The brothers had begun to call out to warn her, but it had already been too late. They both watched as the driver of the car finally realized someone was in front of him and braked. But the woman had been hit by then and had landed in the street, stunned or unconscious.

Both brothers raced across the park knowing they were too far away to help immediately, but determined to do something. They watched in utter astonishment as a few seconds later the woman rose to her knees, then slowly to her feet with the help of a few good Samaritans who had rushed to her side.

They had stopped in their tracks and continued to watch as the driver got out of the car, went to the woman, and gave her something. She shook her head at him, then limped off in the direction she'd been heading.

The brothers looked to one another and made a decision.

"She's the one. She will take the place of the bride Aunt Sara assumes we are destined to find."

As they followed her, they began to speak of the strength the woman showed, and the foolishness they would apparently have to watch out for.

Remembering now, Shan Lin shook his head in wonder. The orgasm they had given Shari at her door was designed to heal as much as to give pleasure. It was a specialty Vincent developed along with the ability to ease the minds of those in need.

Seeing the view in front of him once more, he spoke to Vincent.

"I can see it from here even with the big metal trash recycler in the way. As long as there isn't much traffic at the head of the alley off the next building, we should be able to make the *Tear* we were heading for originally. One hop, one shimmy, and we'll hit home."

"Fine. Let's go."

Looking left, then right to make sure no one was about, Shan Lin opened the door and stepped through, Vincent following with the unconscious Shari.

* * * * *

Vincent stepped through the door with Shari still oblivious to the world. Using his body to hold the door, he followed his brother. He too remembered the scene they had witnessed. At the time, he had longed to follow the driver of the vehicle, which had hit Shari, but knew the more important job was to follow the woman they had found.

Now with all three of them making their way to the *Tear*, Vincent knew it didn't matter. They had what they came for and only needed to make their way through the *Tear* to Aranak.

"We'll make it. Just a bit further and..." Shan Lin's voice trailed off as his arm gestured to the opening both brothers could now see.

"Thank *Riad*," Vincent breathed, relieved.

He looked to his brother, tightening his grip on Shari, and prepared to step into the doorway to Aranak. He was suddenly brought to a halt by a hand on his shoulder.

"I'll take her through."

"What?" Vincent asked in astonishment.

"I said I'll take her through." Shan Lin spoke calmly. "You must be tired having carried her all this way."

Even as Shan Lin spoke, Vincent knew his brother didn't believe his own words. The weight of the woman could have been a mo-go cycle and Vincent wouldn't have complained.

Vincent stood a moment and heard the thoughts running through his brother's head. Shan Lin knew Vincent could carry his own horse across a running river if he needed to and one tiny woman would barely make a hitch in his stride.

Looking at his brother now, Vincent had to wonder if maybe Shan Lin had hit his head on the ground too hard when they'd come through the *Tear*. Deciding it would be prudent to hang onto Shari because of this, Vincent shook his head negatively and continued to make his way through the Realms opening.

"*Freching idjit!*" Shan Lin grated out as he watched Vincent step into the opening and marveled at the new and very strange feelings gripping him. They were foreign and unwanted, but they were there nonetheless.

Disgusted with himself, he followed his brother and Shari through the *Tear* and vowed he would learn to control what ran through his veins at any cost.

Chapter Five

Theresa could not believe her luck. Yesterday, she had been at the local Vid/Sync store reporting the situation to her Commander and a twenty-four hour pass had come through.

Thinking on it now as the transport made its way up the mountain heading for Naralin, she remembered the shouting her crew had done when she'd told them.

"You aren't playing us, are you, Captain? Please tell me this isn't some kind of joke we're going to be the butt of when we wake up?" Corp. Dyden, their resident Medic-Tracker, questioned.

He hadn't received a pass, of any kind, in the last eight months he'd been at Camp Grenlak. They had all been scouting or stopping skirmishes, and Theresa and her crew were more than ready for time off. Even if it *was* only for twenty-four hours.

"No Corp. Dyden. You're not dreaming and it's not a joke. We have twenty-four hours as of the top of the hour. I've synced in our reports from Hetcha and let them know about the fighting that went on, so we're free in about…"

Theresa looked down at her time holder and did the math.

"…eight minutes. In the meantime…"

Before she could finish, Lt. Roberts interrupted her.

"Sorry, Sir. What about the prisoners in the hold car? Are we doing anything with them, or leaving them as is?"

"Actually, we're letting them go."

The disbelief the statement caused was expected.

"We busted our asses rounding those prisoners up! What the hell do they mean…" This was from Lt. Roberts.

"…let them go my ass! I got a *bladestem* cut from the big one that'll ache for days! That's just *frech*…"

Theresa cut off the curse before it finished. She had allowed her team to voice their displeasure, but orders were orders. Holding up her hand in a gesture to silence her crew, she waited for the outcries to cease.

"Those were the orders. Last time I checked, this was the Queen's Guard, and when we're given an order, we follow it." She raised her eyebrow inquiringly and got the response she had come to expect.

In one motion and voice, her team came to attention and answered.

"Yes, Sir!" The bellow turned heads all around them and Theresa saw the looks of respect and contempt. Unfortunately, she had come to expect the contempt, also. The thought stayed only in her mind, but she knew her Aunt Sara had a lot to answer for.

Being niece to Queen Sara through her deceased mother, Gwen, never stopped Theresa from knowing what her aunt truly was. An evil entity to her core.

Theresa had then taken care of the prisoners herself explaining they were all free and it had been a bad misunderstanding. An inquiry would be convened soon, and she expected every one of them to be there. With Queen's Guard, or QG as it was often called, business taken care of, she would allow her team their freedom for the next twenty-four hours.

* * * * *

The following morning, her crew came back on time and ready for whatever lay ahead of them. All five of the men and women appeared to have come back renewed and enthusiastic. It relieved Theresa to see them a little more themselves.

"Next stop—Naralin." The pleasant voice broke into her thoughts. It was a good thing too. She had begun to sink deeper into the memories of just how she had spent the night.

Shuddering in sensual delight, she got up to get her gear. She smiled as she thought fondly of the two men she had spent the night with. Strangers they may have been at the start of the evening, but by the end, she had been making plans to see Kyden and Dylan again.

"Captain. Will we be taking any of this along, or do you want me to sync it up to the Camp?"

The smile fading from her face, Captain Theresa Lawsai became Commander of her unit once more.

"Sync it, Second Capt. Dresden. We've got a long way to travel, and the animals don't need the extra weight." Moving off the transpo, Theresa strode to the livery where they had stabled their animals.

* * * * *

Shan Lin came out the other side of the *Tear* into Aranak and immediately gained his feet. Looking around suspiciously, he spotted Vincent still holding Shari clutched to his chest. Making his way to them, he did his best to keep the expression he held on his face neutral. Knowing he had little hope of keeping anything from his brother, Shan Lin still did his best.

"It's all right, Shan Lin," he heard Vincent say. "You can take her from here. If I didn't know any better, I'd think we'd actually found our mate rather than the bride we were commanded to take. But that can't be as I don't seem to have the same covetous feelings you're showing."

Smiling smugly, Vincent gently transferred Shari into Shan Lin's arms. Immediately Shan Lin's inner-self shifted to a righted position. He could now look at his brother with everything inside him as it should be. There were no thoughts of violence running through him. He was at ease once more.

"Vincent. I wish I could explain..." Grimacing with shame, Shan Lin knew he need not. Vincent had already rifled through his mind.

A look of teasing tenderness covered Vincent's face.

"You have a *trant*, don't you?" Vincent asked, even knowing the answer already. Immediately, Shan Lin's cheeks pinked before tuning vivid red.

Shan Lin stood in front of his brother with Shari held tightly in his arms, and watched as Vincent, the one whom Shan Lin would kill and die for, the brother of his mother's womb and his own heart, began to laugh uproariously at him.

A growl escaped Shan Lin's throat as he took a step toward his brother. Before he could take a second step, he remembered the weight he held in his arms. The scowl curling his lips quickly turned into a look of joy as he juggled Shari's unconscious body to free up one of his arms. The anger drained from him as he cradled the woman's head on his shoulder as if she were a sleeping child, and used his free hand to stroke her face.

"She is truly lovely. I don't think we could have found a better bride for this mission if we had scoured the seventy-five Realms for a decade." The softly spoken voice came from Vincent and had Shan Lin lifting his head.

Smiling now, Shan Lin stopped stroking the woman's face and used his free hand to lightly sock his brother on the shoulder.

"Seems I'm not the only one with a *trant*."

Vincent, loath to admit aloud what his brother already knew he felt, gave a snort and started for the road leading to their horses.

And further on to Naralin. Home.

Yes, brother. It's time our bride saw her new home. Us as well.

His emotions too close to the surface for further conversation, Vincent set off to reclaim their beasts.

* * * * *

Theresa set a pounding pace as she and her crew made their way toward Camp Grenlak. She knew they would pass through the town of Naralin on their way back to the camp, and she also knew she was going to call upon her family to accommodate her and her crew for the night.

Besides, it was not much further, she and her crew were tired, and they deserved a night of fine lodgings and amenities. It would be a long time before any of them got anything better than barracks or a tent. At the rate her aunt sent missives to General Kristoky for battle movements, Theresa knew this war could drag out long after her own grandchildren had left the Realm.

Grandchildren.

Theresa shook her head and grimaced. It was so unlikely she would ever have children of her own, grandchildren would never even enter into her life. Shaking off the melancholy, which so easily crept in with those thoughts, Theresa spoke to her crew through the earmics the team always wore when on duty.

"We ride for another hour. We'll stop in Naralin where we'll find suitable lodgings. In the morning, we should have sufficient time to reach Camp Grenlak."

"Aye, Sir." The affirmatives came as Theresa cleared her thoughts of personal baggage and concentrated on what the report she had sent to the general hadn't said instead.

Yes. Her aunt indeed had much to answer for.

* * * * *

The modest lodge stood before the riders, a fence with a locked gate surrounding it. Shan Lin, barely reaching it before Vincent, spoke a few words, and the gate opened before them.

Still mounted on their horses, Shari tucked securely against Shan Lin's massive chest, both men rode toward the home they'd shared for the better part of twenty years.

I wonder if she'll see it as we do? Vincent asked Shan Lin absently as they rode through the cultivated lawn.

Shells of *tarkey* fish crunched under their horses' hooves along the flower-bordered drive as they made their way to the front door.

Don't know. Shan Lin shrugged causing Shari to mumble, but not to wake.

Hushing the woman, Shan Lin looked once again at his home and wondered just what she would see.

From where he sat, he could see what appeared to be a modest hunting lodge. Spacious, not nearly the size of a palace, it would undoubtedly fit into Queen Sara's personal chambers with room left over.

The outer walls were fortified with steel from the Klakin mines and provided both relief from intemperate weather, but also from invaders. There was more to the house than just what the eye saw, and the temperature could be better regulated in the underground portions of the house.

The windows shone in the afternoon sun, his favorite view of them at this time of day. Looking behind him, he found the sun shone brightly in the colorful sky. Glancing back to the windows, he discovered them strewn with the various colors of their world.

If you start to tear up, brother mine, at least let me take the woman. Wouldn't want you to sob and accidentally drop her.

The sarcastic voice echoed through Shan Lin's mind, but he ignored it. He would remember the words next time he and Vincent sparred. Smiling, he urged his horse toward the solid wood door.

Vincent was the first to reach the steps leading up to the door of their home. Dismounting, he left the reins on his saddle and murmured softly to his horse to find its own home. Patting it gently on the rump, the horse bumped its head against Vincent's chest, then turned and made its way toward food and shelter.

Before he took another step, a bald man dressed in a shiny, flowing shirt, butter--soft leather pants and knee-high boots stepped out of the door and began speaking.

"Ah, my Lords. It's good to have you home. And I see you've brought a guest. Wonderful, just wonderful! I'm always grateful to have company. Will you be wishing a suite made up for her? Near the both of you, of course."

Ignoring the hand stretched out toward him by Vincent, the man strode past Vincent and down the steps toward Shan Lin and his horse.

"Do get down off the beast and let me have her, Shan Lin." Before Shan Lin could protest, the man stepped up to him and grasped hold of Shari. Taking her with a reverence he normally reserved for infants and children, the man cradled the woman carefully, then turned and made his way back up the steps.

"Do be so good as to wipe your feet before you come in. Mistress Lichen has just finished cleaning the carpets and you know how she is about them. Don't forget to bring in all your baggage as Josef isn't quite up to the task. Poor man has suffered from another bout of the grimes."

Even as the man spoke, he continued toward the door, bent down to reach out his hand to the doorknob without jostling the woman he carried, opened the door, and on his last word, shut it behind him.

Shan Lin and Vincent looked to each other, shrugged their shoulders, then went about the tasks they'd been ordered to do. A smile lingered the entire time they worked. Whether the woman knew it or not, the man who had practically raised them, along with their parents before their mother's death, had just accepted Shari as the brothers' possession. Winters had just stolen their bride out from under their noses.

The woman didn't stand a chance.

*   *   *   *   *

Shari awoke slowly, a feeling of contentment running through her as she stretched her body languidly. Remnant feelings of her orgasm tingled through her, while her sleepy thoughts steered toward the wonderful dream she'd just had. Absently, she wondered why she felt so much better. Nearly all the pain had left her body.

Shrugging cautiously, and not about to discount possible divine intervention, Shari remembered the two men gratefully and with benevolent thoughts. Apparently, they had worked a miracle. At least the one beyond the unbelievable orgasm.

Two of the most gorgeous men she'd ever laid eyes on had just finished giving her the best orgasm it had been her privilege to partake of. Finishing her stretch, she reached her hand back under the sheet covering her to run her hand down her naked body.

I'm alone in bed, still slightly aroused from my dream, and it's not as if I've had anyone to share it with in awhile. Might as well indulge.

Following those thoughts, she closed her eyes as her fingers found the springy hair surrounding her pussy and she began to run them back and forth. She circled the hard bud of her clit bringing even more pleasure to herself. The image of two men standing at the door and beckoning to her to let herself come ran through her mind.

Each of the dream men stood stroking their shafts simultaneously as they approached the bed she lay on in her imagination, and her mouth watered at the thought of one of the men coming up to her and allowing her to suck his cock until they both came.

Shari's breathing came faster as her finger traveled rapidly over and into her now wet pussy. Her other hand reaching back up to grasp an abundant breast as she teased and pinched her nipple into a hard bead of aching need. Her sleepy mind awakened further as the heat of her imagination took over. She knew the two men she saw in her mind were going to do anything she asked, willingly be at her beck and call, and make her come at a moment's notice.

"Anything you desire, we shall oblige." The breathless whisper sounded in her ear as a second, then a third finger joined the initial one. Pinching her nipple and stabbing at herself, she barely noticed the voice was actually speaking into her ear of the wicked things it wanted to do to her.

"That's it. My fingers are three times the size of yours and will stretch your gorgeous cunt for my cock. I'm going to thrust it so deep and with such power into your creamy pussy, you'll feel it in your throat."

The voice dropped in octaves and became choppy in its speech, and Shari heard heavy panting, but hardly felt the hot breath on her ear as a second voice spoke into her other ear. Sleep vanished completely as the second voice, just as harsh, deep, and breathless as the first, joined in and began to describe a long list of sexual positions and things it was going to do to her. The orgasm, which had hovered just out of her reach, suddenly crashed through her, resounding and vibrating around the fingers jammed deep into her cunt. She let out a stifled screeching moan as her body went taut and her mind wrapped itself around the pleasures snaking through her body.

When all that remained of the release running through her were pleasant tremors, leaving her feeling relaxed and partially sated, she let the air out of her body and snuggled deeper into the pillow under her head.

"That was beautiful," a deep, gruff, and very excited voice whispered into her ear.

Shari screamed as she shot up in her bed, throwing the now tangled covers off of herself and leapt to her feet, landing in the position of a fighting stance she'd seen recently in a movie. She wasn't a trained fighter, but her male cousins had seen fit to teach her everything they knew and then some. She could, and would, hold her own with the best of them.

Her recently relaxed muscles now snapped instantly into a tense and prepared-to-die stance. She faced the same two gorgeous body-hardened men who had starred in her self-pleasuring imaginings. Her jaw dropped open as her mind took in the two naked men. Her quick glance took in their identical looks, chiseled features stamped no doubt from some genetic perfection running in their families.

Short, sable-colored hair, which looked thick and capable of sustaining many runs of a woman's fingers through it. Eyes, two different colors. Prominent, slanting noses, mouths which begged a woman to run her tongue over the pouting bottom lip and suck on the top one. Their chins rounded and pronounced.

At the moment, those two different colored eyes shone, almost literally shone, with scorching looks of hunger at her presently exposed body. Shari watched in disbelief now as their stiff cocks, strained slightly past their navels, twitched in unison, and seemed to stretch longer before her eyes. Looking up quickly, she saw both men looking once again at her face, their eyes full of lust, as they began to advance on her.

Her mind scattered at the sight of the men who stood before her, her mouth watering at the bulging flesh so readily available. But she hadn't a clue who these two men were.

She put up a hand hoping to, at the very least, stop their forward motion, and at the most, make them magically freeze so her mind could settle into some form of order. It didn't work. Their forward progress continued, and her mind finally realized it would have to order her mouth to speak.

"Wait!" Shari tried to put as much authority into the command as possible, but the word came out as barely a squeak. She tried once more.

Doing her best to look the identical men in the eye, rather than at the more tempting objects jutting from their lower halves, she again spoke.

"Stop!" There were still remnants of huskiness in her voice, but the volume had increased at least. Both men stopped, coming to attention as if to wait for her next command. Their lust-filled eyes remained glued to her naked form, but at least they were no longer bearing down on her.

She cleared her throat discreetly, gathering her thoughts, then tried not to stutter her questions.

"What have you...why are you...and those!" The questions seemed clear enough to understand in her mind as she pointed at the magnificent straining cocks the two men displayed so readily to her.

"Just who are you?" she asked, momentarily taking her eyes away from the men to make a quick glance around the room they occupied.

Finding nothing familiar, she looked to the men once again only to find them advancing once more.

Using the voice and tone she normally would have reserved for a homicidal maniac, if she ever ran into one, Shari bellowed as loud as she could. "*Stop!*"

Startled, the men stopped advancing.

Composing herself as best she could, Shari took a deep breath before beginning the interrogation.

"I'd really appreciate some answers. First, I'd like to know where we are. Second, I'd like to know who you two are. Third, and this is the important one," she paused for a brief moment. "I want to know just who the hell took it upon themselves to take off my clothes!" She meant the last to be menacing but found instead her words sounded more indignant than threatening.

The two smiled at her as they relaxed their stances but didn't advance any further. Shari watched as one turned to the other and casually landed a punch.

"Well, *Kasha*, I am Shan Lin and the ugly one here is my brother Vincent." He gestured absentmindedly. "We're in The Queendom of Aranak, and I," he gestured to himself, "would have been the one who stripped you bare."

Shari watched as he reached down to his still rampant cock and stroked it as he spoke.

"Your *shanti*," Shan Lin began, gesturing toward the bed, "was exquisite and tempted me beyond control. It was all I could do not to wake you by burying myself deep inside your luscious body." Shan Lin's eyes began to shine slightly as Shari's widened further.

Vincent turned toward his brother and gave him a none too gentle nudge in his side. Shan Lin winced slightly and Shari couldn't help but see his impressive erection twitch.

Not privy to Shan Lin's thoughts, Shari blinked quickly, then gave her head a slight shake. There was no way she had just seen the man's eyes glow like some cheap Hollywood special effect.

"Look...um..." The man had said his name was...her brain had gone blank. Something to do with a Sho Lin Warrior... Wasn't the guy's name Kane? No, Bruce Lee...

She rifled through her brain's knowledge of Kung Fu legends coming up with Jackie Chan, Bruce Lee, and Mr. Miyagi from the

Karate Kid movie. Limited though the knowledge was, she knew one of the two guys in front of her had a name that sounded foreign.

"Shan Lin and Vincent..." Both men spoke up in unison as if they knew she had needed their names spoken again.

"Yes, Shan Lin and Vincent. Right. What's a *shanti*, and when did I get one?" Okay. So she'd been about to ask something else. But how was a girl supposed to remember anything when hard-bodied males with large scrumptious erections stood in front of her naked and very willing body? Her own nakedness just reminded her it would be extremely easy to forget any questions she wanted answered, and instead rather made her want to saunter over to the pair and offer up her willing body to them.

Thoughts swirled inside her head even as she fought her body's instinct to let the pair have their way with her while she had her way with them.

Neither man seemed inclined to answer her questions and in fact began once again to advance on her. Shari shook as she thought out her possibilities. Looking left, then right, in hopes of finding a window to leap through, she was sorely disappointed to find nothing but art and unique objects on the walls.

Before either man could reach her, she stiffened her spine and came to a quick decision.

"No. You will not advance any further before explaining just why I'm here and why I seem to be held prisoner for a couple of sex starved men. I want clothing, I want answers, and I want them now."

She spoke quietly, yet authoritatively, as if perhaps these two men could be reasoned with. As if the two enormous penises were not swaying heavily as if to shout, 'Come and get us!'

Holding still and praying her voice had remained calm, Shari waited for the two to stop.

Much to her surprise, they did.

The aura of sexual tension surrounding the three dampened but didn't leave completely as they both came to a halt.

"Shari. We won't hurt you. You're our wife. Why would we want to hurt you?"

"Wife... Yeah, sure, I'm you're wife. I'm not buying it." Shari stubbornly refused to believe any word that came out of either man's mouth.

"It's true, *Kasha*. We've been so terribly worried about you since you fell and struck your head."

"We've anxiously been waiting for you to wake. It was all we could do not to climb into bed with you when we heard you moaning out in orgasm." Vincent moved as if to come closer when Shari held up her hand.

"But, married? What do you...*married*?!? Bullshit! I don't remember this and I think I'd remember a husband, much less two— I'm not agreeing to anything!"

Vincent came up to the side of the bed and sat down before her, reaching out for Shari. Before he could, Shari dodged his hand.

"Don't. I want to know how we met."

"There was an accident. Shan Lin and I followed you home. When we got there, we..."

"We wanted to know if you were all right. We saw the accident and..."

"...worried you would be in need of us."

Shari watched the two men with her mind reeling. They had seen the accident. They were worried. Even now they were telling her she was the only one for them.

"The only what for you?" Shari asked suspiciously.

"You are ours. You are the wife we have searched for. You are the one."

The unison thing. They were both speaking at once.

Shari took a step forward and turning, sat down heavily on the bed.

"Right. I'm the one." She looked suspiciously at the man sitting next to her and shifted a little further away. Snatching a loose sheet from the bed, she hastily wrapped herself in it.

"Is this a joke?" she asked. "Did Karen put you up to this? Is there a camera somewhere and at any moment, some famous celebrity is going to pop out and yell, "Just kidding. You've been caught on 'Film By Jorgio' or something? Or maybe Karen thought that if I was naked and in the vicinity of two well-hung men I'd finally get some? Or maybe I've died and this is..."

She was rambling, again. Shari knew she was yet couldn't stop herself. Talking faster and faster, she finally noticed the second man,

Shan Lin was his name, had somehow found his way onto the other side of the bed. And the other side of her.

Abruptly, her chattering stopped as she got a look at the man who had just climbed onto the bed. His eyes, both different colors as before, were back to shining. Suddenly sexual tension was flying through the room, her body responding to the pull the man was sending out.

"Hmmm." Shari knew she should object, though hadn't a clue to what she needed to object to.

Giving her head a tiny shake to clear it as her body responded to the visions racing through her thoughts, she closed her eyes and surreptitiously squeezed her legs together.

Opening her eyes, she found both men staring at her midsection. Looking down, she knew what they both saw. The filmy sheets surrounding her weren't meant to absorb liquid, and she'd given away just how she felt about the sex.

A vicious growl sounded in her throat, but the two Warriors ignored it and began to close in around her.

"*No!* Stop it."

Both men stopped at once.

Surprise passed for a moment across her face but Shari ignored it.

"Listen…I need to figure out just what you two mean by married."

"*Kasha.* You agreed to marry us when you orgasmed answering the door. When we explained why we had come. Right before you passed out."

"'Scuse me? Wait a minute. The orgasm was enjoyable, and sex is all fine and dandy. And, yeah, it would be frickin' marvelous with the two of you…" Both men practically purred at hearing the words. "But it sure as hell doesn't make us married. I need more than a good orgasm to be married!"

Her voice rose as she spoke and when she finally ended her rant both men seemed to have moved closer.

"Hey… What are you guys… Wait a minute…"

It was too late. Both men had come alongside her and were now taking each of her hands in theirs so they all held each other.

"We're glad you enjoyed the orgasm. We're ecstatic you think sex with us would be extraordinary. But it isn't why we married you," Shan Lin began.

Vincent cleared his throat.

"You have the other half of our hearts. They now beat in time with yours. Soon, you'll know us as no other ever will. You'll be in our minds just as we are in yours. You must know you are our lifemate. You are our bride. And you agreed to the marriage."

Shari listened, unsure if they weren't perhaps escapees from some sanitarium. One look into both brothers' eyes, and she wondered if perhaps she hadn't hit her head harder than she thought. These men were serious.

"You're my…husbands?" Shari asked thinking she had never said anything more ridiculous in her life. Husbands. Plural. Double trouble. Twins. Two of a kind. A pair…

"Shari."

Shari turned toward the sound of her name to find Shan Lin had wrapped his very hot body half around her own.

"What?" she asked grumpily.

"Please, look at me," Shan Lin asked her as he reached up and turned her head to him. Looking into his eyes, she could have sworn he was telling her the truth.

"I am telling the truth. But there are more truths you need to hear."

"Truths? What truths? I still haven't discovered if you're telling the truth about the three of us being married. What more truths could I need to hear?"

Vincent broke in from behind her as she slipped free of Shan Lin's light hold.

"We married you. We also took you back to our home in Aranak. It's where we are now. Aranak is located in a different realm than your own. In Aranak, twins of Royal birth…"

"Different Realm? Royal birth? What in the hell…"

"*Kasha*, listen. We'll answer any questions you have, just let us explain."

Doubting she could keep her comments to herself long enough, she agreed reluctantly, crossing her arms against her chest and waited.

"Twins of royal birth marry one woman, or one man. Very rarely, triplets are born. When a triplet birth happens…"

"What happens when…"

"Shari." Shari quickly closed her mouth.

"You are the woman we chose. We brought you back to Aranak, which is in the Realm of Azaya. There are *Tears*, rips in universes, where people can travel between realms. We were visiting…friends in the Earth realm and were on our way home when we saw what happened. We followed you, and the rest led us to where we are now. Here, married, with you."

As he finished speaking, Vincent brought Shari's hand gently to his lips. Velvety soft lips met delicate skin and left an impression on Shari's skin. Looking down at her hand thinking she would find some tangible proof his kiss had left an impression, Shari noticed for the first time the ring gracing her finger.

Astonishment crossed her features as she gaped at the triple braided ring on her finger. Vincent tugged her hand when suddenly, from behind her, Shan Lin brought his own hand forward. The three hands met together, fingers entwining in a caress and Shari noticed all three hands wore nearly identical rings.

"No…I… But I wasn't… How?"

It was the best she could do. Her mind had been clear right up until the point she gazed into the brothers' eyes. She had been so sure this was all part of some joke, some scheme…something or other than what it actually was.

They were married. Jesus. It was true.

"But why *me*?" she asked, knowing she couldn't be that special. She couldn't have been so special two men would come from another place just to claim her. It couldn't be happening.

It is happening. We knew it would one day. We couldn't have picked a more worthy bride to be ours.

Stunned momentarily, Shari abruptly pulled out of the brothers' embrace, leaping off the bed, and took several steps back from the bed. More importantly, away from the men.

"You're talking to me in my mind! Mother of God, I'm in a spaceship somewhere in a galaxy far, far away from Earth!"

Sinking toward the floor, she landed half-on half-off the cushioned pouf she'd almost backed into. Falling completely to the floor, she ignored the men who scrambled toward her with the intention of checking to see if she had hurt herself. Both brothers came over and lifted her onto the pouf, checking her body as she sat stunned.

"Married? *Fer cryin out loud! I'm married!*"

"Yes." Even spoken quietly, firmly, the word came from two mouths in perfect unison. "We can also read your mind."

Chapter Six

Shan Lin and Vincent watched as Shari opened the door and ran smack into a wall. The wall was currently asking their bride if there was something she needed.

"Good afternoon, My Lady Princess. How may I serve you?"

Winters. Thank you Father for Winters. Shan Lin pathed to his brother, relief in his words.

"What do you want to bet he has her ensconced in a comfy chair with biscuits and drink before she can remember just where it was she was going? In say…two minutes?"

Shan Lin chuckled at his brother and walked toward a seamless door in the wall. Opening it, he began to pull out a set of clothing for himself. Grimacing slightly at the thought of putting on anything to cover his raging hard-on, Shan Lin shrugged, then set his teeth against the pain to come.

The suffering was indeed painful. His cock ached to slide deep into Shari's pussy and pump hard until she screamed out her pleasure and he emptied the full weight of his seed into her.

"Shan Lin…"

The acute longing in Vincent's voice brought him back to the present and sighed deeply. Looking over at his brother sheepishly, Shan Lin did his best to push his craving need aside. He nearly gave into the overwhelming need bombarding them both as he felt the same longing in Vincent.

"Sorry. The bet is too easy. Trust me…" His voice paused as he listened to Winters comfort Shari and assure her he would have clothing brought for her immediately.

"He'll calm Shari down enough for us to speak more about her being our wife." Shan Lin's voice spoke to Vincent from inside the clothing room.

Vincent growled.

"Not that it matters, brother mine. The woman won't be leaving us any time soon, whether she wants to or not."

"No. She won't be."

* * * * *

Shari didn't know how it happened. All too soon she was surrounded by luxury as a sweet old man attended to her every need as if she were the Queen of England, or something.

She'd had it all set. She was going to walk out the door, find her way outside, and run for her life to the nearest police station. Once there, she was going to let them know two crazy men were on the loose.

Married.

Yeah right.

Unfortunately, it had not happened that way. The man, Winters, had gently grasped her arm and escorted her out of the doorway down the long hallway she had spied behind him.

Before she could demand to know where she was going, he had patted her hand in a fatherly motion and told her to leave everything up to him. He would tend to those two. His gesture had been in the direction of the room she had just left, indicating just which two he was talking about. Sniffing disdainfully as if they were scum, Winters had led her to where she now sat.

Shari nearly giggled thinking about it. The aggravated tone of his voice had been mixed with some other emotion she hadn't caught, she was too busy at the time gawking.

The room she currently resided in was a thing of splendor. Four pillars stood floor to ceiling holding the roof up. They were intricately carved with small scenes of what she assumed to be daily life. The chair she sat in now was made of velvety soft material against her nearly naked flesh. The rug she ran her feet back and forth across felt like pure silk.

Lost in sensory delight of the room, Shari almost missed Winters as he walked in front of her.

"Excuse me. Winters, right?"

"Yes, My Lady Princess? Was there something else I can get you?"

"We'll take it from here, Winters." Vincent's gravely voice sounded from behind Shari, startling her.

"That is unless Shari would feel safer if you stayed," this from Shan Lin, making Shari crane her neck backward to watch the two men walk toward her.

The sight of the two men sent her hormones into overdrive. They seemed to have dressed with the qualifications of minimal clothing required. The sight of them with hard-ons stretching above their navels was one thing, and could drive a saint to orgasm. Dressed as they were now in worn, matte-black, leather pants riding low on their hips, they were a sight to send any woman to the floor and worship.

Her gaze tried to take in the whole package at once, but her vision seemed to be stuck in the middle where the men's abs looked as if they would be able to stop bricks.

"Shari?" The rumbled question came from Vincent.

"Ummmmmm...?" Shari all but purred as she felt her nipples tighten and moisture began to form between her thighs. Her plan of escape was forgotten at the sight of the bounty before her.

Maybe she could stick around for just a little wh...

"Here." An amused voice spoke.

"What?"

Shari, lost in a world where those bodies were sliding under, over, and into her, turned dreamily to find Shan Lin on the other side of her chair. He was holding out some kind of clothing toward her. Admiring the rippling muscles in front of her, she absentmindedly took hold of the clothing.

Tucking the material in her lap, Shari reached out to touch the gorgeous skin. So soft and supple, yet granite hard. She hardly noticed the drool begin to collect at the side of her mouth.

It wasn't until a throat cleared to her right she reluctantly turned her attention back to a voice calling her name.

"What...? Oh." She prayed none of the men noticed the blush as she wiped the slobber from her chin. She tried to bluff her way out of it.

"Yes, well... Can you tell me what's really going on? You seem to be the stable one in this bunch."

Winters smiled winningly at Shari and she knew she hadn't managed to pull anything off. He was gentle as he answered her.

"Of course, My Lady Princess. What would you like to know?"

My Lady what? Maybe he hadn't been the one to ask after all. Straightening up in her chair and hitching her covering higher still, she tried again.

"Where am I? Let's start with that and go from there."

Winters nodded agreeably.

"Of course, My Lady Princess. You're in the Queendom of Aranak in the Realm of Azaya."

Shari gaped at the man.

"Was that all you wished to know, My Lady Princess?"

Quickly, closing her mouth, she shook her head negatively.

"Um… The *Queendom* of Aranak? The *Realm* of Azaya? Where on Earth exactly am I?"

"Earth? No dear." Winters reached out, patting her hand with a look of sympathy in his eyes. "You're in Azaya now. Earth is another realm in the universes. Here, in Azaya, you have Aranak, Horrd, Zynthia, Stocklem, Xaneria, Kled…"

Shari shook her head in astonishment at the man. He had to be a loon too. Even though he had stopped speaking, he was nodding his head in the affirmative.

"Yes, My Lady Princess. It's true. There are other realms. My Lord Princes would be more than happy to…"

This could not be happening. It could not.

"Shari."

She turned her head from Winters and found Vincent had been calling her name softly in a tone she would normally reserve for a person in shock.

"Shari, you really are in another realm. If, when we're done speaking, you want proof, we'll show you. But please, hear us out first."

Shari felt a hand grasp one of hers and turned to find Shan Lin on his knees at her side.

"*Kasha.* When we came to your door in the Earth…"

Shari opened her mouth to object to the term Earth, and was quickly silenced.

"...realm we did so to check on you. We saw what happened and were worried."

"But you don't even know me!" Shari cried helplessly.

Shan Lin stroked a hand down her arm again.

"It's true, but we went to check on you nonetheless."

Shari tried to imagine someone she had never met caring for her but couldn't wrap her mind around the possibility.

"It's true. We came to your door to check on you. There is something about you...a strength we sensed in you. We wanted to meet you and..."

"So you kidnapped me, stripped me, and stood over me naked with raging hard-ons until I woke up so you could speak to me?"

Shan Lin winced. *Put that way...*

Vincent made a rude noise. "No. We married you."

Shan Lin looked up at Vincent and tried to keep the smile off his face. The frustration in his brother's voice amused him. He stroked a hand down Shari's arm to gain back her attention. His grin widened as he watched Shari glare at Vincent.

"What my brother is so eloquently trying to say is we have need of you just as you have need of us."

Shari knotted her brows, finally turning toward Shan Lin.

"What do you mean *have need of me*? Outside of a good psychiatrist's phone number or the name of a great psycho ward, I can't think of anything the two of you would need from me."

"We're not insane, Shari. I swear to you."

Vincent's voice, when he spoke, was persuasive, seducing her to listen to the crazy words he was spouting. It was the only defense Shari could come up with to justify continuing to sit here and listen to the two men tell her these lies. Not to mention, to continue to sit there wrapped only in a sheet.

Vincent, who had been standing just a few feet away, suddenly came forward and knelt at Shari's feet. She stared down at him while he lifted her other hand and brought it to his lips.

"I'll make you a deal, *Kasha*. Why don't you get dressed, and afterwards, we'll take you outside and let you see Aranak for yourself. You can go into Naralin, which is the closest town to our home, and find out for yourself. If afterward you still think we're crazy, we'll send you home."

Shari listened and breathed a sigh of relief. If she could get outside, she had a good chance to get away. If she could just slip...

"However," Vincent interrupted her escape plan. "If you find you'd rather stay here a while longer with your new husbands, then agree to sit and listen to what we have to say, and find out that there really are more inhabitants in your Realm of worlds than any human could ever dream of."

Shari nodded her agreement immediately. She was going to be able to get out of this situation. With clothes on no less, and she wasn't even going to have to fight her way out. It was the best deal she had ever been given. The best thing anyone...

Shari forced herself to quit nodding and her brain to cease babbling. If she was going to pull this off, she had to pull her thoughts together and form a plan for when she finally got outside.

"Good. We'll leave you now to dress. When you're ready, Winters will be just outside the door to take you through the house. All right?"

Shari found her head bobbing up and down once more and kept nodding until the two men got up and left the room closing the door behind them.

Not daring to think they might just change their mind and come back in, Shari jumped out of her chair to dress. Fumbling with the clothing Shan Lin had handed her, she began to unravel the fabric and hurriedly slipped on the butter soft material, barely paying attention to just what she wore.

The pants fit her nearly like a second skin seeming to stretch with her every movement without restriction. The shirt sleeves ended below the elbow and came to rest at the top of the pants. The color of both seemed to be a mixture of sea green and teal blue.

All this, she noticed peripherally as she pulled the clothing on as fast as she could.

When the shirt and pants were on, she wondered absently if they'd forgotten to give her underclothes on purpose. Even though she didn't need a bra, even if it was just one more shield of a woman's armor, she would love to have one at the moment.

Thinking of shields, she looked around her chair, praying Shan Lin had left shoes behind and she just hadn't noticed. Even though she went around the chair twice, then got down on her hands and knees and looked under it, she couldn't find them.

She had to wonder. Had they deliberately forgotten to give her some? Did they already know she was planning to escape? Had they read her mind and wanted to keep her here even though they had told her she would be able to leave?

She tried to put some ummph into her words, not whimper if she could help it, but was afraid what came out was more of a frightened squeak.

"Shit! They still managed to only answer one question, and damn it all! I still need shoes!"

Chapter Seven

"You know she thinks we're insane, don't you?" Shan Lin asked philosophically as the brothers made their way back to their room for more clothing.

Vincent grunted moodily as the two brothers reached their room.

"As long as she doesn't hold onto the naive belief we'll let her go, she can think we're *freching lours* for all I give a shit."

Shan Lin grumbled an assent as the brothers grabbed shirts, socks, and boots for their trip to town.

"Why was it necessary to spring the bit about us needing her so soon?"

Vincent pulled the tan, button-down shirt on and sat on the bed to put his boots on before he spoke.

"Because it felt too much like lying to her and I'll be damned if I wanted to do that. It's not as if we have any choice about it. Yes, we've said we married her, but…" Vincent shrugged, "Then there's the Queen to worry about."

"Which one?" Shan Lin mumbled at his brother's words and pulled the leathery boots on. He felt the emotions running riot through Vincent and understood. Since the same emotions started churning in his own gut, he changed the subject.

"I have a feeling Queen Sara will be unable to read her mind. It was a steel trap the first time I tried to get in. You know, before she had actually made eye contact with us?"

Vincent paused in pulling on his own boots thinking on his brother's words.

"Now that you mention it, I had the same problem. Usually we can scan humans without much thought. I can only hope with Queen Sara's track record, your prediction happens to be the case."

Shan Lin stood as Vincent handed him the weapons the brothers had discarded earlier and began stuffing them in various places on his person. Vincent did the same once he gained his feet.

Mentally counting his weaponry, Shan Lin spoke, satisfied.

"That ought to do it. Just remember, treat her as our bride, and things should go well."

Vincent gave his brother a speaking look that said, "Do you think I'm an idiot?", before walking across the room and out the door.

Shan Lin snickered and followed in the wake of the sexual hunger that had yet to leak completely from his brother's body.

* * * * *

The tension in the vehicle nearly threatened to choke Shari. The brothers sat in the back of what Shari assumed was a proto-type car. One on either side of her, she experienced first hand the hold they were keeping on their bodies.

The tension felt sexual and she gazed quickly toward the bodies of the men. Both still had hard-ons bulging against the front of their tight pants. Shivering in response at the thought of just what she could do with one of those hard, sleek, *large* bulges. Shari did her best to push the thoughts out of her mind.

Think of something else, she chided herself, her own body beginning to react to the sexual tension.

She hadn't a clue what make the car could be.

Yes, the car! That ought to do the trick.

It reminded her of a Lincoln Town Car, yet not quite. She couldn't put her finger on just what made the car different, she just knew it was. And what a car it was. Apparently, there was no driver needed.

Dismissing it as unimportant at the moment, her mind began to race with the possibility she had lost her mind. If she could just get loose once the car doors opened...

She was so lost in her plans it took her a few moments to realize Shan Lin had begun to stroke her arm. He seemed to be trying to reassure her. Vincent had, at some time during her racing thoughts, grabbed hold of her hand, laid it in his lap, and begun to caress her palm sensually.

So much for forgetting the sexual tension, Shari thought wryly.

Looking down, she noticed her nipples poking against the material of the top she now wore. Hunching her shoulders in case one of the men noticed, Shari nearly cried out at the stimulation of silky clothing sliding against her aroused nipples.

Sucking in a deep breath, Shari looked from one brother to the other. Finding neither of them had noticed; she slowly released her pent up breath, then decided to ignore what they were doing.

I can do this, Shari thought determinedly. She would only be with them a little longer, and they weren't actually hurting her... In fact, the two didn't seem to realize what they were doing to her. Both men were looking out the vehicle's windows rather than at her. She wondered if either one was asked if they knew what they were doing, if they would have a clue what she was talking about.

Sighing inwardly, she acknowledged she could force herself to live with two delectable, if insane, hunks, fawning over her for a few more moments.

She looked out the window, expecting to find nothing more than what she saw every day in her own town, and gasped. Whatever country they were in was gorgeous.

Lush scenery flew by as the vehicle raced along. Vivid colors streamed past the car windows, interrupted occasionally by breathtaking fauna and flora. Tree branches swayed on standing timber, some as tall as skyscrapers, and flowers bloomed from their limbs. Here and there structures dotted the landscape, but the vehicle was going so fast Shari had little time to get a good look at them.

"Slow down." Shan Lin spoke quietly.

Shari stared out the window as the vehicle began to slow, barely aware of the spoken command.

The Realm of Azaya seemed to be a curiously blended mix of both old and new. Shari found, to her delight, a castle right down the road from where the brothers lived.

We must be somewhere in Europe.

As soon as she had the thought, she was immediately proved wrong. The huts they were approaching were near exact duplicates to ones she had seen in pictures of Africa and South American jungles.

The vehicle made its way past the huts coming alongside what looked to Shari to be tract housing.

Shari found her mouth had been gaping because Vincent reached a hand over, stroked her cheek with the back of his hand right before she snapped her mouth shut.

"We're nearing the heart of the town of Naralin, *Kasha*. From here on in you might see some things you've never seen before. If you have questions, or would like to stop, all you have to do…"

"What the hell is *that*?" Shari cried out as something flew by at an incredible speed.

She'd been trying to listen to what Vincent had been saying, but the blur of fur that streaked by the window had startled her. Even though the car was moving at a pretty steady pace, whatever had passed them a moment ago had zoomed by them as if they were standing still.

"It was a mo-go." Shan Lin said explaining. "It's a hybrid of a rocket and a land cruiser for two. Would you like a ride on one?"

"Mo-go? You can ride a mo-go? What kind of animal is it? A fast horse of some kind?" Shari asked in disbelief.

"No. It was a man riding a mo-go with a shag-rug for warmth." Vincent spoke up.

"He was wearing a carpet for warmth? Don't you have jackets here?" Shari asked, taking in the sights beyond the window.

She flashed back on what Shan Lin had said suddenly.

"A rocket hybrid? Are we in Florida then? Somewhere near NASA?"

Her mind quickly dismissed what she had seen.

"No, Shari. We're heading to Naralin, in the Queendom of Aranak." Shan Lin interrupted her thoughts gently.

"It was a hybrid rocket L/C, model 45 M-Class. It can go from nil to ocht in three seconds flat. It has dual cylendric cart-hars and gets two hundred frit to the coals. I have seven of them in different colors and…" Vincent began quickly, a note of excitement to his words.

Shari tuned him out. If she was in another realm, one thing was surely universal everywhere. Men and their vehicles. Vincent spoke like most of the guys she worked with describing in minute detail all the bells and whistles of their cars and bikes.

The words might not be the same, but feelings were. Even if he had been speaking a language she understood, she would still have been lost.

"What's nil to ocht mean?" Shari interrupted in the middle of his on going enthusiasm.

Vincent started as he stopped speaking, then squeezed the hand he was still stroking in his lap.

"Sorry. That would be...zero to eighty." He smiled lovingly down at her as he explained.

Oh lord, I might be in trouble here if he keeps looking at me like that.

Smiling a little in turn, she turned with the intention of seeing out the other side of the vehicle and glimpsed Shan Lin looking at her too.

Down girl! Shari commanded her body as her heart raced. Thoughts of flight left her mind to be replaced by images of these two men worshipping her body.

There was a fire kindling in Shan Lin eyes that seemed to send a message to her groin for an answer. Heat began to spread through her body at an alarming rate as she gasped then quickly turned back to look out the other window.

Too late, she realized her mistake.

If it was possible, Vincent's eyes held even more fire than his brother's. The heat starting to spread through her body began to pool in one place in her body, directly in the center of her core.

Shari squirmed as she felt the moistness in her pussy, and could have kicked herself. The more she moved, the more intense the feeling got.

"Um..." she began, as the two men suddenly seemed to have grown larger. The feeling of being surrounded, enclosed by a wall of desire, began to overwhelm any thoughts trying to rise to the surface.

Shan Lin no longer stroked her arm. Instead, he seemed to have scooted closer to her in the confines of the vehicle and was now stroking the nape of her neck.

On the other side of her, Vincent was now bringing her sensitized hand up to his mouth and scraping his teeth gently against the palm of her hand. A shiver raced through her body as he then bit down gently upon the base of her thumb.

She glanced over and found the heat in his eyes had turned up yet another notch. He was even closer to her than before. An almost physical impossibility in the small space the three now occupied.

"Er..." There was something she wanted to say, but Shan Lin reached out at that moment and laid his palm on her cheek turning her head toward him.

He was so close their mouths nearly touched, and Shari was tempted to lean just a little bit closer...

"Shari..." There was no need for her to lean in. Instead, Shan Lin moved to take her lips in a scorching kiss.

It began as a questing and soon turned into meltdown. His lips were hot and so silky soft as he began skimming them back and forth over her lips. A touch so light at first that she ended up leaning into him anyway. He opened his mouth and nipped at her lower lip gently with his teeth before slowly soothing the sting away with his tongue.

He skimmed his tongue down the edge of her mouth, trailing heat before the hand now holding her cheek slid down to her chin and opened her mouth.

A whimper escaped her parted lips before his tongue entered her mouth. It had been too long since a man had kissed her properly, and Shan Lin seemed to be making up for lost time.

His tongue touched hers briefly before moving on to explore her mouth in devastating thoroughness. He skimmed her teeth lightly, touched the sensitive roof of her mouth then sought her tongue once more.

The second touch of his tongue on hers roused her into motion. He slid his tongue along side her own, stroking one side, then the other, coaxing it into a dance of slowly dueling partners.

All the while she tried to concentrate on the wondrous kiss before her, she realized Vincent had not just been sitting idly by and letting his brother get to know her mouth intimately.

Vincent's hands seemed to have begun an exploration of her body. While Shan Lin's hands held her face as if she were made of spun glass, his brother's hands roamed her body in seemingly random patterns.

They had started at the top of her shoulders in a kind of massage that seemed to have loosened her body into Jell-O. They had traveled down her spine lightly massaging here and there along her back, and now were on her hips.

The minute she noticed them there, they moved. With a gentleness Shari never suspected Vincent had, he slid his hands toward her bottom leaving a trail of fire in their wake.

He stopped at the rounded curve of her butt and began to knead her cheeks like an expert masseuse.

A groan escaped her throat as Shan Lin's tongue started to pick up its pace. His thrust became vigorous, just as she felt Vincent moving behind her.

Vincent never took his hands from the position he'd taken on her butt, but Shari suddenly felt her ass plastered into the V between his legs.

Shan Lin continued his assault on her mouth as Vincent guided her body backward and Shari found herself sandwiched between the two brothers on the vehicle's seat.

Shan Lin took one hand away from her face briefly to adjust his position so Shari could breathe, but was soon back once again. As he lay nearly fully on top of her, she had her evidence of just what the kiss was doing to him.

A hard bulge nudged at the juncture of Shari's thighs causing her pussy to ache in response. A second bulge nudged the seam of her backside in nearly the same place Vincent's hands had been.

The feeling of two hard shafts nudging the entrances to her body at one time was heady. Her head spun and her hips began to rock back and forth as both brothers pressed their impressive hard-ons into her.

"That's it, *Kasha*. Give in to the fire burning between us."

Once again Shan Lin let her up for air and Shari drew in deep hungry breaths. All to quickly, Shan Lin re-claimed her mouth.

He stroked his tongue, in and out of her mouth in rhythm to the slow rocking of his hips. Shari quickly found the rhythm and matched him when she felt teeth scrape against her neck.

A cry of pleasure escaped but was quickly swallowed by Shan Lin. Before she knew what was happening, both teeth and tongue were nipping and licking at her neck.

Her pussy was on fire when Vincent bit the lobe of her ear.

"Do you like that Shari? Would you like me to do it again?"

Wanting desperately to say yes, she tried to nod her head.

It must have been a rhetorical question because before she could answer, Vincent sank his teeth into a spot so tender on her neck she near came right then and there.

Her thoughts were shattering rapidly now and when she felt the first questing hand on her breasts, she nearly screamed out loud. Shan Lin was making encouraging noises as Shari's hips began to rock faster onto the shaft straining against the confines of his pants.

She wanted nothing more than for him to stop what he was doing and take off their clothes to thrust it…

"You want his hard cock in your pussy, don't you, *Kasha*? You want his cock buried so deep inside your wet cunt he can never leave you. Is that what you want?"

Vincent asked the question, but Shari was too busy reacting to the moment when he closed his mouth once more over the nape of her neck and bit down hard. Shan Lin did his part as he ground his shaft into Shari's pussy, his tongue mimicking the thrust of his hips.

Vincent ground his own hard shaft against her ass, then bit down a final time when Shan Lin wrenched his mouth away from Shari's and the three let out a roaring scream of mutual release.

* * * * *

Shari panted heavily in the aftermath of her orgasm, wallowing in the afterglow. There had been so much light when she came Shari thought for sure she had seen the other side of heaven.

Opening her eyes now when she hadn't remembered closing them, she smiled up at the man looking down at her. His breath still heaved as he looked on, but a smile of tired joy shone back at her.

"Thank you, *Kasha*."

The words, in stereo, caught her by surprise. She turned her head and looked back to find Vincent nearly wore the same look as his brother.

Swiveling her head, she replied, "You're welcome. That was wonderful."

The men managed to right themselves and Shari, and she was grateful for their help. Her body seemed to have become boneless. Her limbs had been infused with Jell-O and hardly cooperated when she commanded them to move.

The brothers didn't seem to be affected as much as she was because they were already sitting up and alert. Shari had to wonder if the men were uncomfortable moving around with come soaking their pants but didn't want to break the mood by asking.

Although they didn't look as if they minded...

"We're here." Vincent's gruff voice interrupted Shari's thoughts. "Would you like to drive through the town, or would you rather get out and walk?"

"Here?" Her mind still refused to work. "Where here?"

It also seemed she'd been reduced to caveman speak. *Where here, indeed.*

When she did remember, she sat up all too quickly.

"We're in Narawhatsit already?" she asked stupidly. *Of course that's where they were. Wasn't it where they told her they were headed?*

"Naralin. And yes, we've been here for about twenty minutes or so."

Twenty minutes? She wondered just how close they'd been to the town to begin with, then quickly reversed the thought.

She didn't really care.

She had just nearly had sex with two completely insane strangers who thought they lived in another Realm. A Realm that wasn't Earth. In the back seat of a Lincoln Town Car. Which might or might not have a driver in a car, which was not a Lincoln Town Car, but sure looked like one. All the while a strange landscape had past by her with strange vehicles and...

Her mind was rambling. Or so she thought.

"Do not worry, little one. You haven't gone completely insane. If you'll look out the window there, maybe it will convince you."

Shari turned blindly toward the window Shan Lin pointed out of and would have surely fallen off the seat if the two men had not caught her in time.

There, for the entire world to see, was something out of a Star Trek movie.

Hell and damn and shit all rolled into one served with a twist! Dorothy, I'm no longer anywhere *near Earth!*

* * * * *

"But...? How did you...? What is..." Shari turned in slow circles as she gaped in wondered amazement at her surroundings. Her mind was having difficulties wrapping itself around what her eyes were seeing.

The scene before her could be Anytown, USA if not for the buildings with spacecraft hovering above them. And now upon closer inspection, Shari could see the strange animals. Cattle type creatures baying like hyenas as children walked them as she would a dog. They were also the size of a Pekinese and sported three tails with twice the amount of hair.

The buildings looked strange to her too. It took Shari a moment to realize why. They weren't brick and mortar as she knew the substances. They appeared to be made of rubber. Shari imagined if she stretched one, it would bounce back as if in a cartoon. Reaching out to try just that, she was pleasantly surprised to find them more solid than rock, but much softer.

"Easier to wash down and more practical. They can withstand a severe catastrophe. We've managed to create material that can withstand what you would term a hurricane." Shan Lin smiled indulgently at Shari as he explained.

"Amazing," Shari muttered.

Do I pinch myself?

"No, you needn't. But if you'd like, I'd be more than happy to show you the areas on your body a pinch would produce the most pleasure."

Shari whipped her head around at the husky suggestion to find Vincent hovering to her left, a wicked gleam in his eyes promising even more pleasure than she had recently found.

Cheeks flaming, Shari stared at him for a brief moment. Her first thoughts were a jumble of immediate escape attempts from this insanity. On the other hand, they were warring with the memories of pleasure she had found so recently in the arms of this man and his brother.

"You need not fight your body's natural response to us. You only have to ask and we will leave here immediately, allowing you to find as much pleasure as you are willing to take."

The purring offer was whispered in her ear by Shan Lin making, Shari shudder. She felt a hand come up to slowly caress her back in slow sensual circles, which left trails of pleasure skittering through her body. A soft moan sounded from her lips as her eyes closed on the amazing sights around her. Two other hands found their way onto her body. One of the hands wrapped possessively around a butt cheek and began a massage of its own. The other cupped the side of her face and turned it toward its owner.

"Anything you wish. Any time you want. In any way you can imagine, we'll give you. You have us until you cannot stand to be apart from us, until you crave our touch more than your next breath of life giving ether. We are at your beck and call for anything you desire."

Shari felt the butterfly soft kisses along the back of her neck and her body's response to them. Her pussy began to pulsate in time to her racing heart as her barely satiated body ached for its next release.

She was at the point of giving into the demands her body screamed for when a loud crash sounded. She tried to pull away abruptly from the embrace of the two men now surrounding her, but found it impossible. Both Shan Lin and Vincent had her locked tightly against their bodies and instead of the relaxed muscles she had just been held against, the two men's bodies had become hard as a stone.

Her head was nearly surrounded by the chests of the two men and when she tried to wiggle out of the embrace, a hand came up and firmly held her head still.

"Easy, *Juanita*. We will protect you. No harm shall ever come to you."

Shari snorted out loud, a muffled response followed.

"What?" a distracted Vincent asked.

"Leeeh hooo!"

"What?" Shan Lin asked as he finally turned his attention to Shari and eased up his hold.

Shari began to struggle harder in their embrace drawing in a deep breath. Glaring back at Shan Lin, then at Vincent, who had finally let her go, she gritted her teeth and answered once again.

"I said, *let go*!"

Straightening her clothing to give her something to do so she wouldn't hit either man, Shari ignored Shan Lin and Vincent and turned to find where the noise had come from. When she finally did locate the commotion still going on, her mouth gaped open once again.

"Everything is fine. One of the local shop owners had just dropped his merchandise." Shan Lin informed her unnecessarily.

"I can see that." Shari replied in an aggrieved tone. She watched as the man ran around what seemed to be a million tiny chicks running in every direction of the street.

Well, maybe not a million, she quickly amended. But there sure were a lot of them.

No one seemed to pay the man chasing the chicks any mind, all eyes stayed trained on the animals scurrying to and fro. In fact, most of the people walking down the street were doing their best to avoid the animals.

"Why are the people not helping him? They're only chicks. The worst they could do to a person would be to peck their hands."

She directed the question to no one in particular, but Vincent answered her in a conversational tone.

"Actually. Those are *krikers*. They're more inclined to open their beaks and take a hand or foot off, than to actually peck at you. The man should run in and grab some protective gear before he touches them."

"Think we should ask if he needs help?" Shari turned from watching the man nearly capture three chicks at once as she asked the question of Vincent. Then watched as Vincent almost hid a grimace.

"That bad are they?"

Vincent shook his head then turned to his brother resignedly.

"Stay with her, I'll take care of this."

Before walking off, he turned back to Shari, grasped her against his body, kissed her roughly yet thoroughly, then sauntered over to the now cowering man.

It took Shari a moment to recover from the kiss, and when she did, she began muttering to herself.

"I've got to get away before I convince myself to stay."

* * * * *

Shan Lin nearly chuckled at Shari as he watched Vincent round up a few of the men and women who were trying to hide from the *krikers*. It would be up to himself and Vincent to convince Shari to stay.

"Look at..." Shari began.

"At what, *Kasha*?"

"I wonder what Vincent said to entice those folks to help round up the chicks?"

"I imagine he asked them." Shan Lin said casually wondering if Shari had missed Winters addressing her by her own title. Shrugging it off, Shan Lin knew she would soon figure it out. Thinking to distract her, Shan Lin began to question her.

"Where would you like to start with the tour? Would you like to go to the top of the port? Would you like to see some of the *Tears* in the town? Was there anything particular about our realm you'd like to know?"

Watching Shari, Shan Lin detected her planned escape attempt retreat from her eyes, and waited patiently for what she would say.

"I...I think I'd like to see a bit more of the town before I decide. Would it be all right?"

"Whatever you would like. We are at your disposal," he said, amusement in his voice.

Watching her nod of acceptance, Shan Lin knew he and his brother had their work cut out for them.

What work? All you're doing is salivating over our bride.

Shan Lin did chuckle when he heard the impatience in Vincent's voice.

"What? What's so funny?" Shari asked as she turned from looking around Naralin once more to face him.

"Just watching the villagers rounding up the *krikers*. Watch when..."

Shan Lin was saved from having to further explain as one of the *krikers* chose to try for a man's foot just then. As the man dodged the *kriker* coming at him, one of the other *krikers* charged the man from behind, and with an enormous leap, latched onto the man's backside.

A howl of indignant pain, the man swatted at the *kriker* to no avail. The little bird hung on for its life until one of the women helpers came over and extracted it from the man's backside.

"He's bleeding!" Shari exclaimed.

"It happens. If they had been *kriker* handlers, they would have flak skin-suits under their clothing for just such accidents. It looks as if the owner of the *kriker* shop neglected to feed them. Or more likely, he's just getting a delivery and they need to be fed."

"What do they eat?" Shari asked suspiciously as she continued to watch the man limp off.

"If left to their own, they'll forage mostly on vegetation."

Shari turned giving him a look of disbelief.

"Those look like they were raised on a farm though." Shan Lin continued, ignoring Shari's look. "If they are, then they'll want meat. They're being bred for the military."

"What exactly could those tiny things be good for?" Shari asked skeptically.

"They do get bigger. In fact, they will eventually get big enough for a man or woman to ride or fly on. They're handy to have in battle when the battlefield is a long stretch of uncovered ground. Easy in, easy out, and if you're good, no damage to the person."

Shan Lin watched Shari as the last of the *krikers* were put back into their cages and knew she wouldn't believe him. It mattered little though. She would be here long enough to see what he was telling her was the truth, even if she thought differently.

She'll leave over my dead body, came Vincent's response to Shan Lin's thoughts.

Shan Lin agreed wholeheartedly.

Chapter Eight

Vincent joined them and they all made their way up and down the paved and unpaved streets of Naralin. Shari marveled at the things she saw. She barely paid the slightest attention to the two men following her other than to listen to their answers to questions she asked.

If she had paid attention to them, she would have noticed how the two men always kept her between them. How they steered her away from anything that would even remotely mar the pleasure she was having in what she saw.

Like now, they had stopped at what she assumed was a type of Radio Shack only to find out it was a Techio Trip.

"It's a what?" she asked for the second time as she gazed into the front window of the building they had stopped in front of. Through the window of the cavernous building she watched men and women of all ages, different races, and some with strange looking pets, prowling around electronic equipment. She watched as one of the animals who looked like a goat crawl directly through what looked like a speaker only to come back out almost instantly staggering on all four legs.

Before she could ask again, Shan Lin explained.

"A Techio Trip. This is a type of hotel you can stay in. Any kind of techno equipment out on the market today is in this hotel. You can spend a week watching nothing but what you want to see. You can spend three days listening to concerts of your choice, you can spend a month using the Pseudo Reality games and take reality trips around the different Realms without ever leaving your hotel room. You can set up an elaborate game of Warrior and Wasted, and slay the enemy without ever leaving your room. The most popular version of the game lasted for four and a half months, seventeen hours, and a couple of minutes."

Vincent interrupted his brother to further explain.

"There was a convention of techies here who took over and blocked off the hotel for six months. When they finally came out of the game they'd booked, they didn't know if the game had been real or if they were the last surviving members in Naralin. They wondered if they had offed every known person in the vicinity. The entire group ended up having to go through a program deprogramming before their reality righted itself again."

Shari shook her head. *Techies. Warrior and Wasted, program deprograms. Huh?*

She might not have understood what they were saying, but she got the gist of the hotel's purpose.

"Why is a goat in there though? Is it for a pretend sacrifice in the game, or dinner?"

Shan Lin and Vincent turned to look into the window for what she was seeing.

"What goat?" Both men asked in unison.

Shari looked once again for the goat going through a speaker.

"*That* goat. The one going in and out of a speaker over there." She pointed at the window and watched the now nearly dead on its feet goat enter and exit the same speaker over and over as it got weaker and weaker each time.

Shan Lin and Vincent began to chuckle and Vincent answered her.

"It's not a goat. It's Aharlin."

"What's a harlin?" Shari asked.

"Not what, who." Shan Lin answered this time.

"Okay. Who's a harlin?"

"Aharlin is a shifter."

"A shifter?" Shari asked inanely.

"Yes, a shifter. He's from Krinmal and vacations here every year. He enjoys staying at The Techio Trip. He shifts into whatever animal takes his fancy whenever he's here. Aharlin enjoys the feeling of orgasming in the vibration chamber as an Earth animal."

Shari nodded dumbly wondering if she hadn't stepped down Alice's hole and gone too far 'round the bend.

"Ok. Ummm… I think I've seen enough."

Before either man could respond, Shari walked further down the street only to come to a halt when she reached the end. Before her were huts made of crude materials. They were the same type she had seen on their drive into the town.

Thinking about the drive she became distracted remembering the feel of both men surrounding her with their bodies, grinding their hard…

"Um… What are those?"

Her question fairly shot out of her mouth and tripped over her tongue as she did her best to stop the reaction her body was having at the remembrance of her trip into town.

"People's homes," was Shan Lin's response. Shari thought she heard a smile in his voice but when she turned to look, his face held a bland expression.

"People's homes? Does that mean this is, what, the poorer side of the tracks?"

She watched as a look of confusion stole over the men's faces before Vincent spoke up.

"No. The tracks are on the west side of town. This is the east."

Shari grimaced before correcting him.

"No. I mean, is this where the people who can't get work live?"

Vincent shook his head negatively.

"No. These people chose to live like this."

Shari thought her jaw might be permanently lodged into the completely open position as she snapped it shut once more.

"But… Why?" she asked, baffled anyone would want to live in squalor. Because that's what it looked like, primitive, crude, nearly caveman-like. The huts were built out of what looked to be whatever the owners could find. Straw, bricks, sticks, metal sheets… Maybe the three little pigs lived there.

A snort sounded behind her and she looked back to find Vincent stifling laughter.

Ahhhh. They were teasing her.

"Very funny. People don't actually live there, do they? You were just pulling my leg."

Shan Lin frowned as he looked down at her legs.

"No, but if you'd like…"

He walked forward and reached out for her leg. Shari thought he might just be trying to really pull it and managed to step back quickly.

Shan Lin straightened, giving her a curious look.

"No. I mean, you weren't actually telling me the truth about people living there."

The curious look stayed on his face.

"No, I wasn't joking. People actually live there. Would you like to see inside one?"

Shari, thinking they might be taking this joke a bit too far, accepted.

"Sure, show me."

The three of them walked across the street and approached one of the buildings.

"Just go up and knock on one of the doors. They'll let you in."

Unsure whether to trust him or not, Shari hesitated. Before she could make up her mind, Vincent walked forward and banged on the side of the shanty.

It took barely three seconds before the entrance was opened and a man, dressed in what Shari could only decide was some kind of business suit, stepped into the doorway.

"Yes?" he asked looking at Shari.

"Er…" She was at a loss how to ask a complete stranger for a tour of his…abode.

"My Lady Princess would like a tour," Vincent growled.

Shari watched as the man's eyes opened wide, then watched as he bowed deep from the waist toward Vincent, before rising to stand proud.

"Anything, My Lady Princess. Please, my home is yours."

Shari looked from the man to Vincent before entering the man's home. Laying a hand on his shoulder, she felt the flinch he tried to hide as well as the shaking.

Without looking back to the brothers, she spoke softly to the man.

"What's your name?"

"Why, My Lady Princess?" he asked in a confused voice. "It's not important."

A low growling sound suddenly came from her right. She ignored it as she spoke to the man.

"Well, I can call you Sir, but if I'm to come into your home, I'd enjoy knowing your name. If you wouldn't mind giving it." Shari added the last hoping to quell the man's fear. Shan Lin's growling wasn't exactly helping.

And why should it? The man had been ordered to let her in, and now he was being growled at. Gently, so neither Shan Lin nor Vincent could hear, Shari leaned closer to the man and whispered in his ear.

"You don't have to let me in, Sir. I can tell them I've changed my mind. If you're afraid…"

"No. Not at all!" The man protested hastily. "I'm proud to have…"

"Get away from him, now."

Shari's head whipped around at the sound of Shan Lin's usually calm voice suddenly speaking in a soft, menacing whisper. She watched Shan Lin struggle to control his anger.

Almost before she knew it was happening, he was advancing slowly on her and the man now visibly trembled. Both she and the frightened man could feel the anger coming off Shan Lin.

Shari came to a sudden decision. Placing herself in front of the man's body, her only thought to protect him, her mind could come up with only one question.

"What the hell is going on?"

Shan Lin! Control yourself now!

The thought was as close to ice water as Vincent had and he prayed it stifled the *Try Nas Ayn* Shan Lin seemed to have developed. Stunned, Vincent made his way over to his brother but found when he neared Shan Lin, his brother, the other half of his near whole, turned on him.

"Back away. She's mine," Shan Lin grated out, stepping closer to Shari in an attempt to block Vincent's advance.

"Warrior Rayan! Control yourself immediately."

Shan Lin suddenly stopped his forward progress and stood still, his body visibly vibrating, as he seemed to fight himself. Several seconds went by as Vincent edged his way nearer to Shari, and when he finally reached her, he watched as his brother's body shuddered.

"Warrior Rayan?"

Vincent kept the command in his voice as he again asked his brother if he was all right.

"I am fine, brother mine."

Vincent held his breath briefly as Shan Lin turned to Shari who stood in front of the stranger blocking him from harm.

Vincent finally realized why this woman felt so familiar, and mentally shook his head in astonishment.

It seemed, she was their one.

* * * * *

Shari had listened to Mr. Freid as he gave her a tour of his home. For all his home looked like a hovel on the outside, the inside was airy as well as welcoming. Sparse as it was, she found it homey. There was no electricity, and when Shari had questioned him Mr. Freid had explained the lack of it to her.

"Technology runs through the realm for any and all who wish to use it. Electricity could be found in huts made the old fashioned way. With whatever can be found at the time. The insides of most of the huts you see here are completely modern with computers running the household. It's all in how we want to spend our money, and our time."

Shari had nodded absently as she listen to him ramble on about the way some people lived in Naralin even as she summoned up some explanation for Shan Lin's burst of possessiveness.

Shan Lin had been contrite, claiming he was overly tired with both his brother and himself just returning from intensive military training. Shari had given some kind of response, then kept her distance, and done her best to ignore what had happened.

She probably needed to get away from these two, and fast. Mr. Freid had just shrugged off Shan Lin's behavior and continued the tour of his home.

"Shan Lin really is harmless. I know you think he may have gone off the deep end, but it's not true. With our kind, twins who marry the same woman, this is what happens."

Vincent had caught up to her as they left Mr. Freid's home and began to explain Shan Lin's behavior. Shari listened reluctantly as they made their way back toward where they had gotten out of the car.

"Shari, Shan Lin's behavior stems from the fact you have yet to accept the truth. You are our wife, but have not acknowledged it. I too will soon start to become overly possessive of you, to the point where I will deny Shan Lin belongs to you also. It is the way of our people. It is how a marriage of three has survived for so long."

"Acceptance and equality are a must in a marriage of three. In any marriage for that matter, but it is essential in a marriage of three."

Shari listened as Vincent spoke and marveled at the fact she actually wanted to accept she was married to these two unique individuals. In her heart, feelings had begun to develop for the two men already, when in her mind, she barely even knew them.

"I know. We're married, but it's all so...sudden." Shari mumbled, wondering if she would ever have any hope of escaping now. Feeling silly, she realized the two men had already become important to her.

Vincent opened his mouth to protest, and Shari quickly waved away his reply.

"Was it love at first sight?" Shari asked in a small voice.

Vincent nodded, taking her into his arms, reassuring her with his presence. Suddenly she was being covered from the back too.

"My apologies, *Kasha*. *Try Nas Ayn* is not a pretty thing to see, and not as easy to recognize as I had thought. I fear it got the better of me for a time. Please, allow me to reassure you it will not happen again."

"Try a whatty?" Shari mumbled into Vincent's impressive chest, vaguely noticing her hands had begun to wander over the magnificent body.

Vincent and Shan Lin tried to explain, but the men themselves were rapidly diverting Shari's attention.

Funny how she had just done some heavy petting with two men she barely knew and didn't seem to be the least bit uncomfortable with them now. Oddly enough, her mind was even beginning to believe they really were her husbands.

Husbands. When she was alone, she was seriously going to have to sit down and examine the word. But for now, the feel of two large, muscled, hard bodies surrounding her was bringing back memories of the ride into Naralwhatever.

The men seemed to be feeling it too, if the evidence poking her from the front and rear was any indication.

The sound of her sharply inhaled breath sounded overloud to her as Shan Lin ground his impressive erection against her ass. Not to be out done Vincent suddenly unwrapped his arms from around her body and lifted her, bracing her legs around his body as her arms went around his neck.

"Vincent...Shan Lin." The huskiness Shari heard in her own voice shouldn't have surprised her. Already she was wet with the heat sparking between the three of them. From behind her Shan Lin began to grind himself deeper into her cleft, biting her neck sensually, as at the same moment Vincent ground his rock hard shaft into her pussy. Shivers of pleasure raced through her body.

Vaguely aware of where they were and the conversation they had been having, and suddenly not caring in the least, Shari made what for her was a bold suggestion.

"I want you inside me. At this moment, I don't care if we're truly married or not. I don't care what Tryyawhatty is, and I don't think I care much if I'm on the rings of Saturn in the Nebula Galaxy on the Millennium Falcon with Centurions following us. I just want..."

A groan sounded from Vincent as her mouth skimmed his chest through his clothing.

"The taste I had of the two of you in the car doesn't seem to have done the trick. I'm so hot...so wet..."

Her voice trailed away and with it thoughts of why she was doing this. Vincent leaned forward into her, his body covering her front as he took her mouth in a kiss that left her breathless.

"You shall always have what we can provide for you," Shan Lin whispered seductively in her ear, his voice heavy with arousal.

"Whatever you command." The words, spoken enticingly by Vincent, moved through her body, inflaming an already raging blaze in her core.

"Please…" The word ripped from Shari's mouth. "I don't understand what's happening… I…I don't usually… You're both strangers…"

It was all the men needed to hear. Sooner than she could ask how, a vehicle pulled up alongside them, a car door whooshed open, and Shari found herself inside, surrounded by the men.

"We're not strangers, *Kasha*. We're your husbands. This is a natural…"

Shari listened as Shan Lin babbled something but quickly cut off his tirade as she leaned her body fully on top of his.

"Shut up. I don't care." The raw aching in her pussy was nigh unto killing her and all she wanted was the pulsating bulge tenting his pants to ease her pain.

"Drive," the terse command was given in a guttural voice.

Chapter Nine

Shari was unsure how they eventually made it home. At the moment, she could have cared less. The drive was a blur of sexual heat and unfulfilled desire, with vague impressions of fuchsia sky steadily growing darker and the occasional greenish red tree whizzing by. Mostly, it was the taste and feel of Vincent and Shan Lin's bodies.

Somehow, the three made it into the men's home.

One moment, sitting in the car on Vincent's lap facing him and using his hard-on to torment her nearly beyond endurance, the next moment, they were exiting the car, Shari still riding his cock for all she was worth.

Vincent gently unwrapped her legs from his waist and let her body slide slowly down his own until her shaky legs hit the floor.

With a snarl of unfulfilled lust, Shari reached out and grasped Vincent by the shirtfront.

"Now. I've got to have you now. One…both…I don't care," breathless and panting with need, Shari did her best to begin divesting the men of clothing.

"If one of you doesn't make me come now…" It was as far as she got. A door slammed behind her and then she was covered in gloriously naked flesh from behind. Closing her eyes against the need coursing through her body, Shari leaned back into the hard muscled frame behind her.

"That's it, Shari. Give yourself over to it. Give over to your need of us. Give us all of you." Hands reached around her from behind sliding from her abdomen to her breast, ripping her shirt easily, then cupping the mounds gently before steadily increasing the pressure. Clever fingers plucked at her tight nipples until Shari felt the answering need in her pussy.

She was so wet she was squirming in her pants.

Tension snaked through her body, heightening her desire. Tiny cries, or perhaps desperate pleas, escaped from her mouth as she suddenly ground her hips backward against the rigid shaft once again aligning her ass.

The clever fingers at her breast continued pinching and plucking her nipples causing Shari to cry out. *God, please...*, she thought.

Her plea was answered immediately. A mouth latched onto her pants and she felt heat scorching through her clothing. The barrier between herself and the owner of the body part was little protection against the insistent mouth.

Shards of half pain and all delight started in her pussy making their presence known.

"Take 'em off." Shari gritted out in frustration. She didn't want the stimulation caused by the mouth to stop long enough for her clothing to disappear, but wanted more than anything for the barrier to be gone.

Suddenly, it was.

"Mine." A voice growled against her curls.

Shivering slightly the moment she felt the first touch of a tongue, a sobbing sigh escaped her lips. The tongue, gentle at first, started with a thorough lick from the bottom of her nether lips progressing upward until it stopped at the top of her mons.

"Such a sweet little cunt. I think I'll just eat it right up."

Shari's body flinched at the raw hunger she heard in Vincent's voice, then ground her ass backwards once more.

"Don't move." The harsh words, spoken once again directly into her mons, caused delightful vibrations against her body as his tongue finally found her clit. At first, the tongue merely gave her clit a few tentative thrusts before the gifted entity plunged into the folds of her pussy.

Leaning into Shan Lin as her knees grew weaker, Shari let the feeling of Vincent's mouth take over her senses. Becoming lost quickly, Shari barely heard the voice speaking in her ear.

"Well if he thinks I'm going to just roll over and play dead, he can get *frechied*. Spread those creamy thighs, *Kasha*, my cock can't wait a moment longer."

* * * * *

With some help from Shan Lin, Shari complied with his demand. Shan Lin gave a growl of his own the moment his cock came into contact intimate with Shari's ass. If he wasn't careful, he'd spend himself like an unschooled youth before he had even sank his cock into his wife.

"Now, *Kasha*. Open them a bit wider and allow Vincent the access he needs. Soon, I'll be buried so far in your cunt you won't know where we start and you end. And when I've had my fill of your sweet pussy, we'll get down to business with your ass."

Riad! If you don't stop whispering sweet nothings in her ear, I'm going to come in my pants. This...gracious Riad! Her pussy is the sweetest elixir I've tasted in my life.

Vincent, his mouth buried between the folds of Shari's nether lips, stroked his tongue in tighter circles around the outer rim of her clit ignoring it as he explored his find.

Hey, you got the first taste, the least I should have is the first stroke. I want her wetter than a Warrior on water detail. Now mind your manners and don't eat it all.

A husky laugh escaped Shan Lin as he let go of one of Shari's nipples. He used the hand to wrap around his cock. Guiding the way, he used his impressive length to stroke Shari's drenched opening. The exquisite feel of her silky wetness brought shivers of pleasure to his frame and he shuddered at the contact. Starting a slow rocking motion, Shan Lin twisted forward, raking the tip of his hot shaft between the folds of her entrance.

"Is this what you want?" he asked, gritting his teeth against the need to thrust deeply into the hot, creamy liquid she expelled.

The barely coherent sounds escaping her mouth assured Shan Lin the brothers had her full attention. Wanting desperately to make their first time last forever, Shan Lin continued stroking just the tip of his engorged cock back and forth, he felt Vincent finally take Shari's clit into his mouth.

The scream erupting from her told the brothers everything.

"May I enter?" Shan Lin asked, his breath coming in pants as the tenuous hold on his control slipped another notch.

The only response he received from Shari was heavy panting. It took three tries before she responded.

"You're asking me, *now*?" The words tore from her throat gutturally. "Yeeeesss! God ye..."

Shan Lin waited no longer. Feeling as if it was his first time, he guided his slicked tip to her channel and thrust into her tight pussy with one steady thrust. He barely heard Shari suck in her breath before she let it out on a scream in the next moment. The taut inner walls of her pussy clenched Shan Lin's already over stimulated cock and he hung on firmly as she milked his cock dry.

* * * * *

Shari's head spun as she found herself abruptly disengaged from Shan Lin. Before she could gather a coherent thought, Shan Lin lifted her up, repositioned her against himself and entered her pussy rapidly from behind once again. Contorting her legs so they were wrapped behind his back and flush with his hips, he left her front completely open to the elements. She felt like an acrobat in the circus, bent any which way needed to achieve the maximum result.

Too heady from her recent release to mind very much about the breeze hitting her extremely exposed body, Shari clung to Shan Lin as tiny tremors continued through her pussy. Shan Lin walked faster, Vincent nearly running ahead of them, as the three made their way to a room on their left.

Shari watched bemused as Vincent stalked through mumbling something about firsts through the door. Smiling lazily, her body beginning to respond to the jostling it received, Shari let out a stimulated keen. Vincent turned at the sound and Shari watched as he peeled himself rapidly out of his clothing.

"Mine. Give her to me." The words commanded immediate obedience. Shan Lin chose to ignore them.

One moment, brother mine. The feel of her channel tightening around my cock is exquisite.

Shan Lin thrust himself once more into her pussy and Shari cried out at the friction. Her eyes closed briefly and when she managed to pry her lids apart once more, she found herself staring into the eyes of a savage predator.

The dual colored eyes of Vincent were glowing.

Managing to swallow the lust brought on by Shan Lin so soon after her recent climax, Shari tried to curl into Shan Lin further. He seemed to instantaneously sense her problem.

"*Kasha*, relax. This is a normal reaction for an Aranakian husband. The glowing eyes are a telltale sign your husband is extremely eager to mate. If you turn and look into my eyes, you'll find the same glow."

Shari swiveled her head around and found Shan Lin's eyes the same.

"You...you're sure yyyy... Not demons...are you?" she asked as the glowing wonder of her climax began to fade.

"Does this feel evil to you?" Shan Lin asked as he shifted his hips to emphasize his point.

Unintelligible words flitted through Shari's mind but she could not grasp hold of even one firmly.

"Mine." A voice growled once again.

"Yessssss." Shari spoke, her mind now firmly focused on the movement of Shan Lin's hips.

Before she had time to protest, Shari's legs were unwrapped from around Shan Lin's hips as he apologized for having to leave her. Quickly unsheathing himself from her warmth, Shan Lin kissed her cheek as he gently handed her to Vincent.

Shari protested, but her words were drowned out by Vincent's tongue swooping into her mouth and engaging her own. Shari returned his thrusts hungrily as her body began to clamor for more of the sexual play it had recently gotten.

Coming up for air, Shari gasped as Vincent's mouth moved rapidly from her lips to her neck.

"More," she begged helplessly as she felt the tip of his shaft nudge the entrance to her painfully aroused pussy. Lips and teeth tasted their way up her neck and bit down on the lobe of her ear before Vincent's tongue soothed away the tiny pain.

"May I enter?" Shari heard Vincent grate out as she squirmed her body in an attempt to mount the thick head of his cock.

Incredulous, Shari shrieked.

"God yes! Stop asking me and just dooooooo..." Once again her breath left her as Vincent slammed his cock to the hilt into her already wet passage and began to piston his hips wildly.

Her oversensitive body shuddered into a climax instantly as she bit down hard on his shoulder. Vincent continued to pump his hips and within moments followed her.

* * * * *

Once again Shari found herself sated, her body still pulsing deeply as Vincent rocked his hips against her body.

She marveled at the turn her mind had taken since the trip into town. No doubt about it, she was a believer. These two men had married her, brought her to their home, and claimed her.

Hell, they were still claiming her.

She felt as if she was a maiden in some medieval romance taken by the knight of the Realm and...

Knights. There were two of them.

"*Kasha*," Vincent rasped as Shari shifted her hips higher.

Shari smiled thinking two could play this game.

"Would you like us to capture you as knights would a true maiden? We would be more than happy to clap you in chains and take your virtue. First, it would be our duty to see you submit. We could command you perform any sexual act we chose."

The words, spoken in a rough timbre, caused a shudder to rip through Shari's body.

"For me, I think you would need to coax my cock into a response with your mouth. To begin, you would lick the tip and swirl your tongue around the head. Then, bit by bit you would have to tease it into responding by taking it into your mouth...slowly...an inch...at...a...time."

Shari could barely countenance it as her pussy began to contract for a third time. No small ripples, only hard, pulsing contractions, held Vincent's shaft as her body undulated in climax.

"That's it." A deep voice purred sounding pleased.

"Brother mine. I do believe she might like it." Vincent grated out holding still as Shari's mind numbing climax continued.

"Do you trust us?" Shan Lin asked a few moments later.

Shari never thought about it before answering in the affirmative. Strangely enough, she already did.

* * * * *

It was sometime later Shari found herself blindfolded and physically restrained.

A length of some kind of nylon had been hung from the ceiling and her hands had been placed into velvet lined cuffs. Her feet had been spread apart at a forty-five degree angle and clamped in metal, lined in the softest fur her body had ever touched. Then the blindfold had been placed over her eyes and she strained to listen for sounds of what was happening.

Nothing. Not a thing had happened for some time. Shari waited in anticipation for the men to come and ravish her, but nothing happened. She waited, her body tense, and still, nothing. It was driving her crazy.

Were they going to leave her hanging here and go off on some jaunt? What if someone came in while she hung there, naked for all to see? Would someone take advantage of her vulnerable position?

"At this point, would you care?"

Shari nearly leapt out of her own skin. Was that her voice, husky from the tension thrumming through her body? She squirmed again and found her pussy was wet enough to begin running down the inside of her leg.

"Christ, I'm pathetic! Give a woman a fantasy and..." When she got out of this, Shari was going to give those two as good as she wasn't getting right now.

To make matters worse, the fur and silk seemed to be alive. Tiny tongues of heat lashed her wrists and ankles as Shari squirmed in their hold.

I agreed to this, Shari reminded herself, shivering at the loss of sight the blindfold took. She could only imagine what came next and her imagination was working overtime at the moment.

Startled by a sound behind her as Shari felt deliciously hot breath on the back of her neck. Lips feathered their way back and forth and Shari strained to listen for some sign of recognition.

"Wh-whooo..." Shari winced, clearing her throat. "Who are you?"

The words whispered out and she mentally kicked herself for being afraid. Of course it had to be either Shan Lin or Vincent. They were the only ones who knew she was here.

Right?

Shari groaned out loud as the lips became teeth scraping along the sensitive nape of her neck. Her nipples tightened, puckering into tiny buds as another set of lips wrapped themselves around one puckered nipple.

"Please." The question came out huskily. "Who are you?"

The only answer was a quiet, aroused chuckle.

Vincent. Shari let her pent up breath release as she thought she recognized his laugh.

A hand cupped the bottom of her other breast and slid upward where fingers grasped lightly at her nipple. The fingers plucked at and rolled the sensitive nipple, squeezing first hard, then lightly. Fingers rimmed the puckered bud, then clamped down and began the process again and again.

The teeth found purchase on her over-stimulated skin and bit down, sucking lightly, then moving on to the next area they found.

A hand behind her, skimmed down her butt cheek, kneading the plump cheek softly. A thumb massaged toward the slit of her ass, then with wider circles it nearly reached her puckered hole before stopping and making its way back to its original position, then starting all over again.

A third callused hand touched her stomach, causing Shari to suck in her breath. As it made its way lower, stopping briefly to circle her navel, the breath she held rushed out.

Fingers slid at a leisurely pace, lightly down her skin, spreading outward as it met springy, wet hair. Barely pausing in their forward progress, the fingers continued their way toward Shari's silky nether lips. Skimming slowly down the outside of her moist folds, the fingers dipped near her bottom before their path reversed and journeyed upward producing exquisite friction along the way.

"More?" a purring voice inquired.

Shari nodded dumbly, her senses reeling from the contact of hands, lips, and teeth. The hand delving through her pussy began to make its way down the inside of her thigh, then back upward, slowly, oh so slowly, causing her to swing her hips minutely.

If I could just get this blindfold off... Shari began.

A fourth hand joined in on her other ass cheek and kneaded in tandem with its partner. Thoughts of losing the blindfold fled.

"More?" Another voice whispered into Shari's opposite ear as the mouth at her neck moved to her other earlobe. The fingers traversing up her inner thigh made their way back up to her pussy and dipped inside briefly.

Shari tried to bend her shaking knees to allow better access but was prevented from doing so when the length of nylon strained to its full breadth.

A frustrated cry escaped before she could stop it. Then, a tiny whimper, as the fingers left her channel and traversed, once again, upward. She stifled her cries as she bit her lip and waited.

She was soon rewarded as fingers began to tickle her clit.

Stifling the moan wanting to escape, Shari quivered in pleasure.

"More?" the voice queried again.

"Please..." It was all she could manage. Thoughts of what could possibly come next overwhelmed her. The pair of hands kneading her ass were, in turn, stretching her cheeks apart, then massaging them. A finger had begun to rim her puckered hole, occasionally scraping against one lip of her pussy.

Just how many hands are there on me now? Shari asked herself as she felt those same hands tormenting her. Logically, she knew there were only four, but damned if it didn't feel like multiple sets were teasing her.

The fingers at her nipple pinched harder as the mouth opposite them sucked harder. Teeth sank roughly into her neck quickly followed by a soothing tongue.

Then everything stopped as suddenly as it had begun.

Shari nearly screamed, her body on fire, her senses reeling from pleasure.

"More," she ground out.

The only response was heavy panting from more than one person.

"Please. Shan Lin? Vincent?"

Her cries went ignored.

Grabbing onto the nylon as best she could, Shari tried to yank the material out of the ceiling. It held, just as she knew it would. Snapping out in frustration, Shari tried again.

"I demand my bridal rights as a maiden. Do me now!"

The heavy breathing slowed before stopping altogether.

Okay. I can do this. It's not the first time I've been denied sex. I can handle it.

How bad could it be? So she would have to wait a bit. No big deal.

* * * * *

Riad! If I don't sink my cock into her cunt soon, I'm damned sure I'll have to go kill somebody!

Vincent pathed tightly as he, and Shan Lin waited. They would give her five minutes before her body calmed; then they could begin their tormenting again.

She is still debating if it is us. I wonder if it would make her hotter to think that we truly might not be Shan Lin and Vincent?

Vincent grinned at his brother's thoughts.

We could always save that game for next time.

Shan Lin nearly laughed out loud.

Deal, brother mine.

Have you noticed she is already comfortable with us? There is no hesitancy in her trust of us. Do you think she knows we truly did marry her with the asking? Vincent asked, not caring for a negative answer but waiting just the same.

Regardless of why we claimed her, she is now truly our wife. We asked entrance into her body and she gave it willingly. The Aranak laws have been fulfilled. She is now our mate.

Vincent agreed absently, his next thought so tight he wondered if Shan Lin might not glean it.

Now she must claim us truly, or we all shall perish.

* * * * *

Shari's thoughts were not nearly so morbid. At least about dying, killing on the other hand... The thought held great appeal.

The thought came out of nowhere, but Shari agreed with it. She had worked herself up nearly as much as the hands, teeth, and mouths had done and her body was still on fire. She wanted to scream out her frustration but knew it would only work her up more.

Panting heavily, she tried to hold her body still.

No dice. Her body was screaming in acute frustration needing immediate release.

"Please..." she whispered, her frustration bringing a tear to her eye and a plea to her voice. She was so horny, one touch in the right place and she would go over the edge.

And then the mouths, hands, teeth, and tongues were back, working her into another frenzy. This time, the fingers did not just rim her asshole, they delved gradually inward, stretching at intervals as if to accustom her opening to the intrusion. Each time she thought she couldn't take another millimeter into her body, the fingers stopped. She nearly groaned aloud in frustration at the cessation but never needed to. Once again, before she knew she was ready to continue, another inch sank deeper.

The fingers, which had previously dipped into her channel, now sank in fully, stroking her, filling her. She began to rock her hips, first forward, jamming them on the fingers in her pussy, then backward, sinking onto the fingers slowly filling her backside. Her mind imagined her body filled with cocks and Shari came screaming her release until the breath left her body.

When the muscles of her body stopped convulsing, Shari found her body truly was filled with cocks. Her mind connected the fact and her body responded.

"More?" Two voices asked simultaneously, passion spilling from the word.

"Fuck me...please."

Shari was too far gone in desire to realize what she said, but the voices took her at her word. Hips pistoned wildly into her pussy and ass, and Shari held on, reveling in the attention her body received.

Her climaxes came one on top of another until finally her mind overrode her body and she passed out.

* * * * *

It was sometime later that Shari awoke surrounded by bodies and immersed completely in warm fluid. Her first and only thought was thanks.

"Our pleasure, *Kasha*. You are our bride. Our life. You are our heart and soul. What you desire, what you command, is ours to give," two gravely voices crooned.

"Did we pleasure you well?" Shan Lin asked as he ran a soapy cloth down Shari's breast.

Shari stretched briefly, wincing at her body's delicious aches and smiled, her eyes closing in memory of the love play the two men had given her.

"Immensely. I'd even enjoy a repeat."

The shaft currently resting against her backside twitched and Vincent spoke in her ear.

"We can arrange it, *Kasha*. All you have to do is ask."

Preparing to lift her onto his lap, Shari forestalled him.

"Just as soon as I have a nap. It's been a long day. It's not everyday a woman leaves…home and finds herself married. To two men. In another realm…"

Shari's voice trailed away as her mind began to think of more than sex. She would have to explore that line of thought further. Snuggling against Vincent's chest a bit more, Shari lay there and allowed the men to tend her.

Just as soon as she had a nap.

* * * * *

Theresa pounded on the door and simultaneously yelled, "Get your lazy asses out here. The night's not fit for beast nor woman, and we need shelter."

Theresa smiled, knowing her crew would get a kick out of seeing their Commander ordering Warriors to do anything. Any one of the people in her unit could stand the rain, and they could have even traveled through the night. But as the Captain had known, the crew would enjoy seeing the Warriors, and she was loathe to let the opportunity to spend a night under part of her family's roof pass her by.

Turning back to the door and raising her fist once more to smash against the wood, she quickly jerked it back when the heavy door opened silently and Winters stuck his head out.

"Ah, my little *Bricka*. Come in. Come in. If you'll give me your gear, I'll store it for you and have rooms prepared."

Theresa smiled as she walked into her cousins' home and prepared to make herself comfortable. Stopping on the other side of Winters as he held the door, Theresa took off her protective head gear.

"Are they in, Winters?" she asked him around the rest of her crew coming through the door.

"Yes, they are. At present, they are making their wife comfortable in her new home. Shall I send for them, or would you rather find them yourself?"

Smiling wickedly, and very curious to see the woman who pinned down two of the most eligible bachelors Aranak had on it, Theresa opted to find them herself.

"I'll go, Winters. I know where they are. Anything you'd like me to tell them?"

Fighting a grin of his own, Winters answered her.

"Please inform their Highnesses dinner will be served in five minutes."

A sound came from one of her crew and had her looking to them. Standing in the foyer of her cousins' home, her crew seemed to be in awe. She couldn't really blame them, and going forward after exchanging a look between herself and Winters, she did her level best to reassure her crew they weren't walking into the enemy's camp.

Hearing the words 'Vicious Warrior' and 'Death Bringer', Theresa held back her smile.

"Ladies and Gents. This is my cousins' home. The Rayan Princes' may be hell on their enemies, but to friends, they are gracious hosts. Please, follow Winters who'll show you to your rooms. I want you back here in five minutes ready to dine with our hosts."

"Yes, Sir!"

Mari Byrne

"Dismissed." Theresa turned and headed in the direction of her cousins' rooms as her crew went in the opposite direction, awe still clearly showing on their faces.

Making her way into the spacious living area of the house, Theresa passed countless objects of her and her cousins' trade. Swords hung on the walls next to priceless paintings that hung beside more objects of a Warrior's trade. She ignored them now as she had when she'd visited the house the last time. They were part of her childhood and had hung there forever.

She continued toward a hallway off to her left that segued to another hallway toward her left. If someone didn't know their way around the house, they could easily get lost.

Coming to a doorway on her right, she opened it to find an airlift. Stepping in, she punched the button marked with three lines, and waited for the lift to engage.

The ride was short, and opening the door now in front of her, she stepped out into another foyer. The door directly in front of her belonged to the apartments of her cousins', Shan Lin and Vincent.

Not bothering to knock, she walked right in. The moment she opened the door she heard a woman's agitated voice and knew she would soon be meeting her marriagecousin. She listened a moment, then continued on toward the voices.

"...don't care who you are. Put some clothes on. While very impressive, I don't go around speaking to naked aroused men every day and I'd..."

The woman's voice trailed off as she spotted Theresa.

"Hello. Sorry to interrupt, but Winters says dinner will be ready in five. Boys, better get a move on and dress like the lady asked."

The moment she'd opened her mouth, the Warriors sprang into action. Both men, naked as the day they had been born, put their bodies in front of the obviously naked woman, protecting every part of her. The looks on their faces told Theresa everything she would have questioned them about. This was their life-mate, their soul-mate, pure and simple. *Riad* help anyone who harmed her.

The smile stayed on her lips even if it dimmed at the thought she'd never have her own set of twins. She relaxed her stance as casually as possible and waited for the bloodlust to leave her cousins' eyes. The wait was not long.

* * * * *

"Theresa!" Shan Lin and Vincent cried in unison and relaxed their stance around their wife. They both started forward to greet her but halted quickly when she held up her hand for them to stop.

"Your wife's right. They're impressive all right," she gestured toward their midsection, "but I agree with her when she says you need to put some clothes on. I don't mind for myself, but my crew might be a little discomfited by your dinner attire."

Vincent watched the smile on her face strengthen into a real one as she spoke, and even though he'd forgotten his state of dress, he was glad Theresa had been able to laugh at their expense. It had been too long since most people had seen a real smile light her eyes, and not just her face.

"Since our wife insists, we'll dress." Vincent heard Shan Lin speaking to Theresa even as he heard his brother silently agree with his thoughts.

"Don't even think if she wasn't here we'd do anything for you. You're just lil' biddy *Bricka* come to torment us all over again." Smiling, Shan Lin turned back to Shari and gently kissed her cheek. Vincent walked toward Shari and kissed her other cheek. Both men walked toward a door in the wall and opening it, went through the clothing hanging inside, ignoring Theresa completely.

* * * * *

Shari stared at the woman standing in the doorway. The woman was beautiful with the same good looks the two men shared. She was obviously part of the family, and someone Shari would be wise to avoid.

The orgasms her husbands had just given her were making her daft. She was still wet between her legs with an ache to once again jump one, if not both, of the men currently donning clothing over their magnificent bodies.

Whimpering mentally at the loss of those gorgeous cocks, Shari stepped forward to play the gracious, if newly appointed, hostess.

Reaching out her hand as she walked toward the woman, Shari plastered a hopefully convincing smile on her face.

"Hi, I'm Shari. We've only been home for a little while, so you'll have to excuse their behavior. They're…"

Her mind went blank as she watched the woman hold out her own hand and shake Shari's. What the hell kind of explanation was she going to give this unknown woman?

"Not to worry, Shari. I'm Theresa Lawsai, a cousin of the two barbarians over there and know just what they're like. Now even more so."

There was a choked sound from the closet as the woman spoke and Shari turned to glare at the two men as they dressed. Turning back to Theresa, she was all set to offer the woman a seat when the word clothing registered in her brain.

Looking down at herself, even knowing what she would find, she found she was still naked.

Completely mortified, Shari choked as she tried to find the words to explain just why she was greeting a member of her husbands' family naked. At the word husbands, she choked again. There were two of them. *Holy Mary, Mother of God. Just what had she gotten herself into?!?*

* * * * *

Theresa watched the knowledge come into Shari's eyes as the woman looked from herself then back up to Theresa. *The poor thing. Yes dear, you're very naked. But as long as you weren't going to comment, neither was I. Just think of it as a custom.*

Theresa willed the woman to hear her words, and had to wonder if Shari just might have. For one moment Shari was white as *snea*, and the next, red as the blood of the *primpate* fruit. Then suddenly, though still the color of *primpate*, the woman seemed to steady herself and asked Theresa to have a seat while she dressed.

The woman went to the closet, balled both hands into fists, and sent them flying in opposite directions. One landed on the shoulder of Vincent, and the other landed on the arm of Shan Lin.

Theresa watched as both men flinched politely for their wife then looked over their shoulder with a wink at Theresa. Then their wife was physically shoving both men out of the closet, and the doors slammed behind her.

"What?" the men asked in unison, speaking as they always had when in some kind of trouble with their mother. Together.

Theresa held the laughter in for as long as she could, but could only hold it in for a few seconds. Suddenly, laughter roared out of her. She laughed so hard she fell over and onto the floor, rolling around as she used to do as a child.

When she could finally speak, Theresa saw the brothers sitting across from where she had fallen to the floor.

"Feel better, *Bricka*?"

Vincent stroked her hair as she sat up. Shan Lin grinned at her from the chair he'd taken while waiting for his wife.

"Yes. Yes I do. It's been a long week and there's much I've still to tell the two of you. But I *did* need the laughter." A look passed between Vincent and Theresa before Vincent turned to look at his brother.

"There will be time later. For now, we need to see to our wife. Out, *Bricka*!"

* * * * *

Brother mine, she may have not been the intended one we chose, but she is the one destined to be ours. Vincent pathed to his brother as they waited for Shari to shriek in outrage. Vincent found it a plus their bride had yet to do more than grumble and demand they allow her privacy.

Shan Lin agreed with his brother, the woman should be delved into further, and in more ways than with just their cocks. He too, was impressed with the way the woman had handled the situation she had found herself in.

Shari was a perfect choice for the Warriors. Both brothers agreed.

Chapter Ten

The summons came when dinner was barely finished. Winters watched a maid walk through the dining room doors, salver in her hands, a note laid folded on the tray. The maid strolled over to Winters who took the tray, dismissing the maid with a murmured thanks.

Winters walked up to Vincent, tray held out before him.

Vincent took the note, nodded his thanks, opened the missive, and began to read it.

"Who in their right mind has dared to interrupt The Queen's Most Vicious Warrior and The Death Bringer at dinner?" Theresa joked as she forked the last of the Tine Chocolate Tort into her mouth.

Her unit members smiled uneasily as they watched for some reaction out of the Warriors. "Why, it's your father, *Bricka*. He's sent a note around to tell you it's past your bedtime and time you toddled on home to bed. Now scat." Shan Lin replied easily and the table at large laughed at the casual teasing between the family members.

"I'm sorry to cut your first dinner in Aranak short, *Kasha*, but Shan Lin and I must attend some business." Vincent spoke casually to Shari.

Shari, who had been having palpitations at the taste of the dessert, turned to her husband with a look of gluttony in her eyes. The tort was as close to orgasm from chocolate Shari had ever gotten, and if she wasn't careful, she was going to embarrass herself in front of the entire table.

Her voice came out husky when she spoke.

"Will you be long?"

The words barely left her mouth before Shan Lin and Vincent stood up from the table suddenly, their movements bringing those assembled to their feet. Without explanation to anyone, Shan Lin bodily lifted Shari from her chair, swung her into his arms, and raced from the room, followed closely by Vincent.

Theresa, the only one who had stayed seated, smiled. Paying little attention to what had just happened, she spoke to Winters.

"The meal was wonderful, Winters. Any chance there's more of this aphrodisiac in the kitchen?"

"Of course, My Lady...Captain Lawsai."

Theresa glanced lazily around the table, finding looks of astonishment on the faces of her crew. She laughed huskily before she explained her cousins' behavior.

"They're newly married. What did you expect?"

Smiles erupted all around as the anxiety drained the room.

"Oh my," Lt. Roberts, Theresa's medic said as she fanned herself. "Where do I find myself a couple of those?"

Corp. Dyden elbowed her gently in the ribs. "Whenever you want me, I'm right here."

Lt. Char made a rude sound.

"You wish! But to be fair, come see me in a few years when you've gotten some experience, and I'll show you what a woman really wants."

Theresa listened as her crew joked and teased each other, just like the family they had become. Advice of a raunchy nature flew back and forth between the tired crew and Theresa ignored it. They were all blowing off steam, relaxing in a way most military troops in combat mode needed after long days, even weeks, spent together in danger.

She would give them their time to unwind, giving Shan Lin and Vincent time to finish jumping their wife, and then she would have to have a quick chat with her cousins. Theresa was nearly positive the missive had been a command from Queen Sara and she needed to tell the twins what had gone on at her last assignment. She had to tell someone, and she knew the twins would keep her counsel.

She had to warn them. Queen Sara, who had never been the best ruler when it came to military strategy, had finally lost it. It might even be up to the brothers to fix it.

* * * * *

Riad, my cock is at attention. What in the Seven Hells did she do to have you shooting out of your chair as if the averon's of Horrd were on your ass? Shan Lin asked as he walked rapidly toward their apartments.

I wasn't paying attention to what Winters served Shari and Theresa for dessert. He gave them Tine Chocolate Tort. All Shari did was look at me, Vincent snarled.

What about the summons from Queen Sara? Are we going to... Stupid question. Of course we are. Forgive me, brother mine. My dick is throbbing in time to the beating of Shari's heart. I can feel it against my chest. She's going to explode all by herself if we don't...

Shari stirred in Shan Lin's arms, emitting a small cry of sexual hunger.

"Too late. It's started." Shan Lin said unnecessarily as the men watched Shari squirm in his arms.

A sigh escaped Vincent.

"To be fair to Winters, he had no idea Queen Sara would summon us. I could only wish he'd said something to us before he gave Shari the Tine Tort."

Vincent reached for the apartment door they had arrived at and pushed it open to allow Shan Lin to carry Shari through, he spoke as he followed them through the door.

"Don't worry about it. She'll be fine once we get her into bed. Besides, Tine Chocolate Tort *is* the customary dessert served to the bride and her female guest on the first night of marriage. He was only following tradition."

Shan Lin walked through the spacious rooms until he came to the large bed that he hoped the three would share for many nights to come and gently laid Shari down. He was just beginning to divest her of her clothing when an inhuman sound came from behind.

Spinning, reaching for the *pryt* lance strapped to his side, he whirled to face whatever danger had suddenly come into the room where their wife lay.

"Mine. She's mine. Get away, now."

The hoarse words grated over Shan Lin's skin as he watched Vincent crouch into a killing stance. Not relaxing his body by an inch, Shan Lin watched Vincent begin his advance, a killing rage in his eyes.

"Vincent," Shan Lin began, gentleness devoid in his voice. "You know she is ours. You must control the *Try Nas Ayn* or you will kill us all. It was you who have been accepting Shari as the one. Regardless of the fact we claimed her as our bride as a ruse. Shari is our bride. We both agreed when we asked for entrance. You must give her time to accept us. It is the only way we three will survive."

The reminder, given in a monotone voice, did little to calm Vincent. It did however get him to stop advancing.

"Warrior Rayan. Use those legendary skills to get control of yourself. That is an order!"

A movement from the bed turned Shan Lin's attention for a split second. It was all Vincent had been waiting for.

* * * * *

Shari sat up suddenly unsure how she had come to be in bed when only seconds before she had been sitting at a table staring into Vincent's eyes. No sooner had the thought flashed in her mind then she watched as Vincent attacked Shan Lin.

The brothers grappled, each trying to find the best possible hold on the other to bring him down. It was to no avail. The brothers grunted, cursed, and went around in circles, but neither went down.

"Stop it." The husky voice came out softly.

Both men ignored it.

"I said, stop it." Shari tried to put more strength in her voice, still to no benefit.

Taking a deep breath, Shari screamed.

"*Stop it!*"

Both men, who had been communicating in grunts, snarls and grappling, suddenly fell to the floor letting go of each other and rolling apart. Panting from exertion, both men turned to stare at Shari.

"What's going on? Last thing I remember, I was sitting at a dinner table, horny as hell. Now, I'm here. You two are fighting, and I'm a bowl of Jell-O. Somebody care to explain?"

Vincent got to his feet and walking around Shan Lin came to stand beside the bed. He opened his mouth to speak and Shari watched as his face suddenly turned red and he quickly closed his mouth.

Shan Lin stayed where he was, but explained.

"It was the dessert. Are you feeling..." He paused as if searching for a word, but Vincent beat him to it by asking bluntly.

"Are you feeling as if you've had a pleasant orgasm?"

Shari blinked up at him.

"Are you serious?"

"Yes. The dessert, Tine Chocolate Tort, is what is traditionally served at the dinner the night of the wedding. It is served to the females only. As we were married recently and Winters hadn't a chance to serve it earlier, you received it tonight."

Shari thought for a moment then remembered the feeling she'd had when she looked at Vincent. She blushed saying in a small voice.

"I guess I did."

Shan Lin got up from the floor and came to stand next to Vincent.

"It is an aphrodisiac. It is used as an enticement for the wedding night. I'm sorry to say I had forgotten about it until after Vincent said something."

Shari nodded not really understanding. She wanted to complain, but at the moment was feeling too relaxed. Maybe when she had some sleep...

A jaw-popping yawn stole over her and she slid down in bed, a feeling of sleepiness descending.

"Okay. But why were you fighting?" Even as she snuggled into the bed, her mind becoming fuddled, she knew the answer was important.

"*Try Nas Ayn.*" The brothers said the words together.

"Umm. All right." Shari agreed around another yawn. Shari should probably ask for an explanation, she knew she should, but sleep claimed her too quickly.

* * * * *

Shan Lin and Vincent made their way to the front door wanting only to get the meeting with Queen Sara over and done. It was not to be. Theresa waylaid them before they could leave.

"I told you. We have to talk."

Vincent made as if to object but Theresa overrode him.

"It's Aranak business and you won't be leaving until you hear me out."

Sighing, both brothers' emotions still highly volatile, they nodded briefly and listened.

* * * * *

"...overheard it at the Vid/Sync depot. Mercs making their way toward a town east of Naralin, but I couldn't hear the rest of the conversation. Something's going down and you two need to be on the look out for it. I can't be everywhere you know."

Theresa tried to make a joke to lessen the tension emanating from the two men and failed miserably. Shrugging, she finished her report.

"It wouldn't look strange for the Queen's favorites to ask around, and I wanted you two to get a heads up about the prisoners I had to release."

The two Warriors waited before speaking.

"It's started, hasn't it?" Shan Lin asked softly.

"Yes, brother mine, it has."

Theresa looked from one to the other perplexed.

"It's been going on for a while. What do you mean it's started?"

Shan Lin shook his head sighing.

"Never mind. We'll keep our ears open. Now, enjoy the hospitality of our home and leave our bride to sleep. Love you, *Bricka*." Shan Lin hugged her and walked away.

"Be careful, cousin and keep your ears open. Love you too." Vincent hugged her to him, then set her away and followed his brother.

"Back at you two!" Theresa yelled, walking after the two men who strode out the front door.

"Even if you are secretive *frechies*," she mumbled, veering off to rejoin her crew, back at the table.

* * * * *

"Well, that went…" Vincent trailed off as the brothers left their home.

"There are the horses. Let's just go and see what she wants. The sooner we get this over with, the sooner we can come back to Shari."

There was no anger in Shan Lin's voice, but Vincent knew he would have to apologize. As they gained their saddles, Vincent made up his mind he would do so now.

"Brother mine…" he began, only to have Shan Lin stop him.

"No. It is the *Try Nas Ayn*. I know it. I felt it. The only thing you have to do is control it. What we both have to do now is convince Shari she is the only one who can stop it. This might have started out as a ploy, but it has become more important than that. Don't apologize for who we are."

Vincent nodded as the brothers kicked their horses into a trot.

"You're right. I know now she is the one. She is our chosen, our soul-mate. But it's been what? Two days? And for those two days, she slept for part of them recovering from the accident. Her feelings may not have been…"

Vincent emitted a sound of harsh frustration.

"You're thinking of Syne and Asnan, the two twins whose mate never accepted them, thus sending them spiraling out of control, killing their intended, and eventually each other."

The legendary tale of Syne and Asnan was told to every set of twins as a warning the moment they were old enough to understand.

Two mighty Warriors believing they had found the woman who would allow them to achieve *juniane*, went into *Try Nas Ayn*. The cycle to claim their mate began quickly and accelerated at a rapid pace. Unfortunately for the brothers, the woman they believed to be their mate, when confronted with effects of *Try Nas Ayn*, rejected the brothers in disgust.

Fleeing in horror, the lady eventually settled down with another man. The brothers on the other hand obsessed about the woman incessantly, continuously heaping physical violence on each other when the *Try Nas Ayn* was at its worse. The destruction they created wasn't always confined to each other. There were rumors started that some of the ruins of Aranak were actually caused by these twins.

When neither Syne nor Asnan could stand the physical or mental anguish any longer, the two brothers went after the woman and her mate. There were patches in Aranak where the ground lay open and bare, no crops would grow there nor would buildings remain erect on these sights. It is said this was the path the twins took to first slaughter the woman they had loved, then turn on each other for a final fight and kill each other in an unstoppable rage.

Vincent nodded closing his eyes, a slight shudder raking his body, as he remembered the gory details his father had gone into. If he and Shan Lin...

"You can't think like that. This may have started out as a means to deceive Queen Sara, but we both knew somewhere inside, she was the one. It was the only way we would have picked her."

"She was the first woman we saw. There was no way we could have known she was ours," Vincent argued.

Shan Lin shook his head.

"No. She was not the first woman we saw. When we left the house on Earth, we must have passed by a hundred women and you know it. For one reason or another, each of us had a reason for not choosing any of them. Too tall, too short, not enough stamina. I touched as many as I could and felt nothing. You know the only one we agreed on was her. It wasn't the orgasm we gave her at her door. It was the fact I couldn't feel anything from her when I touched her. It was the reason we chose her."

Shan Lin's voice had risen in intensity as he spoke, and Vincent heard the surety in Shan Lin's words as the brothers remembered. Vincent had to face facts. She was indeed the one and they had known it from the start.

Sighing in disgust at himself because he hadn't seen it clearly to begin with, Vincent admitted to himself, Shan Lin was right.

"Shari is our chosen. She is the woman we will love for the rest of our days. There will be no other. *Riad* help us if she doesn't realize it herself before we destroy her."

Nudging the horse into a canter, then a flat out race toward Aranak, Vincent tried to ignore the words his brother pathed into his mind.

Riad *already has. He showed us to our soul-mate. What more could you ask of him?*

Chapter Eleven

Both men stood before Queen Sara who was half dressed and lounging on the royal bed surrounded by seven naked men and women in various stages of coupling. Hiding their disgust behind years of training, both Warriors waited to be acknowledged.

A cry of painful satisfaction came from one of the couplings before Queen Sara chose to speak to the brothers.

"That's it, Roola. Make sure the pain is equal to the satisfaction. That's a good boy." Petting the man's rapidly diminishing penis, the Queen turned to her Warriors.

"There's a rumor you've been joined. I've felt the presence of a new mind in Aranak and I've had to wonder what the reason was for your not presenting her to me?" The Queen paused before adding delicately. "Or him."

The brothers stood steeling themselves to show no emotions at the taunting.

"I must say, I'm hurt. I would have thought you could have brought your bride here at least to introduce her to your Auntie Sara. Are you ashamed of me?"

The brothers waited, knowing the question, asked so innocently, would soon be followed by an order. No matter what, the Queen seemed bound to provoke Shan Lin and Vincent.

"Your Majesty. It was not our intent to slight you in the least. As our Auntie Sara, or as our Queen. However, our bride, upon arrival to Aranak, was suffering from a recent accident. We found her in the Earth Realm and a vehicle had struck her. We only wanted her to recover first, thus allowing her to be at her best, before presenting her to you."

Vincent, never one for the diplomatic speeches, listened as his brother spoke so eloquently.

"I see. Has she recovered?" the Queen asked sweetly.

Vincent looked at Shan Lin knowing they would have to present their bride to their aunt before Shari had accepted them, and almost shouted no. Gritting his teeth against the denial, he waited for Shan Lin's answer.

"Mostly, Auntie Sara. Thank you for your concern. If you would like..."

She quickly cut off his reply.

"Yes. It's what this is about. What I would like. Or, if you prefer, what I want."

A scream sounded next to her and their aunt turned to look down at a man under two women.

"That will be enough, Marek. You must learn to turn the pain into pleasure." As she instructed the now whimpering man, she reached over to a small tray next to her and picked up a pair of pincers.

"Clamp these onto his balls and twist them back and forth. If he screams again, gag him. I'm having a conversation with my family."

Her voice never changed from the syrupy sweet tone she had used as she spoke to her nephews.

"Now. Where was I? Oh yes, my marriageniece. When will she be here?"

A look passed once again between the brothers before turning back to their aunt.

"Before you speak, know this. She will come before me and now. I don't care if you must wake her from a drugged sleep. You will present her to me. Also, I have an assignment for the two of you, which we will get into in a moment. But for now, path her and have Winters arrange for her arrival immediately."

Vincent nearly smiled with glee as Shan Lin pathed tightly to his brother.

Thank Riad *for Winters and the Tine Chocolate Torts.*

Bless him indeed. Vincent answered back just as tightly knowing that if they kept the contact brief their aunt wouldn't hear the conversation.

"Your Majesty, Auntie Sara. I'm afraid that won't be possible." Vincent answered, schooling his features carefully into a look of painful denial.

"Just why the *freching* not?" the Queen burst out. "You would deny a command from your sovereign? You would deny me what I asked for? Why you little..."

Both men dropped to their knees, their foreheads in positions of obeisance toward the floor interrupting the Queen's wrath before they began to speak a formal apology.

"Auntie Sara, please. She was given Tine Chocolate tonight for the wedding night. You know she will not function before the morning, if we are lucky. We have truly exhausted the woman beyond her endurance. After all, we are our Queen's Warriors."

Their voices carried through the room. Vincent would not have been surprised if those with ears to the door didn't hear their boast. Both he and Shan Lin were equally glad they had indeed worn out their bride throughout the day with lovemaking. When he opened his mind to allow Queen Sara to see himself and his brother pleasuring their bride thoroughly, the tension in the room dropped appreciably.

The silence that had descended on the room was only interrupted by the occasional groan from one or more of the thrashing bodies on the bed.

"Oh, do get up. As you've been so kind to show me, your boast of your prowess is indeed legendary. The woman is lucky indeed in her choice of you both."

The disgruntled tone of her voice relieved the brothers, but only until she opened her mouth to speak once more.

"Fine. I will give her two days to recover, but that is all. In the meantime, I will send an escort for her alone on the second day. She will see me alone."

The brothers started to protest but the Queen rolled over their objections as they got to their feet.

"No. I have spoken. That is all. I want the two of you to go somewhere else. This is Aranak business and it always comes first."

"Yes, Your Majesty." Vincent and Shan Lin resumed the formal speech as their Aunt once more became the Queen.

"Now. There has been trouble in Hurok."

The command performance had turned into business, and this was one area the brothers intended to pay close attention. There was very little they could do at the moment about the command given to present Shari in two days time, but this business was what they had been trained for. This conversation they would record and burn into their minds.

* * * * *

"Do you believe the woman?" Shan Lin nearly bellowed as the men made their way back to their home.

"What? You mean you weren't yet sure she means to destroy Aranak at all costs so she can retain the right to the throne? I'm surprised at your naiveté, Shan Lin. Really, brother, it was you who convinced me of what your dreams spoke. Why, now, would you think differently?"

The sarcasm so heavy in Vincent's voice, was due to the fact their Queen had finally lost complete control of her faculties.

The conversation the brothers had before leaving with Theresa had only confirmed what they already knew. The conversation with their aunt had confirmed in Queen Sara's words the evidence the men needed to show Queen Stephanie the lengths to which their aunt would go to keep the throne.

"Don't take it out on me. I know you're angry. I know we have been given orders. At the moment, we have to decide if we're going to disobey one Queen's orders to obey the other's."

It was not a hard decision in the end. So their careers as Warriors would be gone forever. Treason would be spoken of. They would need to leave Naralin, probably never to see their home, family, and friends again. It was not a choice at all.

They would do the only thing they could and still live with themselves.

They would protect their bride and survive.

* * * * *

"They think they're so smart, standing there so smug as if I haven't just learned they'd gone to meet that cunt Stephanie. My marriagedaughter. My beloved sons' bride. The woman who would presume to take what is mine."

Sara sat in front of a mirror as one of the men she had summoned off the bed combed out her hair. Admiring its beauty as the man stroked the bristles against her scalp, Sara fumed.

"I am still the ruler of this world. I will soon take over Horrd and demand reverence from another Monarch's people. It is I who has brought Aranak to the notice of the universes. I, who have built up relations with others of power. If the little whore thinks she can just step into my shoes…"

Sara stopped speaking abruptly, reaching up and snatching the gilded brush from the hands of the naked male behind her.

"Stop it!" she shrieked, standing swiftly. She turned to look at the man and began shrieking in a high-pitched voice.

"Vincent thinks I can't hear them. What a crock. I hear everything." Sara began walking around the one who had brushed her hair.

No, you don't. You're lucky if you hear bits and snatches of conversation from them. And you cannot even hear your own sons. The taunting voice mocked Sara.

In fury, she turned on the man behind her.

"Why are you not at attention? Why are you flaccid? Have you not been instructed to be ready to *frech* me at a moment's notice?"

"But Your Majesty… It is…" The man cried in helplessness.

Shrieking still, Sara grasped hold of the man and with a strength born in anger, turned him so he faced away from her. Pushing the man from behind, she began shouting demands.

"Bend over the chair. Get going. You will take your cock in your hand and stroke it to firmness. When I'm done, you'll have learned to have a cockstand any time I look at you!"

Sara, breath heaving in anticipation of what was to come, waited for the man to begin. One hand making its way to her saturated pussy as she used her dominant hand to pick up a flat spatula like paddle.

"Begin." The command was quickly followed by the sounds of metal connecting with flesh.

* * * * *

Shari could hardly countenance it. She had taken to wandering through her husbands' home since they had gone. So far, she had found the most wonderful bathroom was located in the brothers' suite. While the rest of the house had been decorated as if for tours, their rooms seemed made for comfort.

The room she was in now looked to be directly out of a tour guide book.

And next, we'll be visiting the royal home of Shan Lin and Vincent…

Shari paused. Last name. She did not even know their last name. But when she would have gotten angry at the idea she had married men and not gotten their last names, her mind supplied the answer.

Rayan. My name is Shari Lynn Rayan-White.

Where had *that* come from?

But it was all there in her mind. For any thought she had of the men, her mind seemed to supply an answer. She marveled at this fact. Maybe it had something to do with the mind reading deal. Maybe she…

You are our soulmate. This is normal.

Shari nearly knocked over a chair.

"Shit! Don't do that!" she snapped.

My apologies, Kasha. *Are you injured?*

Shari smoothed her hands down her front and settled herself before answering.

"I'm fine. You just scared the crap out of me."

We are headed home. Is there anything you require? Vincent belonged to the voice in her head and he sounded amused. Shari thought about his question and finally answered truthfully.

"Actually there is. I need you both to answer questions. Questions about why I'm really here and just what is happening between us."

Both brothers tried to answer her at once.

"No. This will have to wait until you get home. I'm sorry, but I need to see you face-to-face." The brothers' agreement came through quietly.

* * * * *

Shari went on with her self-directed tour while waiting for the men to return.

There was a burning brazier of hot coals just like any used throughout countless castles and hovels in the days when knights roamed the earth. And yet, a few feet apart from them stood modern conveniences the likes of which she had never seen.

Shaking her head in wonder, Shari marveled at her surroundings. She was indeed in another world, even perhaps another time, but most definitely another place.

She continued to survey her surroundings. Murals depicting scenes of what must have been everyday life in Aranak adorned walls. Some images held children laughing in play, chasing one another across fields of flora and fauna, while others still were of adults, both paired and threesomes, in loving embraces. To be sure, they were each a beauty to behold.

Nearing the other side of the room, still lost in the wonder of images and objects, she didn't hear the footsteps as they came upon her until a voice spoke behind her.

"We are here at your command, *Kasha*. What is it you need of us?"

Startled, Shari turned to find Vincent behind her, a look of bemusement on his face. Schooling her features, Shari smiled and shook her head.

"Yes. Where's Shan Lin?"

"Right behind me." Vincent answered, coming into the room. Shari watched him as Vincent dropped onto the nearest piece of furniture. Noticing his worn out look, the way his eyes closed as his body began to sink into the pliable surface, she wondered just what had called the brothers away.

She opened her mouth to question Vincent but was interrupted by Shan Lin's entrance.

"Shari? You called for us?" His voice sounded as tired as both he and Vincent looked. Shari watched him as she had Vincent and found Shan Lin, like his brother, sinking into the nearest furniture bone tired.

Thoughts of the questions she wanted to ask were pushed back from her mind as she excused herself to find Winters. Taking no more than a few steps out the room's doorway, she ran into him.

"My Lady Princess? How may I serve?"

"Actually, you can call me Shari. My Lady Princess seems so... Anyway. That aside, your...*my* husbands need food and drink. Can you tell me where I can...?"

Shari had wanted to know where she could find them as her tour had not quite made it to the kitchen, but Winters interrupted her.

"My Lady Shari, it would be my honor to procure your husbands' sustenance. Please, allow me to see to their needs."

Shari nearly laughed at the man's concession to using her name. Shrugging mentally, Shari tried asking again where the kitchen was located.

"Please, Winters. I want to do something for my husbands. I..." Shari felt the blush begin, "I want to...take care of them." This time her face was on fire. She had only met Shan Lin and Vincent, what, two days ago? Yet here she was, her emotions surfacing where they were concerned. She wanted to care for them.

An embarrassed laugh escaped.

"I feel silly, but they...they're mine now, Winters. I can't explain it but," Shari shrugged helplessly, "there it is."

Winters nodded solemnly and Shari suspected the man was biting the inside of his lip trying not to laugh at her. Taking a deep breath, Shari tried again.

"Please, I'd like to find the kitchen."

"Of course, My Lady Shari. If you will follow me please." Winters said no more but pivoted and led Shari toward a new part of the house. In moments Shari was guided through the double doorway of the kitchen. Once again, she was astonished at the size of the place. Half the military forces of the United States could easily fit in this kitchen.

Okay, maybe she was exaggerating a bit, but the place was huge. Men and women of all ages and different hues worked side-by-side preparing various foods and the room smelled delicious.

"My Lady Princess." Winters spoke in a loud voice and the commotion in the room ceased. Shari tried not to gape as men and women, their hands full of a variety of items, turned their attention to her. Each individual bowed or curtsied as best they could, then stood at attention.

Shari looked to Winters wondering if she was supposed to do something.

"They are waiting for your approval, My Lady Princess." Winters acknowledged Shari's unspoken question.

Shari cleared her throat and schooled her features. She prayed her voice wouldn't squeak when she spoke, and prayed equally hard to say the right thing.

"Yes, I enjoyed dinner. I especially enjoyed the Tine Chocolate Tort served for dinner. Thank you." *There. That should do it*, Shari thought as she took a few steps in the direction of what looked to be a fridge. If she had stopped to watch the faces of those in the room, she would have seen the smiles of laughter on their faces.

Winters cleared his throat and Shari stopped as she reached for what she thought might be the handle to the appliance. Turning her head in his direction, Shari waited as he came up beside her.

"My Lady Princess. Please, all you need do is ask. Anyone here will fulfill your wants."

Shari almost blushed again before she took in his true meaning. Smiling, she laid her arm on Winters sleeve not noticing the heads turning in her direction.

Before she could remind him again, a voice spoke.

Shari? Is something wrong?

There was tension in the question and Shari sighed. Shan Lin was worried.

"I'm…"

She was interrupted by a growl from the doorway.

"Winters." a voice bellowed and Shari nearly tipped over when Winters yanked his arm away from Shari's light grasp. Shan Lin stood in the doorway to the kitchen, his gaze scanning the room as Vincent came toward her.

Vincent passed the man with a snarl causing Winters to scuttle quickly out of the way.

"Vincent!" Shari admonished her husband, quickly meeting him half way. "What was that for?" she asked even as he reached out and grasped hold of her, pulling her into his arms in a protective grasp.

Before she knew what was happening, Shan Lin had joined them. Shari looked at Shan Lin with a questioning look. He smiled at her and reached down to smooth a stray lock of her hair.

"What is it?" Shari asked, concerned.

"Relax, Vincent," Shan Lin drawled before speaking to Shari. "We were concerned when you did not return immediately. We wanted to assure ourselves you were fine."

Shari squirmed in Vincent's hold until he loosened his grip.

"I'm fine," Shari answered, glaring at Vincent. "I told you two I'd be right back. You both looked tired and I…" She was loathed to admit she had wanted to feed and comfort them, but resigned to the situation, she explained.

"I just wanted to pamper the two of you a bit." The mumbled words fell from her lips as her gaze slid away from Vincent to Shan Lin. A gleeful joy lit Shan Lin's features.

"And if you tell me it's only natural because it's my wifely duties, I'll…" Her words were cut off when Shan Lin bent his head and took her mouth. Shari's knees weakened at the kiss as he coaxed open her mouth and devoured her. Shari wrapped her arms around Shan Lin's torso as her own body began to respond to the assault.

Lost in the kiss it took her a moment to realize Vincent had begun to nibble on her neck and his hands were kneading her ass. Pulling away from Shan Lin gently, Shari nudged Vincent with her butt.

"Guys…" she began, her skin flushed from the sensual encounter, "…we have company." She finished lamely, gesturing toward the men and women surrounding the three of them.

Vincent's husky chuckle sounded in her ear.

"It matters not who is around. If we knew it would not embarrass you, we would sweep the counter behind you free and take you here and now."

Shari's body temperature, which had been peaking quite fine already, shot up another ten degrees. Her pussy, rarely dry around the two men, became saturated completely. Doing her best to control her breathing before she hyperventilated, she reached out to the nearest surface and leaned heavily against it.

"Lord, do you do things to my body. My heart's pounding…" Her heart. Her brain connected the two things slowly. It was what she wanted to speak to the two men about.

Deep breaths, Shari. Just take deep breaths.

"That was what I wanted to talk to you two about." Shari turned to Vincent who still had hold of her hips. "It would help if you two weren't crowding me, too. I just get flustered and…"

"*Kasha*, you humble us." Vincent rumbled, his voice gruff.

"Why?" Shari asked confused.

Shan Lin answered for the two men.

"You have told us you wanted to see to our comfort. Your response to us as your husbands has made our lovemaking extraordinary. Your feelings for us…"

"See, that's just it. I've known you for two whole days. You tell me we got married. Not that it was something I remember, but all right, I'll go with it since you've told the truth about me being in Aranak. I've handled the mind thing pretty well so far. I've pretty much stopped looking for the real royal person who goes by the name of 'My Lady Princess', since who'd ever have thought it was me. I think I've been handling things well. Trynannasuti and all."

Shit! You're rambling woman. Take a breath. She did, but quickly let it out.

"And now, even though I'm not one for love at first sight, somehow the two of you have become extremely important to my well being. I'd just like to know…" Shari thought of all the times she had heard soul-mates, life-mates, and things like it, "…well, if we're soul-mates, life-mates, whatever, how come I've never heard you two…"

Suddenly, she could not bring herself to ask. The 'L' word was not something she had ever thought to experience. Her own emotions had become engaged rapidly ever since she had seen the two men walk through the door of Karen's apartment back on Earth.

"Shari," she heard her name in stereo.

"What?" she mumbled in a small voice.

"*Kasha*." Spoken again in stereo.

"What?" she asked once again, her voice growing stronger.

"Are you telling Shan Lin and myself that you are in love with us?" The question came gently despite Vincent's gruff voice as he turned her body to face him.

"I don't know." Shari expected the words to come out shrilly. Instead, her voice sounded hesitant, confused. She looked into the dual colored eyes of her husband and nearly drowned in the glowing love they held. His eyes were suddenly shining with the golden light she had previously seen when the two brothers had screwed her into unconsciousness.

A hand reached out from behind her and swiveled her body back so she faced Shan Lin.

"*Kasha.*" The husky endearment shot straight to Shari's heart this time. The velvet timbre and longing she heard nearly brought tears to her eyes.

Strangers or not, she had fallen in love with these two men.

Swallowing past the lump in her throat, Shari turned her head to look back at Vincent but her attention was diverted, by a woman staring at the spectacle the three of them must be making. The woman was crying silently, tears streaming down her face as a smile nearly split her face in two.

"Beautiful." The whispered word reached Shari.

Chapter Twelve

Shari came down to breakfast with Vincent feeling content. After the bath she, Shan Lin, and Vincent had taken this morning, some of the apprehension she had about being in an alternate universe had diminished.

"Winters, good morning." Shari called out the greeting as she and Vincent entered the dining room.

"Good morning, My Lady Princess. I trust you slept well last night." He answered her, waiting behind the chair she had sat in the night before. Situated at the head of the curved, ornately carved table, surrounded on either side by two others, was a chair of prominence, something fit for royalty.

Vincent escorted her to it and dismissing Winters, seated her himself.

"As a matter of fact, Winters, I did." Smiling shyly, Shari looked over the elegantly set table to find crystal goblets, gold plates and cups, and discreetly feeling the linen tablecloth. The night her husbands' cousin had dined with them she had paid little heed to what she ate off of or drank out of, and now was amazed she missed the splendor set before her.

"Is My Lady Princess ready to dine?" Winters asked and Shari let go of the cloth she had been fondling.

"Yes, please," Shari answered politely before completely ruining it by adding, "I do believe I could eat this table at the moment. It seems I've worked up quite an appetite lately. I wonder why that is?"

So saying, she turned to wink at Vincent and found him watching her with hungry eyes. Smiling happily in return, she waited as men and women began to bring in the food.

"I was wondering, Vincent. Why are these three chairs at the head of the table? Isn't it a bit strange?"

Vincent shrugged as he looked over the food being set around them and answered absently.

"Not really. It's custom."

Shari waited for him to explain, but apparently he had explained all he was going to. Rolling her eyes, she prodded him.

"What custom?" she asked patiently.

Shari could see she had startled him as he turned to her with a look of surprise.

"Well, I guess you wouldn't know the custom." He began sheepishly.

"No, I wouldn't. As you keep reminding me, I'm not on Earth any longer." It might have only been a few days since she had entered into another universe, but Shari could easily get used to living like this.

Before she could think of the things she had left behind, like her home, her friends…

Pushing the thoughts away before they could overwhelm her, she prodded Vincent once more. He gave her a look mixed with indulgence and understanding.

"It will be all right, Shari." Stroking a hand down her hair, he began to explain.

"I've lived with it for so long I don't really think of it anymore. I should probably thank Winters for remembering…"

"You're welcome, My Lord Prince," Winters piped up from behind them.

Smiling wryly, Vincent went on.

"It is custom for the lady of the house to sit at the head of the table with her husbands. It is she who rules her home. It is her husbands' job to ensure she has all she needs to perform this duty, therefore, it is the woman who sits at the head of the table."

Shari gaped. It was one more thing she would have to get use to. Being the ruler of her home…

"What? Wait. What do you mean? Are you saying I have to be a good wife and stay home like a good girl seeing to the house chores?" *The magnitude of such a task in a house this size would surely take up a woman's entire life*, Shari thought as she waited for Vincent to confirm her thoughts. There's no way in hell Shari could. What if she wanted to work instead? What if she couldn't handle something of this magnitude? What if she screwed it up? This was...

"Easy, my heart. It is not what you are thinking."

Shari took a deep breath, almost grateful the brothers could read her mind. Almost.

Vincent chuckled.

"You can close us out. If you don't want us listening, close the door."

Surprise and uncertainty showed on Shari's face.

"It's true. But back to the woman ruling. I mean it literally. When Shan Lin and I took you to wife, all we have, all that is ours, became yours. What you see here before you, everything in this house and those others we own or hold through our titles, became yours. You could say we were merely stewards awaiting the return of the rightful owner. It is the law of the Queendom. It is the law of the land of Aranak. It is one reason we are at war with Horrd."

Shari sat in astonishment, her thoughts racing and chasing each other. She owned this magnificent home. She reverently touched the plate in front of her, the tips of her fingers skimming the edge before pulling her hand back abruptly and setting it in her lap.

"No." she said.

Vincent turned looking at her questioningly.

"No?"

"No."

"No, what?" he asked, reaching out to pour clear red liquid into a gold rimmed goblet.

"No. Just...no," Shari said stubbornly.

"All right. No. But it all still belongs to you whether you want it or not."

Shari shook her head as Vincent downed the contents of the glass in one swallow.

"Yes. There is nothing you need do. Winters, runs all the houses. Shan Lin and I are... We travel a lot. You remember us telling you we were in the Queen's Guard?" He waited as she nodded. "We mostly live out of barracks and there's little we need beside our weapons, clothing, and mounts. It will change now that we're married. We'll be allotted sufficient quarters as befits the marriage-niece of the Queen..."

"The Queen…" Shari said, only now taking in the memory of the twins telling her their aunt was the Queen of Aranak.

"Yes. The Queen. She is…" Vincent added carefully.

"Your aunt, the Queen of Aranak," Shari repeated.

"Yes." Vincent turned to Shari once more, carefully setting down the crystal pitcher he had just used to refill his glass. Picking the glass up he brought it to Shari's lips, offering her a taste. Accepting the liquid absently as her mind reeled at all she was taking in, Shari quaffed the liquid he poured into her mouth.

Swallowing the drink automatically, Shari took in the taste.

The taste was somewhere between heaven and orgasmic. A sound of pleasure escaped her mouth and her thoughts centered on the surprisingly refreshing drink. She could not quite decide the exact flavor of it though. It tasted as if it was a mimosa, but there did not seem to be alcohol in the drink. The drink was also sweeter then a mimosa. Whatever it was, it quenched a thirst as no other drink she'd ever had. With the exception of water, which had no taste at all.

"Lord, that was wonderful. What is it?"

"It is the juice of the *primpate* fruit. We have them in the garden and Winters sees we're supplied with an ample amount of the juice every morning. Do you like it?"

He was teasing her as he must know she had liked it. At the moment, she was busy draining the contents of his glass. Swallowing the last of her drink, she nodded her answer.

"You have the same look on your face now as you did last night after Shan Lin and I…"

Shari's hand reached out covering Vincent's mouth and cutting off any reference to just what the two men had done to her last night before Winters could hear. Looking back at Winters and then to Vincent, she tried to use her eyes to tell Vincent not to say anything while Winters was in the room.

Chuckling behind her hand, Vincent snaked out his tongue and began to lick her hand sensuously before Shari could snatch it back.

"Hey!" she gasped out loud, before snatching her hand back and rubbing it against her now pounding heart. Using his tongue had been only one of the things Vincent and Shan Lin had done to Shari last night.

"Do not fear Shari. Winters is a very discreet man. He'll never listen to our conversations. Will you, Winters?" Vincent asked, laughter visible in his eyes.

"Hmmm?" Winters started comically. "Did you say something, Sir? I can't quite hear you, My Lord Prince. My hearing has suddenly gone. Would you mind speaking up, Sir?"

Shari glared at Vincent, her heart finally slowing its pounding at the memory of what had gone on between her and her new husbands the night before.

The night before had been... Wonderful, magnificent, fabulous, stupendous... She could barely think of an adjective good enough to describe her feelings of the love and caring the two men had shown her last night, and given time, she could get very used to this kind of treatment.

"I'm very glad you enjoyed yourself, *Kasha*. It was my pleasure."

And mine also, heart of my soul.

Shari froze as Shan Lin's voice sounded inside her head. The business of speaking in her mind would take some getting used to.

"It's all right. We've lived with it all our lives. It's only natural you'd have a time of adjustment, at first."

Vincent leaned over, casually stroking his hand down her back reassuringly, then straightened in his seat and reached for the food in front of him.

* * * * *

"I'm afraid we're going to have to leave you for a day, maybe two. We've been given orders to report to Hurok by tomorrow."

Vincent spoke casually from beside Shari as they sat down to breakfast the next day.

"Is there trouble?" Shari asked wondering why she would think so.

"Nothing, which hasn't been going on for sometime now. It's mostly routine. The Queen thinks if she sends heavy reinforcements in now, there won't be a need for mass forces later."

Do not worry. Shari. It's routine at this point.

Tell her the rest.

Shari turned to Vincent with a question on her face.

"The rest of what?"

Vincent, in the process of scooping his breakfast on a plate, paused momentarily before continuing to fill his dish. Shari waited as he prepared his breakfast, set the plate in front of himself, then began to eat.

Tell her.

Why don't you tell her? You're in such a hurry for her to know, get your ass in here and tell her.

"Hey. I can hear you guys just fine now. Why don't you just tell me Vincent?"

Vincent squirmed in his chair, clearly uneasy.

"Well…that is to say… Look…" Shari nearly smiled into the glass she had just lifted to her mouth but fought the urge. The notion of this large and in-charge man in acute discomfort somehow reassured her as nothing else the two men had done, could.

Setting her drink on the table, she did her best to help him along.

"Maybe if you said it really fast and got it out, it wouldn't be so hard for you."

That's good. Why don't you give it a try.

Vincent snorted.

"Why don't you come in here and stop hiding. You tell her."

Shan Lin strode in, looking refreshed after having lingered in the bath, leaving Shari and Vincent to find breakfast together.

"Good morning, Shari," he said as he bent down to give her a lingering kiss before taking a seat on the other side of her.

Looking between the two men, Shari wondered why Vincent would be having such trouble telling her whatever it was he had to say.

"That's easy. What he doesn't want to tell you is our aunt has requested…"

"Demanded, you mean," Vincent interrupted.

"Fine. Our aunt, has demanded an audience with you. She wants to meet her marriageniece."

Shari's eyebrows drew together in concern.

"And this would be bad, why?" she asked the brothers as she felt tension seep into the room.

"It isn't a bad…" Shan Lin began only to be interrupted once again by Vincent.

"Not if you want to feed our wife to the *averons* so soon after we've finally found her."

Shan Lin frowned at Vincent.

Vincent. We don't want to frighten…

"Frighten? Why would you be worrying about frightening me? Is your aunt an ogre? Is she a…" Shari could not think of anything bad enough she was willing to say about another member of her husbands' family. Well, actually, her family now.

"An ogre? That would be putting it mildly." Shan Lin said reaching for what Shari thought might be some kind of meat.

Shari stared at him wondering why they would even think she would go to meet the woman if she was so bad. Queen or not.

"So I just don't go to see her. End of story. It's not as if she could force me to. After all, I'm an American…" She stopped her speech right there. Was she still an American?

"Can she force me? Just how does this kingdom work anyway?"

Vincent was nodding his head.

"Yes, she can. This is a Queendom. She is the Queen. She can do whatever she wants." As he spoke, Shari heard a thread of bitterness in his voice. Thinking it might just be a problem of a ruler ruling a bit too long, Shari sought to reassure him.

"I can be diplomatic when it's necessary. I have to be…had to be…in order to survive in the corporate world as long as I have." Another reminder of what she had left behind.

"Shari," Shan Lin started, reaching out to grasp her hand. "It is not as simple as that. I'm afraid things have gotten more complicated with our aunt then any of us would like. There are things…"

He stopped mid-sentence as if searching for the right words. Vincent beat him to it.

"There is a power struggle going on at the moment. You see our cousins, Mitch and Kristain, the Queen's sons, have taken a bride."

Shan Lin picked up the conversation and the brothers took turns telling her the tale.

"In the succession of the throne of Aranak, the throne is passed to the female of the line. In the case of only male children, usually twins, being birthed by the ruling Queen, the throne is then passed on to the wife of the male twins the day of the marriage."

"In the case of Mitch and Kristain, the woman they chose as their bride, Queen Stephanie… Here's where it gets complicated."

"Queen Stephanie is from the Realm of Earth, just as you are…"

"But that's…"

Shari had been about to say it was a wonderful thing. Someone she could actually sympathize with, commiserate with, but Shan Lin held up his hand to forestall her.

"Wait. It gets worse."

Worse? Shari wondered. How could being from Earth be worse? Her eyes narrowed as Shan Lin continued.

"Since Queen Stephanie knew nothing of our ways, she chose to learn all she could before actually coming here and taking control of her throne. Minor details had to be taken care of before she could come. Those aren't important now. I only bring it up so you'll understand just how seriously she is taking on the mantle of leadership."

Shari nodded, understanding only too well. In the other woman's place, Shari would want time to learn all she could so as not to make mistakes with an entire world she knew little about, rather than jump in and learn as she went. She shuddered to think what might happen if…

But it was exactly what she was doing now. If Vincent had explained correctly, she was now in a position similar to what this Queen Stephanie must be facing.

Shari's body began to shake.

What if I screw something up? I don't know the first thing…

"Be at ease, little one. It's close, *Kasha*. But not quite." Shan Lin tried to reassure her. "We are here for you."

Vincent and Shan Lin each reached out to comfort Shari, coming out of their chairs to surround her. Shari felt waves of comfort emanate from the pair, and the pounding of fear in her heart, which started at her thoughts, eased gradually.

Taking a deep breath seemed to indicate she was calmer and the two resumed their seats and the discussion.

"The problem is this. Our aunt, Queen Sara, is not ready to have her position or power taken from her. She has barely acknowledged our new Queen except inside the palace where she resides. She makes no concession to the fact she must vacate her position as soon as Queen Stephanie deems it necessary to come and reside in Aranak, and from what my brother and I know, it won't be long now."

"You see Sara is very addicted to the life of a monarch. At the moment any and all are at her beck and call. When she says jump, there is no asking how high, you just do it. She is cruel, she is a tyrant, and she is slowly driving the world of Aranak to its knees for no greater reason than she can."

At those words, Shari watched Shan Lin bow his head in an attempt to hide his growing anger. She reached out her own hand and comforted him by stroking her own fingers down his cheek. She wanted to get out of her chair and take him in her arms and lay his head on her breast. Anything to ease the ache she was now feeling in her own chest as if it was hers.

He looked up out of eyes awash in anguish and gave her a lopsided smile.

"It is we who comfort you. It is the way of our people."

"Then the ways of your people need to shift a bit," Shari said as she got up and went to him, taking his head in her hands and giving him a gentle kiss on his lips. She saw Vincent come up beside her and reached a hand out to his brother. Reaching out one of her hands, she gently guided Shan Lin's head to her breast and awkwardly leaned into Vincent.

"I'm here now. Anything you two need, I'll see you get it."

A choked sound came from Shan Lin.

"It is our duty…" he began.

"It is all of our duty to see the three of us get what we need. You are my husbands now. No matter how it came about, it is a fact. If I need to see your aunt, we'll figure something out in the end. Don't worry. I can hold my own with the best of them."

Shari did what she could to comfort her husbands as they began to tell her about their aunt.

* * * * *

It was sometime later in the evening as Shari sat awake in bed, her husbands sound asleep when she began to think she might have bitten off more then she could chew with their aunt.

Shari shivered between her sleeping husbands as she thought of the things they told her their aunt had done. Two arms, one from each man on either side of her, reached out to enfold her in their warmth as murmurs sounded in stereo.

"Ssssh. I'm fine."

Twin grunts of acceptance sounded and Shari smiled at the sounds. Even in their sleep her husbands worried for her.

It didn't matter. If it was a command performance the woman wanted, a command performance the bitch would get.

Mari Byrne

Chapter Thirteen

Shari awoke gradually to find herself lying on top of Vincent, her back to his chest, her body on fire. Shan Lin lay between her legs, his head dropping forward absently as his tongue darted out teasing against her clitoris. Vincent's shaft was burrowing itself slowly into her pussy before receding just as minutely. A rapturous groan escaped Shari, sounding husky with sleep as well as desire.

"Does this please my wife?" Vincent whispered into her ear as he thrust, then retreated with small circling movements of his hips. First he thrust into her from the left side, sliding negligently out again, then reversing sides and repeating the process over and over again until Shari nearly begged him to go faster.

Shan Lin busily lapped away at her clit, alternately sucking on it, then biting down gently before his tongue laved deliberately at the burning bud. He lifted his head and smiled wickedly at Shari before returning with a vengeance to his task.

"Do your husbands service you well? Is our loving to your liking?" The sensual words whispered in her ear caused her pussy to contract and Vincent to moan sensually against her neck.

"Again, *Kasha*. Again." Shari moved her hips lower, her mind beginning to catch up with her body. Vincent thrust his hips upward just in time to catch her downward movement. The result caused Shari to use her channel muscles to grip the hot cock buried deep within her.

"That's it, love. Do it again." The words were gritted against Shari's neck as Vincent brought a hand upward and began to knead her breast.

Shari gyrated her hips faster, seeking release. It made no difference. No matter how briskly she moved, neither man would be rushed.

In the end, she resorted to pleading, begging in the worst way possible. The men played with her as if she was their personal toy and they had been denied her for a long time. Shan Lin gradually increased his licks and suckled her faster as Vincent's cock rammed harder and harder. Grinding her hips, Shari whimpered in gratitude.

On the verge of an orgasm, crying out in sheer relief at finally being given what she sought, she neared the edge, her hips pistoning in counter rhythm to Vincent's strokes and Shan Lin's tongue, she tasted the climax waiting just ahead. Shari rose off Vincent's chest, grasped onto Shan Lin's hair and pushed his head further into her pussy. Swiveling her hips, she simultaneously ground her pussy against Vincent's thick shaft.

Breath coming in pants and wheezes, Shari listened as Vincent encouraged her to fuck him.

"Harder. Your pussy is so tight, so wet... *Riad! Frech* my cock." His voice trailed away as he sucked in his breath hard.

The words sent her into her climax screaming out as her pussy convulsed and pulsations ripped through her body against Vincent's thrusts. Moments later, or perhaps a lifetime later, Shari felt Vincent's release. As his cock jerked and his body rode out his release, her pussy joined him in another, softer orgasm.

Shari lay panting as Vincent kissed her neck and Shan Lin nuzzled her nether lips occasionally licking her sensitive clit, sending an answering jolt through her body.

When her breath returned, Shari thanked the men.

"Now that's what I call an alarm clock. Any chance I can get the entire performance replayed while I'm fully awake?"

Both men chuckled as Shari disengaged herself from Vincent and collapsed on the bed.

"You're an insatiable woman, *Kasha*, but it's fine with me. I do believe I'll enjoy it in my wife."

Smiling seductively, or hoping she was, Shari tried a come hither look on Shan Lin.

"Are you pained, Shari?" Shan Lin asked solicitously, tilting his head checking her body from head to toe. She rolled her eyes and wondered if perhaps her husbands weren't as in tune with her as she thought.

"He understands well enough, *Kasha*," Vincent said from beside her as he turned his head and bent to kiss her. His tongue made its way into her mouth as his fingers came to rest in her springy curls, playing with her clit.

Shari moaned into his mouth and hung on. Before he had released her mouth, Shari had another climax.

"Now, if you'll excuse me a moment, I'll be right back." Vincent spoke as he climbed from the bed and made his way to the bathroom. As Shari lay in a hedonistic stupor, she heard water running. Turning her attention on Shan Lin she noticed his cock still hard as ever.

Can't have that, now can we? Shari roused herself, demanding her liquefied body answer her commands.

Not if you say so, we can't. The answer slipped into her mind and she smiled knowing Shan Lin agreed completely with her assessment.

"Come here, husband. I must see to your needs. Now."

Shan Lin obeyed her command immediately and with great pleasure. Shari rewarded him by taking his engorged shaft deep into her mouth. Coming upward, she used her teeth to scrape against the bulging veins and wringing a low moan of pleasure out of him. She used her tongue on the tip of him and rimmed the tiny opening before bathing the entire circumference with her tongue, licking her way backward and forward then lifting his swollen, heavy sac with her hand and using the other to stroke his cock up and down.

She repeated the process slowly at first, then faster and faster until her pussy began to pulse in time with the veins of his hot shaft. Just before his release, Shari took him completely into her mouth and down her throat to the hilt, and grabbed onto his naked, silky ass. His hips pumped faster and faster and with each thrust of his cock, Shari's pussy answered with a throb of its own.

"*Frech!* I'm going to come…" Shan Lin barked out. Shari beat him to it, coming first. The vibrations in her throat along with moans of her pleasure set off his climax and a hot stream of salty liquid poured into her mouth and throat. Shari did her best to suck him dry, as she rode her own maddening orgasm. When he tried to pull away, she held on, making sure she had gotten it all.

When she finally released him, he twitched and Shari smiled knowing this was one incident her husband would remember for a while.

"Yes…I will," Shan Lin gasped.

Shari smiled in satisfaction and fell back on the bed once again, a yawn surprising her.

"That was lovely. What time is it anyway?" Shari looked around wondering why she had yet to see clocks in the house.

"Our bodies let us know what time it is. Right now, it is very early. The sun has yet to rise and you can go back to sleep if you'd like." Vincent came out of the bathroom speaking through a towel as he dried his hair.

Shari looked him over and reveled in the power of his beautiful body. His shaft stirred and began to rise, and Vincent chuckled.

"It is always this way with mates. I only have to think of you and I'm hard as a tree. Unfortunately," he paused giving Shan Lin a "hurry up" look then turning his attention back to Shari, went on speaking, "we must leave."

Shan Lin bent over Shari and kissed her soundly before rising and bounding off the bed.

"Thank you, *Kasha*, that was the most wonderful gift I could have received."

Shari breathed heavily after the kiss and barely managed a thank you of her own.

"Thank you...both." Her heart raced and she wondered if they had time for just...one...more...

Both men moved rapidly toward her, Vincent tossing his towel and Shan Lin reversing his direction.

"*Kasha*." The men rasped as they climbed toward her.

Apparently they did.

Chapter Fourteen

Shan Lin and Vincent loaded their horses into the transpo lift they would need to reach Hurok by early the next morning as Winters directed their packs and accessories to be loaded into the cargo bay.

"Easy, Demond." Shan Lin soothed the annoyed horse as he led Demond up the ramp into the ship. The horses rarely protested the trip, but Shan Lin's horse, Demond, and Vincent's, Talana, had been in the middle of breeding season when Queen Sara had ordered the brothers to infiltrate Hurok.

Mate. The word skittered through Vincent's mind as the horses' hooves pounded up the load ramp.

Shan Lin grunted agreement with the word the horses spoke but knew there was little the two men and the two horses could do about their interruptions from their mates.

"Leave it to an animal to remind us where our priorities should lie. It's bad enough he and Talana had to leave their breeding grounds for this sojourn, but we had to leave our bride as well."

The grumpiness Shan Lin heard in his brother's voice echoed in his own heart as well. A resigned sigh escaped Shan Lin.

"Brother mine, if you think I'm in any better of a mood for having to leave Shari curled so sweetly in our bed, then you've lost more of your mind than I thought."

Vincent harrumphed as he threw the last of their gear in behind the horses and prepared to board the ship.

"Orders are orders. But I'm damned if I want to follow these. Don't newlyweds normally get two weeks before they have to face the world? Isn't there some arcane law which would allow us to stay and…"

Vincent looked hopefully at his brother who was already shaking his head.

"We're still in the service of both Queens and we have little choice but to obey. Let's just get on with this and get back as soon as possible.

Leaving a warm, wet woman waiting for the two of us to return is not my idea of a good start to a mission."

Vincent grunted his agreement and climbed into the ship, his boots ringing against the metalloid floor of the cargo transpo. Shan Lin climbed in after him, unhooking the ramp as he looked out the doorway.

"Winters is finished and has secured the hold's door. If we've got everything, let's get this fiasco finished and get back to our wife."

* * * * *

Shari stirred in bed, shivering at the loss of remembered warmth that had recently surrounded her. Stretching, she reached out absently waiting to contact with a warm body and coming up empty handed.

Lifting her head to look around, Shari found she was alone in the cavernous bed.

"Shan Lin? Vincent?" she called out softly at first and receiving no response, called more loudly.

Shari? A gentle voice came into her mind.

Looking around wildly for the source, it took Shari's sleep clogged mind a few moments before she realized the voice was coming from inside her head.

"Well, hell. A couple of glorious nights of uninhibited sex and I'm hearing voices." Shari shook her head at her schizophrenic thoughts and mumbled aloud about losing it. *It*, being her mind.

"I'm in la-la land, trapped in a sexual haze of orgasms, and losing my sanity in the process." Shari started to get off the bed, untangling the coverings as she scooted across the behemoth her husbands called a bed.

Shari?

"What?" she asked querulously.

Are you all right? You seem distressed.

Shari growled at the voice, still not quite able to realize where it came from.

"Look. I'm not even awake. So if this is your idea of a joke..."

Great! Now she was talking to herself.

A sleepy snarl sounded as she began to taunt the voice.

"Little voices in my head, makes me think I am dead. Why do you not go away, come again..." No, it wouldn't work.

Shari! Two voices spoke her name in unison, command inherent in their voices.

Shari jolted, tumbling from the bed directly into the pile of coverings she had just extracted herself from. Coming up fighting through her trappings, Shari looked around the room expecting her husbands to be looking on the scene of her fall and laughing uproariously at her.

"What? Shan Lin? Vincent? Just where the hell are you?"

Not finding the men in the room, though she had gotten up and began to prowl through the enormous room, Shari made her way toward the door to see if perhaps they were on the other side.

I'm sorry, Kasha. *We're pathing to you in your mind.*

The words brought Shari up short on her journey to the room's door. Suddenly she remembered the two men's particular ability.

"Thank God! I thought I had lost my mind." Relief relaxed the muscles that had tightened at the thought of the loss of her faculties.

"I thought I was losing... Wait, does this mean you can listen in on my thoughts anytime you want?" Shari asked, her eyes narrowing in suspicion.

A chuckle sounded in her mind and she felt a soft caress run through her body.

Shivering at the intimate contact, Shari shuddered.

"Hey, knock it off." She meant to speak forcefully but the words came out on a moan.

Vincent. Leave it be. It's not as if we can finish what you're starting in person...

Shari listened to the words, barely hearing them over the sensations beginning to course through her body. Massive heat began to pool in her pussy and her hand began to make its way down her torso toward her naked curls.

Do you want me to stop? Vincent's voice asked, a caress stroking her mentally.

"Are you going to come ease the ache?" Shari asked, her body betraying her need to give in to the stimulation causing her body to undulate.

A sense of disappointment pathed into her mind and the stimulation eased into a feeling of comfort. A snarl sounded briefly and was quickly cut off.

My apologies, Kasha. *I will make it up to you when we return.*

Shari's breath escaped through trembling lips as her body's control was once again returned to her.

"You had better." A snarl of her own sounded and Shari winced as she made her way to the bathroom.

Entering the spacious bathroom, Shari felt something about the room put her off. As gorgeous as it was, it didn't quite give her a feeling of…ownership? *Perhaps all the room needed was her touch. Things in it, that belonged to her.* It was gorgeous in and of itself, but it wasn't quite *theirs* yet. Thinking absently of just how she might be able to accomplish this as she took care of business, her mind wandered to just where the men had gone.

We're headed to Hurok. The Queen has ordered us to…

Shari nearly came off the toilet as she yelped in surprise.

"Hey! Can I have a little privacy here? I'm trying to pee for cripes sakes!"

Mortified at having the two men in her head as she used the bathroom, Shari finished in record time and nearly dove into the shower stall. Waves of contrition pathed into her head as she tried to hide under the waterfall which seemed to be the 'spigot' for the brothers' shower.

Kasha. Please…

Shari listened to Vincent's voice, the humor threaded through it and she let out a stifled scream.

"Just tell me when you'll be back and let me clean up." Frustrated by the aborted seduction, not very happy about waking to find the two brothers gone after she had practically become another limb to the two last night, Shari used the soap she had found and began to scrub viciously at her hair.

"And tell me how to block the two of you out of my head for a while!" Shari sputtered soap out of her mouth as she spoke.

There was silence for a moment before Shan Lin's voice came through.

That is something you must find on your own.

Vincent cut in.

You must find a way in your own mind. But you will also need to find a way to turn it back on. Listen, Shari, it was not my intention…

Shari ignored what the brothers were saying and conjured up a switch in her mind. Mentally turning it off as she would a light switch on a wall, she rinsed her hair and waited.

No voices spoke in her mind.

"Shan Lin?" She spoke tentatively.

No answer from his smooth voice.

"Vincent?" She waited.

Nothing. No growlly snarl replied.

A relieved breath left her as Shari suddenly smiled.

"Fixed those two good, didn't I. Smarter than the average bear, eh Boo-Boo?" Shari snickered feeling much better. Now she could finish wallowing in the luxurious shower, the wonderfully steamy waterfall she had been waiting to try since she had first seen it.

A tiny bubble of joy sounded as she hummed a tune from Gypsy Rose Lee in her mind. It sounded suspiciously like, "Everything's Coming Up Roses."

Now that should drown out those two and allow me to find a real body to speak to.

Thinking she would just round up Winters after her shower and grill him on the brothers' whereabouts, Shari lathered up the floral soap she had found and finished washing her body.

* * * * *

"What the hell did you do that for? We needed her to be in contact with us when she went to see Auntie. You know she hasn't claimed us yet and we have no idea if she'll be able to turn it back on."

Shan Lin snapped at his brother, as Vincent prepared to dock by guiding the ship into the port of Hurok.

"She wanted to know and I would deny her nothing." Vincent spoke calmly ignoring Shan Lin who grumbled in his seat.

"You are not her only husband. I too am entitled to give her what she needs. If you hadn't let her know how to shut off the pathing, I could have…"

Shan Lin never finished the sentence. Vincent watched his brother out of the corner of his eye and was doing his best to keep the ship level as he docked using the latch that would keep the ship attached to the docking bay.

He had no sooner managed the difficult task when a metal case came flying at his head from the opposite side, where his brother had been. Ducking quickly as he had been taught during Warrior training, Vincent easily avoided having his head caved in.

"Tantrum, brother mine?" Vincent asked as an adult speaking to a rebellious child.

An inhuman sound came from Shan Lin as Vincent saw his brother prepare to launch himself at Vincent.

Vincent, never one to pass up the opportunity for a good fight, knew he should put a stop to this. Knowing *Try Nas Ayn* had its talons sunk into Shan Lin, Vincent did his best to talk his brother out of the fight they both knew could kill them.

"Think about it brother mine. Shari is not even…"

"Do not speak the name of my bride! *She is mine!* Do you hear me? It is my right to give her what she needs. You have no rights where she is concerned."

Panting heavily, Shan Lin picked up the closest object in the ship to himself. A *pryt* lance.

Vincent raised his eyebrow questioningly at his brother, willing him to see the absurdity in the situation.

"Shan Lin." Vincent spoke calmly, a sense of unreality seeping into his body. "Shari is my wife also. She is the other half of us. She cannot have one without the other."

Vincent watched Shan Lin fiddle with the switch on the *pryt* lance, flicking it on and off. Vincent began to send waves of love toward his brother wanting to kick his own ass for allowing his feelings for Shari to overwhelm good judgment.

"Brother mine." The words came softly. "You are right. I should not have allowed our wife to learn how to block us out before we have been accepted. *Our* wife will be without our aid. We must have faith in her ability…"

Vincent felt Shan Lin's mind shift into rage. Resigned, Vincent knew the coming fight might just take the edge off the building *Try Nas Ayn* spreading through both the brothers' rational reasoning. Praying silently to *Riad* not to let the two kill each other, Vincent advanced at the sound of his brother's blood curdling war cry.

* * * * *

Vincent limped slightly as he led Talana down the ramp of the ship's docking bay. Glancing back at his brother, Vincent smiled as he watched Shan Lin flinch when Demond bumped into his head playfully asking for affection.

"Knock it off, Demmie. I don't think my head can take much more pounding. My loving brother has only recently knocked some sense into it."

Fight? The horse pathed reproachfully into Vincent's mind.

He was claiming the filly as his own. You know we share. Vincent's child like speech had the horse snorting and throwing its head up jerking the lead line out of Shan Lin's hold.

"Hey! Come back here." Shan Lin mumbled as his horse flicked its tail in Shan Lin's face and walked down the ramp on its own.

Vincent laughed good-naturedly at the scene.

"Serves you right. Even your own horse knows the laws of twins."

The misery suddenly coming off Shan Lin as he gathered up some of the brothers' gear to take off the ship brought a quick halt to the humor Vincent was trying to impart.

Directing his own horse to join Demond, Vincent went to help his brother.

"Shan Lin. It's not your fault."

Shan Lin ignored the comfort Vincent tried to give and continued to gather their things.

"*Try Nas Ayn* kills. We both knew it was a possibility. Granted we didn't really think we would take her to wife for real, but we both knew it could happen. There is no shame…"

Shan Lin straightened quickly throwing the gear he had just gathered from him violently before turning to look Vincent in the eye.

"I tried to kill you! Don't you understand?" Shan Lin ground out.

Vincent shook his head.

"No, you did not. If you had wanted me dead, I would be. You pulled your…"

Vincent wanted his brother to know the truth.

"No! I didn't pull anything. I wanted to kill you and would have. There was one thought in my mind and one thing only. You—dead. I would then have Shari to myself and…"

Shan Lin's voice trailed away as he turned once again to gather the gear he had roughly thrown down.

"Shan Lin. Brother of my heart. Look at me."

Shan Lin stopped, shoulders heaving from the feelings of guilt running through him.

"Don't. There is nothing to feel guilty over. Only know when it is myself in *Try Nas Ayn* I wish you to prevent me from killing you. It is all I ask and all I did for you."

Shan Lin bowed his head.

"Put it behind you and allow us to complete our mission. All will right itself when we return to our heart."

Shan Lin nodded not bothering to turn around. Vincent accepted the quick agreement and left his brother to gather himself a moment. He needed a minute of his own. The memories of the fight were too fresh. The fact was Shan Lin *had* nearly taken Vincent's life. It had to be buried deeply so his brother never found the memory nor the feelings.

Vincent cursed the *Try Nas Ayn* and went to find the brothers' animals.

* * * * *

Shan Lin watched Vincent as they rode toward the small town of Hurok, population twenty-five thousand. Their intelligence had told them of a coming attack from the Horrd border thirty-five miles away. Being this close to enemy lines it would have behooved Shan Lin to pay closer attention to the surrounding area than to his brother.

Snap to soldier! Shan Lin ordered himself as thoughts of the fight on the ship began to make their way back into his thoughts. *Just get on with it. You've got a wife to escort out of the Realm since the Queen ran roughshod over you and Vincent. Oh. And have you forgot the little thing called* Try Nas Ayn *you've both got to get through? Concentrate on what's most important.* Doing his best to bury the memories, especially the exact moment he had nearly ended Vincent's life, Shan Lin drew on all the training he and Vincent had gone through to become Warriors and pushed them aside.

Do you see it?

Vincent's voice brought Shan Lin to attention and the fight was immediately shoved out of his mind.

To the left. Recognize those two?

Shan Lin looked around him casually as if to take in the lay of the land nearly missing the two figures camouflaged into the terrain.

I see them. What are they doing here? I thought they were hot on the trail of Capt. Lawsai?

Vincent shrugged mentally before bringing his horse to a halt speaking in a casual voice out loud.

"I don't know Shan Lin. It might be an ambush. Do you think we should be frightened?"

Shan Lin struggled to make his voice nonchalant as his heart began to pound in anticipation of a fight not with his brother.

"You would think we should be, Vincent. After all, these same Warriors once thought to get the drop on us. They probably would have if we hadn't spotted them first as we've no doubt done once again."

Vincent chuckled, the adrenaline snaking up his spine giving him nearly the same pleasure he got when thinking of Shari.

Don't go there, brother mine. Keep your mind on the situation.

Vincent's smile was closer to an *averon* barring its fangs than something meant to be reassuring, but Shan Lin knew it was the best he would get.

"Why don't we just go over and see if those two are in the mood to dance with us. It's got to be more pleasant for them than the mess of kicking their scrawny asses would be."

This time, the smile lighting Vincent's face was more in tune with laughter.

"I think you're right, brother mine. After all, aren't we The Death Bringer and The Queen's Most Vicious Warrior?"

The bragging note in Vincent's voice did it. From behind Vincent, Shan Lin watched as shapes rose swiftly out of the terrain and quickly became forms of men.

"Hardie, *freching*, har." The one on the left spoke sarcastically.

Shan Lin nodded a greeting as Vincent turned in pretend surprise.

"Why, Shan Lin! Look who it is." The feigned pleasure in Vincent's tone had Shan Lin laughing. "It's Aranak's dirt surveyors all decked out in their finery. I tell you, brother mine, I never thought I would see the day I could proudly say I watched as they wallowed in shit. I must admit they are braver than we. Look at how serious they take their jobs. It's not every man or woman who would allow themselves to be covered in *averon* dung as they crawled through the fields."

Shan Lin laughed harder as his brother bent down and asked the two men in all seriousness if they had to taste samples of the excrement to determine which *averon* hailed from where.

He knew Vincent was pushing his luck with the two men but couldn't help himself. The tension he was feeling from the earlier fight he had with Vincent was slowly draining out of him as Vincent waited for the two men to answer.

"Really, Warrior," the second man drawled as he threw off the ground covering and dusted himself off. "As if you have room to talk after the last place we found you."

The first man to speak nudged the second as they began to snicker.

"Or was it perhaps, you were enjoying yourself in middle of the *freching krikers* and were just patiently waiting for your turn with one of them?"

Shan Lin watched Vincent scowl at the memory. His brother had been sent on reconnaissance to intercept a Horrd missive intended for a highly placed military commander when a family had waylaid Vincent in need of his assistance. The stranded family had been transporting grown *krikers* during mating season and Vincent had made the mistake of getting between a male and his male mate. Something any child knew, just as the child knew *kriker* male organs could become inverted to allow another male *kriker* to impregnate a similar male. The gestation process could, and often did, kill the impregnated males, which was why *krikers* were born in masses.

The *kriker* in discussion had not taken kindly to the interruption of its needs and had sought to take Vincent instead.

"Oh, sure Vincent. You resisted their affections at first," the man went on taunting Shan Lin's brother, "but I had to wonder as I came on the scene if I should just allow you to be taken. You had a look in your eye saying you might just have enjoyed it."

The second man was now howling in laughter, and Vincent looked as if he was ready to get off Talana and teach the man a lesson. It was definitely time for Shan Lin to intervene.

"Okay Kyden. As much as I enjoy seeing Vincent brought down to size every now and then, I think it's time you told us what two Horrdian Warriors are doing on this side of the border."

Even as Shan Lin spoke, he heard Vincent mumble.

"I could have taken them both. Those damned *krikers* would have been good eating if they hadn't already sprouted wings."

Kyden laughed.

"I know Rayan. I thought I was helping another Horrdian Warrior. If I had known it was you, I would have just let you take your chances."

The second man had gotten himself under control as the men spoke and piped up.

"It's a damned shame I didn't have my Vid/Sync cam running though. I think I could have made a lot of creds from the sale of the stills alone."

Vincent gave a snorting laugh.

"So long as you would have split the proceeds with me, Dylan, I would have given it a go."

The four men laughed good-naturedly. All too soon they knew they would have to get down to business. It was Kyden who reminded them of it moments later.

"As much as I'd like to reminisce, we have a bigger problem on our hands at the moment."

Shan Lin and Vincent came to attention.

"What do you mean?" Shan Lin asked.

Kyden looked to Dylan and the second man sighed heavily.

"It's a pain in *Riad's* ass I'm going to be, but we've got intelligence which says a Horrdian war party is going to strike the town of Hurok today."

"Yeah. So? It's why we're here." Vincent quickly spoke up.

But Kyden was already shaking his head.

"Well, that's the problem."

"What's the problem?" Shan Lin asked, wondering why the two Horrdian brothers would come to warn them.

"Aren't the two of you supposed to be somewhere on the other side of Aranak? Like somewhere near Camp Grenlak, putting an end to the skirmishes going on there daily?" Vincent narrowed his eyes suspiciously. "Or have you already done it?"

Dylan looked up at Vincent with a look of pain in his eyes.

"Those skirmishes were called off over four *enons* ago. We told you your armies have been fighting mercenaries. Horrd superiors deemed it a waste of man power to engage the border due to the heavy casualties we received."

Shan Lin's lips flattened in anger. He knew something funny had been going on near the camp for a while. If these two could be trusted, and he had learned the hard way they could, Shan Lin now knew it was true. He just had no way to prove it.

We'll find proof. We have *to find proof. It's the only way we can get evidence to Queen Stephanie.*

Shan Lin nodded.

Dylan seemed to take it as a good sign the brothers believed him because he went on.

"We infiltrated Kilian two nights ago," he began speaking of a larger town nearly sixty miles from where the men now stood talking, "where we overheard a band of mercs making bets on the number of Horrdian's they could take down without blood shed. Now in itself, the statements were harmless. But as they got drunker, a few of them let slip bits of info for anyone within hearing."

Kyden picked up the tale here.

"It seems they had been paid by the 'Queen Whore' herself to instigate a massacre in the town of Hurok two nights from that time, meaning tonight, and lay the blame on the Horrd. Make it look as if our Warriors snuck in and slaughtered the town while it slept. After all, there was little the town could do as it's out of the way and is afforded very little protection from the palace of Aranak."

Shan Lin made a slashing motion with his hand cutting off Kyden's words.

"Are you telling me Queen Sara, the Queen of Aranak herself, paid these…"

"Yes." The Horrdian brothers spoke in unison.

"Bullshit!" Vincent shouted from atop his mount causing Talana to step sideways before he could control the animal.

"Hold, Talana." Vincent spoke harshly at the knowledge the Queen had finally given them something tangible to present the court of Aranak. If what the two brothers said was true.

"No, it's true all right. Matter of fact, we've been waiting here for most of the early hours of morning for you to show. The mercs were bragging the fight was going to give them the chance to take on the Queens' Warriors. She would be sending in a squad behind her initial Trackers…"

"Trackers?" Shan Lin asked incredulously. "Now, we're *freching* Trackers? When the hell did we get demoted fourteen ranks to Trackers?"

Vincent grunted.

"Better than promoting us to dead as it appears she wants."

Shan Lin could only agree.

"Look. As much as it delights me to see the two most bragged about men in Aranak being belittled, there's still more you need to know."

Kyden looked between the Warriors to see if he had their attention. If the menacing looks on their faces were any indication, he did. If he had not been sure they would not kill the messenger, Kyden would have been afraid he might have to fight his way out.

"Well then…" Kyden rubbed the back of his neck absently then cursed as he felt the foul clods of shit roll down his back.

Shan Lin laughed easing the tension.

"Thanks, Horrdian cur. I needed that."

Kyden grimaced.

"Yeah. Glad I could help in your time of need." Reaching around, Kyden untucked his uniform shirt and released the dirt beginning to grow legs of its own.

"As I was saying, if you two would quit interrupting, Dylan and I managed to convince the mercs it would be in their best interest to take the Queen's gold and run."

"And did they?" Vincent asked sweetly just for the pleasure of interrupting the Horrdian and aggravating the man.

"Shut up." Kyden said equally as syrupy.

"As a matter of fact, no, they protested," Dylan said.

Shan Lin stared at the brother. "And?"

A smile of unholy glee lit Dylan's features as he turned to look at his brother who now sported the same evil grin. Turning their smiles on the brothers, they both spoke at once.

"It was the best fight we've…"

"…had in a millennium. You should have seen it. Their leader was…"

"…this little thing from the Warrian Pride over near Tecla, on the far side of Moonla Sid. You know the one? With great big…"

"…muscles piled nearly to her forehead and an ass to make a man weep." A remembered sigh of satisfaction slipped from Kyden's lips before he continued.

"She was the one we took down first. And make no mistake, it took…"

"…both of us. She was a sweet little thing the last time I was between her cheeks, both sets mind you, but this was business she had shouted as I reminded her of our earlier acquaintance."

The Horrdian brothers had slipped into the same twin speak of Aranak twins. Shan Lin had learned it was taught to the Warriors of Horrd for infiltration of Aranak.

Dylan smiled reminiscently.

"*Riad,* but she was sweet this time telling both of us why she would have killed us. Though she did say she would proudly display our cocks on her wall of honor as she had the only other men who had made her come."

Shan Lin looked at Vincent and winced before speaking up.

"It was a good threat, but that's all it was as my brother and I both still have our dicks, thanks very much."

The wry note in his voice had the other set of brothers losing their silly grins.

"*Frechie!* You're as bad as your Queen when it comes to fucking. You take on anything." The words were said in a conversational voice, a hint of jealousy in the words.

Vincent shook his head.

"Not any more. Our wife would have something to say about it." He tried to sound grumbly but knew he failed when the other men laughed uproariously.

Smiling good-naturedly, Vincent let them have their laughter.

Kyden was the first to control himself and continued the tale.

"Anyway, we managed to subdue about thirty-seven of them, and I'll admit because more than a few were so damned drunk. Then once we could convince them to leave with the gold in their pockets, they did so. Those we couldn't convince to leave remain secluded and unconscious down the way there." Kyden ended pointing toward the town of Kilian.

"Good. I'd love to ask them a few questions. You didn't by any chance get the one the Queen paid the gold to did you?" Vincent asked.

"As a matter of fact," Dylan cut in, "we did. You're going to love this. She got it on Vid/Sync."

Shan Lin let out of shout of joy startling his grazing horse and controlling it easily before he was unseated.

"Proof! Finally! How the hell did she get it past the Queen's Guards?" Shan Lin asked happily.

Kyden smiled. "She used a man. Your Queen doesn't think men have brains above their dicks."

Vincent smiled at Shan Lin, knowing the man's answer was true.

"The man stood there looking blank-eyed as the Queen came up to him speaking as if to an idiot. It was a risk worthy of Earth's Trojan Horse maneuver. I mean as much disrespect as I can say when I tell you your Queen is a menace to your Aranak army. If Horrd wasn't in the middle of its own upheaval, I'd revel in Aranak's destruction. At this moment, it would be a slaughter."

Shan Lin and Vincent took no offense at Kyden's words. They knew all too well he spoke the truth.

Vincent opened his mouth to ask how Kyden had known what happened but was interrupted by Dylan.

"We saw the Vid/Sync. We've also got a copy. As much as we trust you two..." Dylan shrugged. "Insurance."

Vincent nodded at the man. He would have done the same.

Thoughts? Vincent pathed his brother.

Too many to count at the moment. Let's just make our way into town and see what happens.

Are we taking them with us? Vincent asked, his voice neutral.

Riad! Shan Lin gave a heaving sigh. *I supposed they earned the right.*

"Do you have any Warrior clothing with you?" Shan Lin asked the two men out loud.

The two men exchanged incredulous looks at Shan Lin.

"Did you think we strolled in to Aranak in full Horrdian dress?" Dylan asked bitingly.

"Yes," Kyden spoke, nudging his brother with his elbow. "Let us clean up a moment and we'll get our mounts. Meet us in town as if we've come from scouting in the opposite direction in..." Kyden opened a flap in his dirty shirt and consulted a hidden time piece there, "...one hour."

The four men agreed, then parted, two going toward the town of Hurok, the other two, back through the stinking field they had crawled into to wait for the Aranakian Warriors.

* * * * *

"Winters." Shari called out to the man as she stepped from the lift and making her way toward him wondering how long it would take her to get used to the house. She had gotten lost twice already and would have missed finding her way back to the elevator if she had not seen someone exiting the machine only seconds before her decision to turn left.

"Yes, My Lady Princess? How may I serve you?" He asked formally.

Shari stood there in the large room she had followed the man into and suddenly stopped. It was exquisite. Family photos hung on the walls and tiny holographic pictures bleeped messages into the air, greetings and love. This was where the brothers had enshrined their family.

"It's magnificent." Shari breathed as she grasped Winters' arm and dragged him through the room. Names adorned faces as messages sounded when Shari brushed the frames. She walked through the room demanding Winters tell her as much as possible about the people in the pictures.

Shari quickly learned her husbands had a sister many years younger than them. She also learned of their father and his grief over the death of his brothers Dain and Larik, Consorts to the Queen, and the death of his wife Evelyn, her husbands' mother.

"Dead?" Shari asked as a queer sense of grief gripped her briefly. "How did she die?"

Winters made a gesture for Shari to sit and then sat down across from her. A young man hesitantly came forward, drinks and refreshments on a tray he offered to Shari.

"Well, where'd you come from?" Shari asked the young man as she accepted the refreshment.

"Winters summoned me, My Lady Princess. Do the refreshments meet with your approval?" The man asked as Shari took a drink.

Swallowing quickly, Shari nodded her head wondering when Winters had summoned what she now noticed must be lunch.

"Yes. Thank you..." Shari wanted to thank the man by name but was at a loss.

"Andrews, My Lady Princess. My name is Brent Andrews."

Shari smiled, suddenly feeling ravenous and could not remember when was the last time she had eaten.

"Thank you, Andrews." She said, then shifted to thank Winters. "And you too. I didn't realize just how hungry I was."

"That will be all, Andrews. Please thank the cook for the fare." Winters dismissed Andrews who left with a smile.

"It was nice to meet you, Andrews." Shari called after the man speaking around the meat she had just bitten into. Seeing Winters smile, Shari rolled her eyes.

"This is delicious! Sorry. I don't usually talk with my mouth full. My mother did teach me manners."

Winters smiled indulgently.

"It is your home. Do as you will."

"Speaking of mothers..." Shari began before stuffing her mouth with more of the scrumptious food.

"Ah, yes, My Lady Princess Evelyn. She was a gentle woman not taken to following the laws of Aranakian society. She enjoyed listening to her husband and what he thought best. In our Realm that is unusual."

Shari ate while she listened.

"As you can see here, she wasn't necessarily a woman of great beauty, but she was gorgeous inside. She adored her children and doted on her sons. Their father, My Lord Thaddeous swore she would mollycoddle them to death if he let her. My Lady Evelyn would only smile and allow her husband to rant. When he was done with his tirade, she would smile and do as she always did. Shower the boys with love.

"When My Lady Princess Lyssa was born, the boys, older than their sister by seventeen years, doted on the little one. It was My Lady Evelyn's turn to complain they were spoiling their sister."

Winters paused smiling in fond remembrance of the memory.

"But their mother still continued to dote on her sons. Their father loved them but knew if anything happened to Queen Sara or her children, it would be Shan Lin and Vincent's bride who would inherit the throne."

At this, Shari sucked in her breath completely forgetting the bite of food she had just taken. The food lodged painfully in her throat, and she hacked and coughed plenty before dislodging the item.

Winters had risen and come to offer his aid, but Shari waved him away as she quaffed at her drink. Recovering quickly, Shari asked the obvious question.

"Does it mean I'll become Queen one day?" The thought nearly made her panic.

Winters shook his head. "No, My Lady Princess. Queen Sara's sons have apparently taken a wife. It is she who will assume the throne."

Shari breathed a heartfelt breath of relief as she muttered thanks.

Winters smiled and continued.

"My Lord Prince Thaddeous wanted his sons to be the best. It didn't matter what they did, they had to be the best at it. To this end, My Lords' father had been sending their mother, My Lady Evelyn, away to her sister's for one month of the summer to ensure his sons were made to train properly in anything they started. The summer of their mother's death, My Lord Princes' Shan Lin and Vincent were to begin training as Warriors. They had already gained their titles and lands their wife would receive upon their marriage, as well as acquired the rank of Generals in the Queen's Guard."

Shari raised her eyebrows at this bit of information.

"I told you, My Lord Princes' insured they were the best at anything they did. It also amused their aunt, Queen Sara, to see the young men in her elite guard."

Now *that* Shari could understand. Partial nepotism, part parental ambition. The same thing went on where she came from. Nodding with understanding, Shari motioned for Winters to continue.

"Yes, well. The Princes had been training night and day for three weeks when the message came out over the Wired News. There had been an attack on an Aranakian village. Men, women, and children had been slaughtered viciously. Horrdian warlords came in and slaughtered the entire village, raping men and women alike, pillaging and burning anything in their paths as they went."

Shari swallowed hard at the description of what Winters described; she set down the food she had been devouring and waited for the man to continue.

"The town which was attacked was named Trantn. My Lord Prince Thaddeous had sent his wife to Trantn for the month to visit her sister. Both women were sisters to the Queen of Aranak and took it for granted the women would be protected at all times. After all, his wife had been visiting her sister for the last twenty years with little trouble. Why shouldn't it be so this time?"

Winters paused, Shari reached for a glass on the tray in front of her and offered it to the man. He took it gratefully and drained half the cup before setting it down to continue.

"All three men abandoned what they were doing and raced to help the village. Their mother was in the village. They had family in the village, all who needed their help. They raced with all speed and arrived in record time but it was too late. Evelyn Carrucci-Rayan was dead. She lay next to the bodies of her sister, My Lady Princess Gwendlyn Lawsai-Rayan and her sister's children, My Lady Princesses Christina and Anna Lawsai-Rayan."

"But Lawsai? Isn't that…" Shari asked recognizing the last name. Winters nodded.

"Yes, Captain Lawsai's mother and sisters. My Lady Princess Theresa Georgia Lawsai-Rayan. Or if she preferred, Anaksup. Both she and My Lord Princes are niece and nephews to the Queen. If they wanted to use the royal name, it is within their right." He paused before saying. "As it is now yours."

Shari shook her head in wonder.

"Their mothers were… How long ago was this?" Shari asked.

"Sixteen years ago."

"But, didn't you say Shan Lin and Vincent were seventeen years older than Lyssa? And if so, where was she? Why didn't Theresa die too? Why in hell weren't royal members of the family being guarded?" Questions backed up in Shari's mind as she waited for the answers.

None came.

"My Lady Lyssa was left in my care. Her father did not wish to be parted from his daughter, and Lady Evelyn acceded to his wishes in this instance. Though why he would have sent his wife away and not…" Winters caught himself before finishing the thought and went on as if the comment had not been made.

"My Lady Gwendyln also had the first set of triplet girls born in the Realm of Aranak in the last one hundred and eighty years. Her girls were local celebrities. When one wanted something, the surrounding area had trouble denying it to the girl. *Riad* help them if all three wanted something at the same time."

Shari heard the bittersweet happiness in Winters voice and felt for him as well as her husbands. What the families had to have endured must have been staggering.

"Theresa, her father and twin brothers, Jonas and Damien were out of the village. Theresa had wanted to accompany her father to town and My Lady Evelyn had managed to talk her sister into letting the girl go. She once confided in me Theresa was her favorite but I was to never let on to the other girls. They never heard a word from me, nor has Theresa."

Shari digested all she had learned and sipped at the remains of the last glass on the tray. This was part of her husbands' past and she was glad she had been told.

"Thank you, Winters. The tale must have been very difficult to relate to me. I'm sorry for any residual pain it might have caused." The heartfelt thanks was rewarded.

"It hurts less with every telling, My Lady Shari. Thank you for listening." Shari nodded absently pondering all she had learned.

"What was your intended purpose for summoning me?" Winters finally asked,F rising from his chair.

"What?" Shari asked, still thinking on some of the things Shan Lin and Vincent had gone through before meeting her.

"Oh. Yes, that." Shari stood taking one last look around the room before she hooked her arm through Winters and made her way out of the room with him.

"I was just a bit lonely. I wanted company. Thank you." Shari leaned forward and kissed the older man on his cheek. "I'm sorry to have interrupted you." She left him to do whatever it was he did.

Chapter Fifteen

"I do believe it's time to meet my marriageniece. Why don't we send her an invitation she can't refuse. Officially, of course."

The smile stretching across the aging Queen's face sent a shiver of fear snaking up and down the spine of the eight servers in attendance.

"Brashon. Send the Lady Princess Shari's escort with an invitation to lunch."

Expecting immediate obedience, the Queen turned to look back at the spectacle playing out before her. An amused smiled played across her face as she watched the three women overpower the strapping man on the floor and proceed to tie him up. The first woman, homely at best, bared her teeth to the man in savage satisfaction.

"Mine. You will see to *my* needs first."

Sara strode toward the woman, pride ringing her smile and stroked the woman's hair absently.

"Now I'll find out exactly what has been going through the minds of my supposedly loyal Warriors. *Riad* help them if they've betrayed me, for I will not."

The words, spoken in such a casual manner, sent one attendant quietly from the room. She would need every second she could find to locate her contact allowing the woman to inform the Warriors of Queen Sara's plans.

* * * * *

"Thank you, Krystal. That will be all." Sara said in her best imitation of imperial sovereign. "You'll be amply rewarded for your loyalty. You may go now."

Sara did her best to hold in her anger as she waited for her spy to leave the room before letting out a snarl of anger. Panting in outrage, the Queen made her way through the official rooms of the palace ignoring greetings and questions alike. Her mind was focused on one thing.

Someone would pay for their betrayal, and that someone would soon be attending her.

* * * * *

"It's such a lovely land. I don't know when I've ever felt so relaxed. The surrounding areas I've seen so far have been the most picturesque places I've seen. I can't imagine ever living anywhere else."

Shari spoke of inconsequential things knowing what the pounding on the door meant. All Shari was waiting for was Winters to come in and inform her that her husbands had been killed, she was now a widow, and he'd come to take her back to her own world.

Turning back to Dorian she listened for footsteps to approach her door. A moment went by, then another. When the door to the covered patio continued to remain closed, she gradually relaxed her body and giving a sigh of relief, relaxed against the back of the chair she sat in.

"My Lady Princess, is it true on Earth there is land and food aplenty for all?" Dorian asked casually.

Shari thought for a moment before answering.

"I could tell you yes, Dorian, but it wouldn't necessarily be the truth. You see, we have people starving on earth and no place to live. There are some who have a preference to wander the Earth for whatever reason they have and not live in one place. They're homeless, but by choice."

She paused to think of a few of the people she'd come in contact with that actually preferred this way of existence. Shaking her head in wonderment, she continued answering Dorian's questions.

"Then there are those who have no choice. Be it from tragedies in their lives, not being able to find a job, lost in the system… Well, I could go on forever. Earth isn't a perfect haven. The grass isn't always greener in someone else's yard." She looked to Dorian to see if he understood her euphemism.

"Do you understand?" She asked hopefully.

"I get the meaning if not the actual saying. Basically, just because it sounds better, doesn't always mean it is better." Turning to look at her, he smiled.

"Exactly. Guess I could have said it that way. There are those who try to change the bad things about Earth. Even if it's a different part of where I come from, there are those who want to help. We haven't quite united the entire planet, and it sure won't happen in my lifetime, but I have hopes it eventually will."

Still watching Dorian, Shari observed as the smile slowly left his face.

"I'll be happy if we ever get the chance to just reconcile with our neighbors. I want an end to this war. It's been dragging on for so long, I wonder sometimes if we aren't just fighting each other because it's what we have always done."

The wistfulness in his voice as he spoke of an end to the Aranak-Horrd War came through loud and clear. As war had only touched her life from a distance, there was little she could do to commiserate with him.

War on television was one thing. Living it day in and day out wasn't something she ever wanted to experience. She'd be glad when this charade was over.

The thought stopped her cold and made her sit up straighter. *No,* she thought. *She sure would* not *be glad.*

Before her thoughts could wander into a time when she might have to leave Shan Lin and Vincent, the door to the patio opened distracting her. Both she and Dorian turned to see who had interrupted them, and her body went rigid at the site of Winters. As best she could, she rose from the chair, her knees shaking nearly so bad she couldn't stand. She stepped toward Winters only to come to a halt when she spotted the two men behind him.

There was no time to reach out for Dorian. Suddenly he was there beside her. Admonishing herself to remain calm, she greeted Winters.

"Hello Winters. I see we have company. Please, invite them in and offer them something to drink."

Winters face remained passive and when he spoke, his voice was crisp and precise.

"I'm afraid they are not staying, My Lady Princess. These...*men,*" he nearly sneered the word, "Walkins and Lith, have come to escort you to the palace. The Queen wishes an audience with her new marriageneice. I have taken the liberty to lay out some of your clothing, if it meets with your approval."

Even though Dorian had grasped her arm with his hand in case she received bad news, it had taken all her strength to refrain from clinging to him. Now, she turned to Dorian and smiled, grasping his arm in return.

"A visit with the Queen. What an honor, Dorian." Turning back to Winters, she smiled brilliantly.

"Of course, Winters. If you gentlemen will excuse me, I'll just freshen up, change, and meet you in a few moments." So saying, she walked into the house, Dorian following in her footsteps and Winters brushing the two newcomers out of her way.

Before either of the new men had come through the door, Shari stopped and looked back at Winters.

"Oh, Winters?"

"Yes My Lady Princess?" He stopped immediately blocking the men behind him from entering.

"If my husbands come home before I return, please give them word of my whereabouts. I wouldn't want them to worry."

"Of course, My Lady Princess. I shall see to it myself."

Smiling her thanks for real this time, Shari made her way through the labyrinth of a house to the suite she shared with her husbands.

A soft, but relieved sounding sigh escaped from Dorian.

"What?" Shari asked, quietly glancing back at Dorian startling him.

"My Lady?" Dorian asked, following closer to Shari but still maintaining a discreet distance.

"Why the relieved sigh, Dorian? Did you expect someone to come here with the intention of harming me?"

"Of course not!" Dorian cried softly.

"Then why the relief?" Shari asked turning left at the intersection the two came to.

"I was... That is, they didn't... Um..." Dorian's words trailed away.

"What? Did you think they were here for you?" Shari asked turning back to once more look at Dorian.

"Yes." Dorian whispered.

Shari stopped so quickly Dorian nearly fell in his attempt to avoid bumping into her.

"I don't understand. Explain." Shari demanded.

Dorian bowed his head momentarily before lifting it again, squaring his shoulders, and staring Shari directly in her eyes.

"My *aunt*," The word was spat out savagely, "the reigning Queen of Aranak, enjoys her family. Enjoys her family so much, she uses them in whatever way amuses her at the time. I made the mistake of thinking I could use this to my advantage." Bitter laughter sounded.

"Queen Sara treated me the same as any other peasant in from the gutters. She used me for her own depraved purposes then discarded me. Which wouldn't have been so bad except instead of having me thrown out of her palace, banned from ever returning, she sent me to her prison and had me treated as a traitor to the crown." Dorian's voice hitched on the last word and Shari gave him a moment to recover.

"The beat...the torture was bad enough, but I could have healed from that. As it is now, I find I suffer from some of the injuries from time to time. It was the healer's hope that in time... That isn't relevant at the moment, even though the telling of my disgrace is."

Shari began to disagree shaking her head in a negative but Dorian stopped her.

"You wanted to know why I was relieved. I was worried either of the two men would recognize me. I'm shocked they haven't yet."

"But... Well, why haven't they?" Shari asked assuming the two men back with Winters were well known to Dorian.

"Because the healer was forced to replace my face with another one. I'm, even now, still healing from the effects."

"Sheezuz, Dorian." Shari blanched. The bitterness Shari heard in the young man's voice was fierce. Whatever price Dorian had paid for his naiveté, it had been too high. She would have never known if he hadn't revealed any of this. His appearance was perfectly normal for... *But was it?* Shari thought. *I never knew what he looked like before...*

"It doesn't matter at the moment. You asked; I gave you an answer. Come. You must hurry."

Putting action to words, Dorian propelled her forward. As they approached the suite, Dorian made as if to hang behind, but Shari grabbed his hand unobtrusively and forced him to come with her.

"After hearing that, there's no way I'd leave you out here. What if those two came down here to check what was taking so long? I'd never forgive myself if they caught on." Shari mumbled the last.

"They would not dare to invade Shan Lin and Vincent's private rooms. They may not be the sons of the Queen, but they are still privileged members of the royal family."

"Well, come on in. I don't want to take the chance today is the day they change their minds."

Dorian nodded and followed Shari.

When they finally reached her room, Shari immediately saw the clothing Winters had laid out for her on the dressing chair. It was the outfit she had seen hanging in her closet, the one she'd exclaimed was fit for a Queen. The very one her husbands had insisted she wear for the arrival of the True Queen.

Shrugging aside thoughts of her men, Shari hurriedly began to strip off what she already wore not caring Dorian was with her. If she could greet a woman perfectly naked, she shouldn't blanche at a man watching her simply dress. There wasn't anytime to dither.

"My Lady Princess! I must…" Dorian began to protest the moment she started to undress, but Shari overrode his protests.

"We don't have time! Just listen to me. No matter what the Queen is up to, and you know she's up to something, make sure you get my husbands out of here. That woman knows what they've done. I know she does. If they get back alive, tell them I've left for Earth, and not to… Damn it! Help me here!"

While she spoke, Shari slid into the luxurious clothing. She had no clue what the outfit was made of, but she did know the only other thing to come close to the feeling of this material was silky smooth skin. Problem was, the outfit did not seem to be cooperating at all. She could not get the back to meet where she needed it to close.

Dorian made his way to her and managed to seal the opening in back.

"My La…Shari. You know there's no way either of your husbands are going to believe me. They'll know the moment you let them inside your head. If the Queen is going to use you as leverage of some kind, she is going to torture you in the hopes of learning everything about what Shan Lin and Vincent have done through your link with them."

Shari nodded her head in agreement knowing Dorian had been in a position to know this first hand. His beating was supposed to have killed him. It was only through Queen Sara's greed and love of finely honed men that saved the man from certain death.

Adjusting her clothing as best she could, she patted Dorian's scarred hand absently then sat to slip into the shoes she was to wear with the outfit.

"I've already thought of that. It doesn't matter what she does to me. There is no link. Apparently I've shut it off and have to find a way to turn it back on. I can't give her what I haven't got."

Shari heard the words she spoke and a feeling of loneliness engulfed her being. Even now her mind prayed something had just gone wrong in her head. The feeling of wholeness she had experienced with the twins was now gone. There *had* been a link between the three of them, there just wasn't one any longer. Shari prayed it was only her mind with the problem.

Dismissing her thoughts as unproductive, not to mention depressing the hell out of her, Shari moved to face the vanity mirror.

"Just do what I've asked. They need to be safe. I'm not important now. They're the ones who must survive. They're the ones who are vital to bringing this bitch down."

"Shari. You are vital to the survival of the twins. Didn't they tell you? Didn't they explain? If you die, so do they. The same goes for them dying. You can't live without your life-mates. Oh, you might survive for a while, but it will be nothing. You'll want to die every day you still live. There are so very few who have ever survived without their life-mates, and the ones who have usually end up insane, or killing themselves."

Shari, in the midst of tucking and smoothing her hair, paused at his words and sank back into the chair.

They had not told her. There had not been time for the little details when she had arrived in Naralin. First, they had the job of getting her to cooperate with them and their plans. Then Theresa had shown up with her crew, the Queen's calling them, and so many things in between...

Why hadn't those two made the time?

"I'm so sorry, My Lady Princess. They should have been the ones to explain. Right now, the Queen's men await your..."

It was the gentleness in Dorian's voice that brought her out of her thoughts. Even as her head reeled with the possibility she might eventually go crazy, or even kill herself, if there was a chance to stop the Queen from learning of her husbands' possible treason, she knew she had to take it.

Standing, she straightened her clothing, then her shoulders, and faced Dorian.

"Tell them I love them. I will do what I can for them, but they are to leave Aranak and Azaya for their True Queen as soon as they can."

Holding her head high, Shari walked from the room.

* * * * *

The three-story ride from her room was too short. She made her way back to the living area where the Queen's men waited, dread and fear in her every step and the mantras *For Vincent and Shan Lin* beating in every footfall.

Arriving all too quickly into the living area, she waited for the men to notice her. Winters, was the first and gave her a surreptitious smile before he announced her arrival.

"My Lady Princess, Her Royal Highness, Shari Lynn Rayan-White. Wife of My Lord Princes, Shan Lin and Vincent White-Rayan, Their Royal Highnesses. Marriageneice of Her Majesty, Queen Sara Annalise Anaksup. Marriagecousin of Her Majesty, Queen Stephanie Anaksup-Armand, and My Lord Princes, Their Royal Highnesses, Mitchell and Kristain Armand-Anaksup. Marriagecousin to My Lady Princess Theresa Lawsai, Captain. Marriagesister to My Lady Princess, Her Royal Highness, Lyssa Carrucci-Rayan. Marriagecousin to…"

As the list went on to name three more cousins and a few other titles Shari neither understood nor cared about at the moment, though she understood what Winters was doing. He was giving her all the protection he could give her at this time. Emotion clogged her throat and threatened to escape before she ruthlessly fought back the urge.

When at last he had finished, both men the Queen had sent, and Dorian were bowing at her feet, their foreheads to the floor in the positions of obedience. While normally she would have been appalled, in this one instance, she wanted to run to Winters and hug him for doing the best he could under these most difficult conditions.

"My Lady Princess, your conveyance awaits."

"Thank you, Winters." But still she waited wondering when the men would arise.

When thirty seconds had passed and they still had not risen, she looked toward Winters for some clue.

He mouthed to her, "You may rise now."

Covering her mouth to stifle the nervous laughter threatening to escape, she quickly cleared her throat before speaking.

"You may rise now. The Queen is waiting."

Dorian was the first to rise, and quickly came to her side offering her his arm.

"May I escort My Lady Princess to her awaiting transport?" The offer was given with such politeness, if Shari had not known better, she would think she had never met the man.

"Yes. You may."

The two other men had risen and were striding toward the door, but soon stopped and waited for Shari as Winters cleared his throat from the doorway. With a look they apparently recognized, the two practically stood at attention as they waited for her to pass them.

"At your convenience, My Lady Princess."

Shari nodded her head in what she hoped passed for a regal movement toward the pair of obviously embarrassed men. Walking ahead of them now out the door, she gave Winters a wink, then went down the stairs toward the waiting vehicle.

It was a thing to behold, and something Shari had never seen before. The vehicle could have passed for an ostentatious royal coach on Earth if not for the air tanks visible below. Outside was the color of mother of pearl and seemed to sparkle. Even with the tanks underneath it, there were still four horses pulling it in front. For a moment, Shari wondered if they flew, then dismissed the idea as unimportant. She'd find out soon enough.

The Queen had obviously wanted anyone who cared to know she was summoning her newest family member.

Dorian, who had remained silent with the exception of asking to escort her, led her to the opening of the carriage. Once she was inside and seated, he leaned his head in as if to adjust her dress and whispered his own assurance.

"Please. Do not worry. They will come for you." Before she could respond, he backed out of the doorway and shut her inside.

She watched out the window in front of her as the two men, Lith and Walkins climbed onto a high front seat and each took up reins for a pair of horses. Climbing up to sit with the pair the Queen had sent, was another man Shari had never seen.

Not wanting to think too hard about it, Shari turned back to the window at her side and watched as Dorian walked back to the porch to stand with Winters. A small smile crept onto her face as she noticed they made a beautiful pair of sentinels. She hung onto the thought until she could no longer see either of the men.

Sitting back, she tried one last time to reach out to her husbands. Bringing up a wavering image of the light switch from earlier in its off position, Shari concentrated on flipping it upward. She hoped her nerve-wracked mind could hold the image long enough.

Please God, let this link business work!

* * * * *

Shan Lin made his way toward the entrance of the tavern intending to gather their crew and leave.

Shan Lin?

The voice startled Shan Lin momentarily before his heart accelerated excitedly. Shari had found her on switch!

Shari! Thank Riad. *This is great. Now we can listen…*

I'm sorry. This is not Shari. It's Stephanie.

Shan Lin's excitement died but his heart continued to pound, just for a different reason.

Your Majesty. He nearly dropped to his knees before remembering she was only pathing into his mind.

Please. Stephanie, remember?

Shan Lin did his best not to blush at the reminder of Queen Stephanie asking him to call her by her given name.

Yes, Stephanie. How may I serve you?

There was a moment's pause before Shan Lin felt a weighted hand settle on his shoulders.

I'm learning still. Forgive me. A commanding voice echoed through his head.

I am sorry to intrude but I couldn't help…hearing, about the Vid/Sync having been found. Is it true?

Shan Lin's attention wavered between astonishment and awe. Queen Stephanie was actually "touching" him through her mental link. This woman, so very new to the ways of Aranakian monarch powers had been able to rifle through *Tears* in the universes and mentally gather information.

Shan Lin? Are you still there? The volume of the question intensified as Stephanie must have assumed she had lost their link.

"My Queen." He spoke out loud as this time he did go to his knees, his head to the floor in obedience. He actually felt waves of embarrassment pathed through their link.

Please, get up.

Shan Lin did as he was bid and rose ignoring the questioning looks from those around him.

Do you have the Vid/Sync?

Shan Lin nodded. "Yes, My Queen."

Good. Stash it in a safe place. I think it's time I visited my soon-to-be home. Excellent job. Satisfaction radiated in the words as praise rang inside his head.

Please inform your brother I will arrange a meeting place with the two of you soon. Mitch and Kristain…yes dears… Well, they're ready to see Aranak again. They think I'm ready to assume my throne.

Happiness threaded her words when she spoke of her husbands and Shan Lin knew his cousins had chosen wisely.

"Yes, Your Majesty. Please know you are always welcome in any of our homes."

Thank you, Shan Lin.

Shan Lin spent a few moments informing Stephanie of what had occurred in Hurok since his arrival before his attention focused once again on the room he occupied now. The tavern was crowded though when he glanced around, there was no sign of Vincent.

Wanting to inform his brother of the contact from Queen Stephanie, Shan Lin started out the door. Suddenly, directly in front of him was one of their crew, Turing. Even though they both saw each other, it was already too late to stop the collision both knew was inevitable.

Accidentally bumping into Shan Lin, Turing did his best to make the contact brief, apologizing to Shan Lin for the encounter. Those watching on from the nearby tables watched on in puzzlement as the newcomer seemed to have gone inside of himself to look at things, which only he could see.

Shan Lin heard his brother curse directly behind him and knew Vincent would reach out to head off the inevitable contact, even knowing it was futile. Vincent would be left to watch helplessly and wait as Shan Lin had his vision.

Minutes passed as everyone stared at Shan Lin. Suddenly, with a quick inhalation of breath, Vincent's brother came back to himself.

Turning, he reached out blindly for Vincent.

"We have to go back." The statement, given in so calm a manner belayed the sheer terror looking back at Vincent through Shan Lin's eyes.

* * * * *

The blows continued to land and Shari still couldn't believe this was happening. Any minute, she expected to awaken from this dream, but then the pain set in, and with her arms tied behind her and her legs equally helpless, all she could do was struggle through the pain.

It continued unabated for what seemed like days, and she screamed through the gag that had been thrust into her mouth by the gleeful woman.

All her concentration was focused on staying conscious and forming a plan, when the blows would eventually stop until suddenly, even that was snatched away from her.

A searing pain started in her leg and eventually made her aware this could go on until she died.

Suddenly, it stopped. Through the red haze obscuring her vision and hearing, she finally heard the high-pitched laughter coming from above her aching body. Opening her eyes, she looked up just in time to see Queen Sara leaning over her leg and thrust her hand into the aching leg.

With a scream of inhuman pain, she lost consciousness.

* * * * *

The men bolted out the doorway leaving shouted questions in their wake. They had barely reached their mounts when the screams of their wife finally entered their minds.

"*Shari!*" The name burst simultaneously from the Warriors, anguish and pain ringing in every syllable. The Warriors ignored the darkness trying to suck them in as they felt the connection once more abruptly disconnect.

Panting with the effort already, both men mounted their beasts and tore out of the town leaving murmured whispers of death surely coming for someone.

* * * * *

The pain was unbearable, both the physical and mental anguish she endured at the hands of this woman people called Queen Sara. It was all Shari could do to draw air between each blow that had landed. As it was, the fear that came at the mention of the rape of her body was nothing to what was actually taking place at the moment.

Every part of her body ached as she did the best she could to stop the bleeding in her leg. Her left eye was swollen shut and she was sure that at least one of her ribs had been broken.

At the moment, she had other priorities. Tend to her wounds and pray help came soon.

Chapter Sixteen

Shari awoke to the throbbing in her body and waited as long as she dared for the pain to subside. When it didn't, she knew she had no choice. It had been hours since she'd been floating in and out of consciousness waiting for rescue, and the Queen would soon make good on her threats of rape. Shari knew it now.

Not knowing if her earlier attempt to contact her husbands had worked, Shari began the mental process once again, wondering how effective it would be through the pain she was now in. She hadn't wanted to contact Shan Lin and Vincent. She had done her best to blank her mind of all thought where the two men were concerned. But the words Queen Sara had whispered in her ear during one of her more lucid moments had sent an icy spear of terror running through Shari.

"Once you're gone, they will die. Do you know what madness a mated trio feels when one link is severed?" Shari had shuddered at the joyful malice in Sara's voice. "No? Oh goodie! I not only get to break this lovely body, I also get to enjoy the fear you'll writhe in as I enlighten you." Sara had mockingly straightened her clothing and gracefully sank into a kneeling position directly in front of Shari.

Shari could barely manage to still the twitches her body involuntarily made from the pain the woman had inflicted. A sudden determination came over her to still any reaction to the words as the Queen began to speak.

"At first, you grieve just as any other person would who has lost their loved one. The hours of, I should have... I could have...why didn't I just...if only I had the chance to do something differently. To once more hold a beloved, to have them with you one last time, selfish as you think it is, you would give anything to have them with you once again. You pray to your maker, you make deals, you beg. I'll do *anything* if you'll only return them to my loving embrace. Then the anger sets in. You feel betrayed by the one entity, who has in effect, taken your life from you. While this is supposed to help you through the steps of your grief, it never does. You slide deeper and deeper into your anger. You vacillate between why have you forsaken me, *Riad*, and how dare you take from me! And that is only the beginning."

Sara had shifted slightly reaching her hand out to stroke it through the blood sliding down Shari's left hip. Shari had had to bite her cheek to stop the painful hiss from escaping.

"And just when you think nothing could be worse, the mate still living turns on you. How long do you think highly trained Warriors would survive trying to beat each other to death hourly? Hmmm?" the Queen asked in a falsely pleasant voice. "Especially the most advanced trained Warriors. From my knowledge of the two, I can tell you they would literally tear each other to pieces. Sharp blades hacking at limbs. The mental pain the two could inflict upon each other..." The heavy pause from Queen Sara had the weight of sexual tension strumming through the room.

Shari lifted her veiled lids in time to see the lust sliding through the other woman's eyes. It had been all she could do not to vomit on the woman. Swallowing back the rising bile, she quickly dropped her eyes back to the floor she had been staring at.

Remembering it now still had the power to make her gag. It was all she could do to stifle the urge and focus her mind on finding a way to contact Shan Lin and Vincent. There was no way in hell she would allow Queen Sara to destroy her husbands. To prevent that from happening, apparently, she had to live.

It took more than one try for her pain-wracked mind to focus as she lay on her side, panting from the effort.

Standing was painful, but out of necessity, she bore the pain. If there was any way out of this cell, she would find it or go down trying.

* * * * *

Shan Lin and Vincent both cursed loudly, simultaneously, and with great effect, if the stares and snickers sounding around them were anything to judge by.

Both men were wishing the direst actions on their aunt and in the most inventive ways they could conjure. Queen Sara had demanded their presence at her behest for the last time. They would never again be taking orders from the woman.

The men were making their way to Shari with all possible speed when they met up with Dorian. Exhausted and barely able to speak, Dorian had told Shan Lin and Vincent how Queen Sara's retainers had come to their home and demanded Shari come to the Palace.

Knowing he could do nothing to stop it, Dorian had done the only thing he could. He had sent Jolan with her and admonished the young man to follow Shari and make sure nothing happened to her. If something did, he was to send a message to Dorian, who would then find Shan Lin and Vincent, and inform them while Jolan did everything in his power to help Shari escape Sara's clutches.

"Why didn't you see this earlier? We could have prevented it!"

Even as Vincent spoke the question, he already knew the answer.

"You know I can't foretell the future of our lives. I've never been able to. Only those around us."

Frustrated, Shan Lin did his best to inject a note of calm in his voice he wasn't feeling.

"I wouldn't even have seen this if Turing hadn't bumped into me. It was a fluke, purely accidental. They all know they shouldn't touch me if they don't want to have knowledge of the outcome of their lives. Turing especially. He's been with us the longest and is always most adamant about not wanting to know what's going to happen. "

Shan Lin swallowed visibly. *The image of their wife passed out on the floor of the palace. Bloodied, broken, he and Vincent raging in despair and futility at not being able to help their wife.* He shuddered in horror.

"We're damned lucky it happened period. Just give thanks to *Riad* it *did* happen. Now we no longer have to deal with this wild goose chase. Let's move on."

Sighing in frustration, Vincent did his best to stop his feeling of sheer terror from over riding his common sense. Shari would be fine, and they'd get there in time to prevent anything from happening to her.

"You're right, and it's no fault of yours. My apologies, brother mine. It's just…"

Seeing the contrition in his brother's heart, Shan Lin did his best to reassure his brother.

"I know. It's only… Queen Sara now has power over the one who has become our life. I feel the same as you."

Nodding his agreement, Vincent urged his mount faster, for once not caring what had to be done to insure the safety and well being of their wife.

"We should never have left her. We should have just taken her with us and to Hellios with what we knew was the right thing." Vincent railed at his brother as their mounts rode hard toward the castle.

"And you know what would have happened if we did. The Queen would have taken her anyway." Shan Lin shouted back.

They were less than half a mile from Aranak and would gain the town soon. Their ride through the streets would undoubtedly cause speculation and possibly panic, but neither brother cared. Let the whole damned town know what their Queen had finally done. The depths to which she would stoop to keep a throne that no longer belonged to her.

Within sight of the city, the brothers, along with five other riders from the Queen's Guard who had ridden into the small village along the coast with them, pulled up their horses and stopped.

"There it is. You know what must be done. At all cost, the Queen must be driven from power so the True Queen can assume the throne." Shan Lin spoke with a certainty the others around him never doubted. This hadn't been the first time Shan Lin had seen the outcome of something the others had no notion was happening. There were very few who questioned the man anymore when he told them of events soon to take place.

Quietly, the men watched as Vincent turned to them and stared each one in the eyes. "The Queen's Most Vicious Warrior" now stared back at them. The look in his eyes was one few ever saw up close and lived to tell about it.

"Not one of you needs to accompany us. You are free to do as you see fit. I'll not ask anyone to go against what they believe is right. If I hadn't seen what I did and known that Shan Lin has never been wrong, I'd be questioning this move myself." Pausing again to let them take in his words, Vincent turned to look at the structure that towered over the modern city.

"But know; if you stay, you'll have to hunt us both, and if you go with us, you'll be hunted too. The decision has to be your own."

Vincent turned to Shan Lin, and both men nodded once in unison then kicked their mounts into action never looking behind them.

* * * * *

Shari's body shook and her head reeled with pain, but she never stopped pulling at the boards she'd found in the side of the wall, all the while thanking all those Hollywood producers for having secret passages hidden in the walls of castles in their movies.

She had been desperate when she began to knock on the walls of the cell. There was no way out of the room short of producing a key, or blowing the door off. Since she had no explosives, key, or lock picks, this was the only other thing she could think of.

She had begun by pounding a fist every few inches against the wall and making her way around the room. Positive she was grasping at straws, she had been stunned when one area had suddenly rung with a hollow sound. Scraping her hands and nails bloody, she had used every bit of the last of her strength to get this far.

Now she could feel the board finally giving way, and at the sound of a snap, she gave out an exhausted yelp of joy.

Panting and drawing breath from her effort, she closed her eyes momentarily before finally opening them to peer through the opening she had revealed. But the more she looked, the less she understood what she was actually seeing.

Just on the other side of the broken plank she had struggled with was a square opening sealed shut with concrete. Closing her eyes once more in disbelief, she brought her hands to her eyes and rubbed them. She had to be hallucinating due to all the pain she was in.

Opening them once more, she knew at last there was no escape out of the room.

Dropping down the wall suddenly in defeat as her weakened legs gave way, Shari put her head in her hands and became resigned to what was about to happen.

Sitting there, she could only thank her divine maker for the chance he had given her to meet two of the most loving, giving, and strongest Warriors it had been her pleasure to know.

She was so lost in thought it took her a few moments to realize she was no longer alone. Taking her hands away from her face and looking upward toward the door expecting the Queen to be there gloating about what was to come, she barely registered it was a friend.

"My Lady? It's Jolan. Please, My Lady, you must get up and come to me. I cannot enter the room or I will be discovered. There are sensors in the room." The words were whispered, but urgent as well as apologetic.

Unbelievably, someone had come to help her. At least she hoped it was the case. She had to believe he wasn't here to take her to her own version of Hell.

She opened her mouth to answer when Jolan put his finger to his lips in the universal sign for silence. Painfully, and with the last of her strength, Shari used both hands against the floor and the wall to brace herself and slowly, very slowly rose to her feet all the while screaming to her body to cooperate.

She gained her feet and began to talk to herself to get them to move.

Just a few more steps, then you'll get help and it will be easier. Promise.

Looking down, she ordered her injured leg to take a step and found the measly piece of cloth she'd used to staunch the flowing blood had barely slowed the tide. Her head reeled from the blood loss, but she ignored it as best she could.

Finally, after what seemed like hours but was actually only as few seconds, she both felt and watched her legs move. She sent encouragement to herself as if she was urging on an exhausted marathon runner.

That's it. You can do it! Go little feet, go!

Before she knew it, she was at the doorway and through it. As soon as she had cleared the doorway, she felt Jolan's arms come around her.

"We have to hurry. I'm so sorry, but we have to move fast. Even as small as you are, I can't carry you through the halls. There would be too much talk and we don't want any help from those inside."

"Wha…what-t-t do you me-e-ean?" Shari stammered the question through the throbbing in her face.

"What? I'm sorry, I can't understand you." Jolan barely stopped as Shari tried her best to use a mouth that felt as if someone had shot it full of Novocain, then took away the pain killing sensation, leaving an inability to use it.

"Wh-why can't you-u-u hep' me?" She said carefully as she continued to concentrate on putting one foot in front of the other.

"Oh, because if I was to carry you, we'd be headed the other way, toward the healer. Since you're still on your feet, the inhabitants of the castle will assume you've been told if you can walk, you can leave. It's the normal procedure of the Queen's."

Shari thought about nodding her head to signal she'd heard him, but her leg chose that moment to buckle. The only thing keeping her upright was Jolan, who continued to hold onto her.

"Keep going, My Lady. Lean on me as much as possible, but keep going."

Even through her pain, Shari knew she had only minutes, if not seconds, and she was going to pass out. But she kept going with one single litany running through her head.

I'mgoingtokillher.   I'mgoingtokillher.   I'mgoingtokillher.
I'mgoingtokillher...

Just then, a man holding linens and two women holding pails of water rounded the corner about ten feet in front of them. Behind them, Shari actually saw sunlight and knew she was going to make it. Even if it was just to the front door. She *would* get out of this place.

She didn't know how much farther she would have to go next, but she at least would make it out the door. After that, she would worry about getting off the grounds of the castle.

No sooner had the thought entered her mind than the three people she had just seen coming toward her were startled by a loud commotion behind them.

The pails the women had been holding flew out of their hands to land on the cement floor. The water sloshed out of the buckets and ran across the cement toward Shari and Jolan as a sound like alarm bells came up from the stone floor. The linen held by the man flew into the air and spread itself out in an arc of white as if a curtain had suddenly come down on a stage.

The screams of startlement sounded unusually loud to Shari, but she was beyond caring. Her body chose then to make its demands known. Even as she fell toward oblivion, she could have sworn she saw through the sheets her Warriors, looks of vengeful wraith, coming up from Hell itself to slay her demon.

* * * * *

Shan Lin and Vincent burst through the double doors of the entrance to the castle's prison and vowed they'd tear the place down to find Shari if they had to. Swords in one hand, laser guns in the other, both had come loaded for a battle.

Hearing stifled yelps and the sounds of steel against the floor, both sprinted toward the sound. Rounding the corner, they saw a bed linen fly through the air obscuring their sight of the corridor they needed to go down. Swinging out with his blade, Vincent quickly sliced the sheet as if it was air. Then looked beyond it to the two figures, who seemed to be making their way towards them.

"Jolan!" The exclamation sounded from behind him. Shan Lin had spotted the pair too.

Running toward the two, Shan Lin and Vincent looked to the figure, who was at the moment, sliding down Jolan's side. Immediately, both men let out a bellow of pain and rage the inhabitants of the castle would later swear had come from the ruling demons of *Burnhad* itself.

Both men dropped to their knees as soon as they reached Jolan and Shari. Vincent, having gotten there first, threw his weapons to the side and picked Shari up, cradling her to his chest.

Shan Lin, dropped down beside them, took them both in his arms and surrounded them, one side of his body in contact with each.

I know, I know. We must go. Both brothers pathed to each other.

Getting to their feet, Vincent made a move to gather his weapons, but found them in the hands of Jolan instead.

"My Lord Princes', we've got to go. She wasn't far behind me when I left to find your wife. We've got to go, now!"

Both brothers knew he was right, and the Warrior in each demanded they get her to a secure place first. But the men, the husbands, in them both wanted to do nothing more then find the person or people responsible for this atrocity.

Yes. But first, our wife needs us.

The brothers looked to one another in agreement, then jumped into battle mode with Shari between them when they heard the horrified gasps from behind them.

Turning as one unit, Shari still cradled in Vincent's arms and clutched tightly to his massive chest, the brothers faced the soldiers who had followed them. Body radiating barely suppressed anger, Shan

Lin stepped aside to allow the other guards to see Shari's appearance in Vincent's arms.

Battered and bloody, face swollen, cuts and bruises visible on nearly every part of her body, clothing in tattered rags, Shari lay as if dead.

"Look! Take a good look!" The shout, from so close and filled with such venomous anger, nearly pushed the soldiers who stared back a step.

Shan Lin, pointing toward his badly abused wife, looked at the soldiers, then at the inhabitants who had dared to come investigate.

"*Look at what your Queen has done!*" Shan Lin's shouts brought even more people at a run. Even those who normally stayed hidden, hoping not to incur the wrath of Her Highness, came out at the shout of the Queen's most honored guards.

"She did this. The *freching* bitch did this to our *wife*! To those who were once the royal heirs! Do you believe now? Can you finally see what she is capable of? Can you not open those terrified eyes and realize she is no longer our sovereign who rules with a gentle, but iron hand. It is a fist of steel to whoever opposes her reign, even though her reign is over! *Look at our wife!*"

* * * * *

The inhabitants listened to the Warrior as he bellowed to all who would listen. They heard the grief in his shouting, as well as felt it. The two most loyal and victorious heroes of the Realm stood in front of the people of Aranak and did everything they could to convince those same people their Queen had finally gone too far.

Soon, Shan Lin stopped speaking as Vincent came up beside his brother and both men began to walk down the hallway toward the doors. Vincent carrying their wife in his arms, her body either unconscious or dead, her arms dragging down at Vincent's side.

Before they gained the outside door they passed a myriad of closed doors. Jolan was the one, however, who discovered the door hadn't been closed all the way, and something inside happened to catch at the corner of his eye, enough to stop him.

Even in their haste, Shan Lin knew the room had to be investigated.

Vincent. Hold one moment.

Shan Lin and Jolan cautiously approached the door. Grabbing the short *pryt* lance at his side, Shan Lin powered up the lethal weapon even as he handed a second one to Jolan, before the two advanced. Putting his outstretched hand against the not completely closed door, Shan Lin stood to the left as Jolan took up a position on the right. When Shan Lin caught Jolan's eyes, he gave a hard nod once then gave a cautious shove to the door.

The sight, which greeted them inside the room, confirmed Shan Lin's suspicions of what happened to Candice. She lay impaled onto the wall, her body nearly unrecognizable to what he saw in his memory. Her face however was nearly untouched.

He heard Jolan's horrified gasp and turned to find a look of horror on the young man's face.

"Did you know her?" Shan Lin asked quietly.

The young man shook his head then contradicted himself.

"She helped me out of here a few months ago. She was a trusted friend, if a brief one."

Shan Lin silently closed the door blocking Jolan's view of what remained of the man's friend. They made their way back to his brother and wife quickly. It hadn't taken very long to check the room, but since there was nothing to be done for the poor woman now, it was his duty to see to his wife's welfare.

Quickly, and yet all too soon, they came upon the other soldiers who had followed them through the doors. Together the brothers, Vincent carrying their wife, their fellow soldiers, and Jolan, who had been accompanying Shari when they'd found her, left through the now useless front doors.

The inhabitants stared after them for a long time after the group had gone, then as if one conscious mind had spoken, all roused at once and began to form a plan.

* * * * *

Once outside, Vincent hurriedly walked toward his waiting steed. Praying he wouldn't jostle Shari too badly all the while, he knew it was a matter of her life or death if he didn't get her to a healer soon. Having come even with his horse, Vincent turned to find his brother right beside him. Carefully clutching Shari, Vincent gained his mount.

Follow at as slow a pace as you dare. I will ride ahead and drag the healer back this way. Whatever you do, don't...

Vincent only nodded as he watched his brother mount his own horse and ride off.

Riad *give your mount wings, brother mine. She is our life.*

Chapter Seventeen

Shari woke to darkness, wondering if she was in her grave awaiting Death to escort her to her next plane of existence. The moment she tried to move, shards of pain racked her body and she knew her existence was still based on earth.

A door opened spilling light into the room illuminating two figures coming through the doorway, and Shari tried to relax her stiff and aching body. For an instant, her body flinched then froze in an attempt to fool her captors into thinking she had disappeared. Shari knew somewhere in her mind that she wanted to prevent those who had escorted her to see Queen Sara from noticing her.

Shari? Shan Lin's anguished voice spoke into her mind.

Taking stock of her body quickly before answering, Shari found she could live through the pain as long as Shan Lin and Vincent were all right.

I'm fine. Where are you two?

There was a brief moment of silence before Vincent answered. *You found your trigger when Sara…* Vincent shook his head, closing his eyes in pain. *That's not important right now. At the moment Shan Lin and I are attempting to locate another doctor. It seems neither of us wants any man to touch you. The first doctor was only able to stabilize you before Shan Lin went berserk.* There was a moment's pause. *I confess; I might have helped him in his endeavor to oust the man from your side. But it's all I'll admit to.*

Amusement sounded in Shan Lin's voice.

Yes, brother mine, you only assisted.

Shari thought for a moment.

Then who's standing in my doorway?

She finally asked, puzzled.

A snarling growl sounded before the answer came.

Jolan, Dorian, or Winters. And if they don't shut the door now I'm going to rip their freching *heads off!*

A bellow followed this comment and Shari smiled at the sound of Vincent's voice shaking the home. The smile quickly turned into a grimace as she heard her door suddenly slam shut.

You're not fine, are you? Dammit Vincent. Go drag the woman healer here. I don't care if you have to force her from another's side, get her here now!

Shari listened as the two brothers bickered between themselves until she finally wished they would both just shut up. Once again, her head was hurting, and all she wanted was for one of them to do the mind orgasm thingie and…

The mind-blowing orgasm. Just thinking about the orgasm and what happened next brought a lopsided smile to Shari's face.

It was how the brothers found their wife. Beaten, bloodied and smiling.

"Why are you smiling? Tell me you're fine. Tell me that vicious bitch didn't harm you permanently."

Startled as the men spoke in unison, Shari looked between the two.

"I…I'm a bit sore still, but better, thank you."

She lies for our benefit, brother. She is thrice more damaged now then when the vehicle hit her in the Earth Realm. Vincent pathed angrily.

"Fix her." Shan Lin snarled at the healer who was making her way slowly into the room. Fully robed, a hood covering the healer's head and concealing her face, the healer approached Shari silently.

"May I ask why either of you cannot heal her yourself?" The woman's soft voice asked.

"There is too much damage to be healed without the claiming." Shan Lin and Vincent spoke calmly and in unison. "She has yet to claim us." There was no censure in their voices, only fact.

Shari stared at her husbands in astonishment. Anger gave her voice strength even as her body protested the distressed movements Shari made.

"I have to claim you. I accepted, with barely any protest at all, that you…that I was your wife. How could you say…"

"If you are ready, My Lady Princess." The healer reached out to Shari, but Shari eluded her touch.

"Hey, I'm peachy here. Matter of fact, you can leave. I need to straighten this out with my husbands." But the woman was insistent.

Before Shari could move again, the woman reached out and laid her hands on Shari's shoulders.

"My Lady Princess. I am Annya. I have come to heal you. I'm sorry, this will hurt."

The words had barely left the woman's lips before Annya's hands slipped down and grasped hold of Shari's wrists. The next thing Shari knew, she lay on the floor, panting and shivering, her body-wracked with more pain then anything Queen Sara had inflicted on her during the torture.

It was over quickly, and Shari waited for the pain to return, laying as still and stiffly as she could manage. When the pain did not return, Shari gathered herself and tried to stand. Her legs refused to cooperate.

It took her a few moments to realize she was stark naked once again.

"It seems I am destined to live my life in Naralin naked," Shari tried to joke as she gathered herself up. "What did you do to me?"

The healer looked down through her hooded robe, a neutral expression on her face.

"I merely became a conduit between yourself and your husbands. I took the art of healing, which runs deeply through Vincent, and applied it to your wounds. The healing properties strengthen when a *juniane'* has been established."

A delicate hand reached down and lifted her by the arm, guiding her exhausted body to a chair near the bed. Shari sat, gathering herself before preparing to strip some skin off the woman who had brought such pain to her so recently abused body.

"You are welcome. If you had already claimed your husbands and allowed them to heal you, this would not have been necessary. I enjoyed it no more than you did. I detest inflicting pain on others, but it was inevitable."

"Could have fooled me." Shari said petulantly.

"It is the quickest way to heal and between your husbands and Winters, they insisted you wanted it this way."

Shari glared up at the woman. "You mean I could have been healed without pain? Why the hell didn't anyone tell me?"

Shari turned her glare on Shan Lin and Vincent.

"As we are not yet joined completely and you have not claimed us…" Shan Lin answered, sadness inherent in his words.

Annya calmly made her way out the door, closing it softly behind herself.

Shari gazed at the closed door for a time before turning her attention to her husbands.

"I won't say it was a pleasant experience. I will say since you didn't 'fix me' as Annya suggested you could, you two owe me. I'll show you claiming..." Shari muttered, the last said with an overwhelming urge to do just that.

Suddenly, claiming her husbands was all that filled her mind. She turned her attention to Shan Lin; the only thought running through her head, *MINE*. She pointed at Shan Lin, then to the chair she had been sitting in and barked out, "Sit!"

Shan Lin complied immediately but the feeling of wanting to dominate him persisted. Shari stalked forward and climbed on the chair, and knelt over Shan Lin.

"Take out your cock," she demanded, her attention directed solely on him until a slight whisper distracted her.

Whipping her head around quickly in search of the distraction, Shari spotted Winters in the room.

"Out." She barely recognized her own voice. Two octaves below a smoker's rasp, she commanded the man and watched as he averted his gaze and left rapidly.

Satisfaction snaked through her briefly until she turned her attention back to Shan Lin. Her eyes dropped to his lap and found to her delight he had an impressive erection.

"Oh goodie. Mine." She purred as she balanced herself one handed on his shoulder and used the other to reach down and grasp his cock. Lowering her hips slowly, she guided his thick shaft toward her pussy taking him deep inside herself, grinding her hips to ease the fit.

Shan Lin stuttered incoherently before giving up completely on any attempt at speech. His breathing became shallow pants as he held himself stiff. His wife had finally deemed him worthy. All he could think about doing was to scream in joy and ram himself upward, taking control from her at the same time. He was barely half way in and ready to come. His hips scarcely moved with the intention of doing just that when Shari snarled in his face, her hips stopping completely.

"Mine!" she roared, her voice rivaling an *averon* trumpeting its fresh kill, "Move again and I'll leave."

He held still waiting, praying she would continue. Eventually she did, closing her eyes and concentrating. She was wet now, her hot moisture running quickly down his pulsing cock and he squeezed his eyes shut praying he did not disappoint her.

She was breathing heavily now, her mouth open wide as she mumbled to herself. Shan Lin caught a few words and translated the few foreign phrases into something he could understand.

Shari had gone into *Ty Na Ran*. It was the act of claiming the mates and Shan Lin tried to path the information to his brother. She was claiming him in the true fashion of Aranakian mating.

He opened his mind and waited for Vincent's reply only to find the link cut by Shari. Her mind pulsed through his brain and overrode any objections he had to not being able to connect to his brother. All he could think of was her.

Shari rode Shan Lin and ignored his attempt at pathing Vincent. Somewhere in her mind she wondered just what she was doing but that thought too quickly faded as pleasure suddenly snaked through her.

Even once sated, she could not stop her hips from grinding past the point of pain. It was sometime before she realized Shan Lin had finally come and she had the skin of his neck between her teeth lapping at the blood trickling through his skin.

The blood seemed to soothe more than the orgasm, and when her body felt sated, she climbed off Shan Lin and left him sitting where she had ordered him.

"Shari." She heard her name spoken in a worried and angry voice but ignored it and turned her possessiveness on Vincent.

"Strip," she whispered harshly, possessive feelings thrumming through her previously sated body.

Vincent swallowed nervously, angry at his wife for choosing Shan Lin instead of him and tried to reach his brother through their mind link. It was no good. All he could feel was Shari, her will forcing his mind out of Shan Lin's and back into her own.

"Imagine, a big, strong Warrior like you afraid of little ole' me." Shari laughed, a chilling sound, raising the hairs on the back of Vincent's neck and arms.

"*Juant...*" Vincent began only to have Shari rush toward him knocking him backward to the floor. She stood above him, an unholy look coming into her eyes as she pointed to his crotch and again demanded, "Strip."

Vincent quickly obeyed, his eyes glued to his wife's hips as they continued to undulate back and forth. He quickly shucked his pants and found to his astonishment he was hard as a *pryt* lance and equally extended in length.

His wife wasted no time as she knelt over him, and bending at her knees, grasped hold of his cock as he had seen her do to Shan Lin and sank fully onto him. Vincent sucked in his breath at the heat he felt riding her channel. It was enough to make him come right then.

"Do so and I stop," Shari grated out. "Mine. You are..." But her eyes closed before she finished speaking and she turned inward.

Ty Na Ran. Vincent lay in awe at the feeling of the mate claiming. He tried once again to path his brother and allow Shan Lin to share in his delight but still found his way blocked. He gritted his teeth at the pleasure snaking through his body and dug his fingers into the short carpeting he lay still on.

All that seemed to be required of him was a hard-on and if it was what his wife needed...

His thoughts flew from his head as Shari picked up her pace, grinding her hips in circles, up and down, side to side, then back and forth. He was lost in sensation for what seemed forever when all too soon Shari screamed in frustrated rage. There was no way he could have avoided her bite and knew he would not have tried if he could.

He let her suck his neck even as he felt her teeth break skin and she began to drink his blood. In moments, he suddenly felt Shan Lin once again but the sensation was quickly overridden by his orgasm. He screamed in happiness and gratification as he came.

No sooner had his orgasm subsided then his wife leapt off him, her hips still pistoning as she walked back to Shan Lin and began to ride him once again. Vincent lay exhausted on the floor and waited for his turn to come again. The night was still young and he knew it could go on for sometime.

Chapter Eighteen

There was no warning before the door to their chambers was thrown open with great force against the wall. The bang sounding against the wall wrenched Shari out of the deep sleep she and her husbands had fallen into after the claiming.

"Seize them!" An angry voice shouted.

"What... Who... Huh?" Shari's mind grappled with the shouted command as she looked left, then right wondering who had invaded her bedroom.

Shan Lin and Vincent had leapt from the bed the moment the door began to open. Watching them now, both Warriors were in full kill mode. Or so Shari assumed.

Both men stood at the foot of the bed, several weapons at the ready, all pointed in the direction of the door. Again, her husbands were naked. It seemed to be the dress code for Aranak. Shari started to turn her head to see who had entered the room when her stomach made itself known.

Barely scrambling out of the bed in time, Shari looked around frantically for a bucket. Finding none within reach and her stomach protesting all the movement, she turned her back on the newcomers and vomited next to the bed.

Blood mixed with the small quantities of food she had eaten the night before poured from her nose and mouth. The sight of the blood brought back the memories of what she had done last night and her stomach heaved again and again until Shari was sure she knew what puking up your guts really meant.

It took a few moments to comprehend that hands held her in comfort, stroking her back, and holding her upright. Disoriented and still unsteady, Shari wiped her mouth with the back of her hand.

"What is this?" an imperious voice asked from in front of her.

Doing her best not to look up at the woman who hovered over her, Shari rasped out an answer as she prayed the Queen took little notice of the fine tremor the woman's voice had caused.

When scared, bluff your way out.

"Exactly what it looks like. Vomit. Nasty, smelly, disgusting, vomit. And if you'll excuse me a..." Shari could not speak further as her stomach heaved again.

When it had passed, Shari knelt panting, the arms surrounding her, somehow easing her. Looking down, Shari saw a familiar ring adorning one hand and knew her husbands had abandoned their Warrior stances to aid her. For the moment there was no threat that could touch them. No telling how long it would last, but Shari was very grateful for it.

"Better?" A gentle voice asked as Shan Lin handed Shari a wet cloth that she used to wipe her mouth.

"Try this." A glass of orange liquid was put in front of her mouth.

"Ugh. I don't think I..."

It will ease the cramping in your stomach, Kasha. Please, trust me.

The voice was Vincent's as was the hand that held the goblet.

Shari knew she would and tried to take the goblet from his hand.

It will quench your thirst. Allow me to aid you, my heart.

A smile spread across her face. Her husband was taking his duties seriously. Quickly swallowing the liquid from the glass Vincent helped hold steady, Shari let the taste of the liquid soothe her sore throat and prayed the fluid would stay down.

We would never allow harm to come to you, Shan Lin's voice sounded nettled.

I know. I just want to make sure nothing comes back...

Shari froze, stunned.

"I'm talking to you in my head. I can hear your thoughts. How the hell..."

A strangled sound came from in front of her.

"So. You've truly mated. It makes little difference. I am the law in the Queendom of Aranak and I will have my traitors under my control. Seize. Them. Now!" Relish sounded in the woman's voice as she made her command.

"No! Wait..." Even as Shari protested, she knew there was little she could do to stop what was about to happen. The tremor taking hold of her body started in earnest now. Controlling it as best she could, Shari's mind raced for possible ways out.

Shari! Two insistent voices sounded in her head simultaneously.

Coming to attention, she listened.

"Please. You can't do this." Shari begged pitifully, knowing as she did that Queen Sara would enjoy it. But it would also give Shari more time to think.

There is something. You can claim mate rights. As you have only just claimed us last night, there is a clause stating you have the right to stay our execution until you have determined you carry no children of ours.

The Queen disagreed sweetly as Shari listened to the words in her head.

"Ah. But I can. I rule, therefore, I can."

Shari watched as Shan Lin and Vincent struggled against their captures as she heard the words the men nearly rocketed into her mind, but didn't quite understand. *Children?*

Yes. Children. Please.

"But you don't actually rule, do you, *Auntie Sara*?" Shan Lin sneered the words.

"And you sure as hell don't rule well!" Vincent snarled at his aunt.

Shari! The insistent voices sounded again. *Demand Consort Claiming rights!*

Rage infused the Queen's face as Shari watched the smugness leak away.

"How dare you! How dare you speak to me…in that tone…those words…"

Shari knew, the Queen would soon erupt if something wasn't done. Shari would know best as she had been on the receiving end of this woman's anger.

Just as the enraged woman began to speak again, Shari opened her mouth and shouted.

"*I demand consort rights!*"

The room stilled.

"What did you say?" The Queen grated out, teeth clenched in fury.

Calmly now, Shari did her best to be heard around her now scratched and sore throat.

"I said…" The fear just bled away. Suddenly, it did not matter if this woman had tried to kill her, and failed.

"I heard what you said." The contempt in the woman's voice came through clearly.

The Queen turned her wrath on her nephews.

"Do you think this will save you? Do you think you're so clever I won't kill you the instant we've found she does *not* carry your children?"

Shan Lin and Vincent stood proud facing their Aunt's anger. Naked, hands haphazardly bound behind them, restraints trailing from their wrists, the two men faced whatever their aunt threw at them.

"You are traitors. You were seen in the company of two Horrdian men who are known spies. You deliberately disobeyed direct orders from your Commander in Chief of the Military of Aranak. Do you think so little of this land you would deliberately…"

Shan Lin and Vincent were quick to interrupt her accusation.

"How dare *you*, Aunt Sara!" Vincent and Shan Lin roared in unison and Shari flinched waiting for the Queen to have them killed outright.

"How dare you accuse us of treason when it is *you* who has been using your position to manipulate circumstances to your own agenda. Those two men we were seen with have proof of the times you've conspired with our enemies in the hopes of taking over Horrd and other surrounding areas."

Breathing heavily, Vincent's voice rang through the room as his emotions leaked out.

"It was you who had those people in Hurok killed, making it look as if Horrdian soldiers had done it. Our spies watched as you had a meeting with those mercenaries that you hired to slaughter those people. It was only by luck the two men intervened, paying off the mercenaries with more gold then you did. It saved the village of Hurok."

A gasping sound came from beside Vincent as one of the men who had just moments before attempted to arrest the brothers, cried out.

"My Queen. Please…Tell me…" But Shari watched as the knowledge of what Vincent had said rang true in the man's eyes.

Shari watched as the Queen ignored the man and didn't deny the charges.

"I am *Queen*," was her only answer, and the man who had protested dropped his weapon and walked dejectedly out the door.

Shari waited, breath held, for what the Queen's next move would be.

"We have proof." Shan Lin and Vincent spoke quietly and in tandem into the void.

The Queen studied the brothers with suspicion in her eyes before she answered them.

"Well, nephews. It seems you have a few secrets of your own."

* * * * *

The fury she so recently held had disappeared.

"What is it you want?" Sara asked, command still in her voice even as she tried her best to sound giving. Her anger had evaporated rapidly once Shan Lin and Vincent had shown her a copy of the video that showed her dealing with the mercenaries. She had become the men's aunt once again, not necessarily affable, but no longer the imperious ruler commanding her peasants.

"We want you to step down from the throne. Queen Stephanie is the rightful ruler and you know it," Vincent ground out.

Both men had dressed sparingly to sit down with the players in this continuing saga. Shari wanted very badly for the whole thing to be over but sat between her husbands and waited as they laid out their demands.

Melodious laughter flowed from the Queen.

"You must be joking," she said when she had herself under control once again.

Both men emphatically shook their heads.

"No, Auntie. It is no longer *your* Realm. Aranak now belongs to the rightful monarch, Her Majesty, Queen Stephanie. Your sons have married her in good faith and by the laws set forth through succession, laws which have been upheld for millennia..."

"Bah!" Sara scoffed. "Laws are meant to be changed. I have a mind to do just that. Now ask me for something that I'm willing to give.

At the moment, you've been charged with treason. As I am still the ruler here now, it would behoove you to remember I could have you killed because I say so."

Shari waited as the men measured their aunt and listened as they pathed each other.

It's not going to happen. Shan Lin pathed tightly to his brother.

I know. She is too ensconced in her position for us to merely be able to convince the whole of Aranak of her duplicities.

Shari, tired of the whole thing, jumped into the discussion wanting only for it to be over.

"Banish them. Send them to my Realm and allow us to live our lives in peace. No threats of death, no sending assassins after us, no nothing. You get what you want, them gone. I get what I want, my soul-mates alive, happy, and mine."

Shan Lin and Vincent started to protest but Shari quickly cut them off.

"Politics be damned! You are my life. Let the whole of the universe die. It is you two I care about now, no one else."

Shari's voice was brittle, her face showing what the death of the two men would mean to her. Whatever arguments the two brothers could come up with, were nothing compared to what Shari wanted.

"As you wish, *Kasha*."

The Queen spoke up, suspicion in her words.

"And how do I know you all won't just send the disc through a *Tear* for anyone to find it? I'd much rather kill you now and deal with the consequences which arise."

"Because. You have *my* word we'll never show the disc in Aranak. I can't guarantee someone else doesn't have a copy, but the three of us will *never* use it to blackmail you. My word as a Woman. As I understand it, in Aranak, this vow is the equivalent to signing my name in blood. Correct?"

Queen Sara nodded, a spark of respect gleaming in her eyes before she squelched it.

"I want your word in the same promise about my husbands' safety, and those of any family we have."

"And your life, *Kasha*." Her husbands echoed each other.

Nodding acknowledgment, Shari turned once again to the Queen.

"And my life."

Their Aunt Sara sat in silence for so long, Shari suspected she was about to be turned down.

"Very well. My word as a Woman." The Queen reached out and offered her hand. Shari took it and the two women shook on the promise.

"As if signed in blood," the Queen murmured.

Shari dipped her head in acknowledgment of the promise.

"I, Queen Sara Anaksup, do here by banish the Warriors Shan Lin Rayan-White and Vincent Rayan-White from the Realm of Azaya. Their bride, My Lady Princess Shari Lynn Rayan-White hereby invokes Consort Claiming rights. It is with the greatest of pleasures she be banished from my land forever or the three be killed outright."

Shari shuddered.

Though I'd much rather kill you all here and now. But you have chosen the one thing I can respect. One-upmanship. Queen Sara's words, full of cruel laughter, slithered through Shari's mind.

One-upmanship? Shari thought incredulously at the word. *The woman is a fucking psycho.* Clenching her fists to keep from acknowledging the parting words, she waited for the woman to leave.

The Queen left quickly, the door to their chambers crashing as it closed, and Shari couldn't take a deep breath until Winters finally came back and announced the woman's departure from their home. Shari's breath wooshed out in relief.

"Your plan, Shari?" Vincent asked, hope in his voice.

Shari looked to her husbands, love shining in her gaze.

"It was a whim." Shari murmured to herself. Shaking her head in disbelief, she answered Vincent.

"To protect my family. After that, I'll tell you once I've gotten the two of you home."

* * * * *

Winters oversaw their packing and assured Shari he would handle everything.

"My Lady Shari," Winters said only to have his voice break on the last syllable.

"What is it, Winters?" Shari went to the man, concern for him evident in her demeanor.

"My Lady, please. One moment," he asked and Shari allowed him to compose himself before he continued.

"Shari. I cannot tell you how proud I am. The Queen…" He scowled as he spoke her title, "…she would have slain my…they are like sons to me. You have saved them from themselves. They would have gone up against that woman and…died." His voice trailed away, his eyes taking on a look of fear Shari knew rarely came into this man's eyes.

"Winters, I will protect them now. It is the way of your…our people." Even as Shari spoke, she knew it was the truth.

Winters turned his head, staring deeply into her eyes.

"They could break you into tiny pieces with a look if they were so inclined. They truly are what their nicknames imply. Most inhabitants of the many Realms fear those two men and their reputation for ruthlessness is legendary. There are those here in Aranak who would gladly slay them as soon as look at them. And who is the only one who offers to protect them?"

Shari smiled as he shook his head in wonder.

"It's as I told their aunt. They are my life. If they die, I die. Their pain is my pain. Their hunger, mine. It is who I now am."

Shari hugged the man and waited as she felt Shan Lin and Vincent come up behind her.

"If you two are ready, I am too."

"*Kasha*. Shari." Shan Lin walked up and enfolded her into his arms. Vincent went to Winters and embraced him in thanks. Then Vincent held Shari as Shan Lin went to Winters.

"Have no fear, Winters, she will keep us safe."

Winters gruffly cleared his throat.

"It is you who had better protect her. Otherwise I will be making a trip through the *Tear* and dispensing my own set of justice."

The three laughed as Winters had intended and Shan Lin, Vincent, and Shari's parting was complete. The three left through the door of the inconspicuous home, and on foot made their way to the *Tear*, which had brought Shari into Aranak.

* * * * *

Shari walked toward the large home of Queen Stephanie and her consorts, Princes Mitch and Kristain, with the reminder they were family.

"It's true. They are our cousins." Shan Lin tried to reassure Shari as the three made their way to the front door.

Vincent pounded on the whitewashed door as he also reassured Shari.

"They're two fluff balls who tremble at our feet. Don't worry about it. We are welcome here."

The door opened and a woman with flowing brown hair and eyes of deep, midnight blue smiled out at them. An aura of serene grace surrounded her and the inviting grin she wore told Shari immediately the three of them were welcomed. The woman took in the appearance of the men before quickly turning to study Shari.

"You are as beautiful in person as these two have told me. Please, don't pay any attention to the lies they tell you about my husbands. Gentle with me they may be, but be wary of softly spoken men."

Shan Lin and Vincent immediately dropped to their knees, heads bowed.

Shari stared at her husbands, her mind bewildered by their actions. She turned back to ask the woman why they were kneeling to her when comprehension came.

"Er..." Shari began to go to her knees when the woman slipped out the door leaving it open behind her.

"Don't," she said laying her arm on Shari's. "Get up, you two. I know I asked you *not* to do that."

Shari watched as Shan Lin and Vincent rose to their feet, their attention going between the woman in front of them, and the two men now close behind her.

"And pay no attention to the two hulking figures behind me. They've been dogging my steps ever since I told them of your banishment."

"Mitch, Kristain," Shan Lin and Vincent grumbled.

"Vincent. Shan Lin," replied two equally grumpy voices.

Shari shook her head.

"Behave you two. As soon as you introduce us properly, the four of you can go play."

"My Queen, Your Majesty. May I present our wife, My Lady Princess Shari Lynn Rayan-White. Shari, My Queen, Her Majesty Stephanie Anaksup-Armand."

The words were spoken so fast Shari nearly missed her own name.

"Now. What's this I've been hearing about us being 'fluff balls'?" one of the twins asked, challenge in his voice.

Another Queen. Shari digested this quickly.

Easy, my love, Vincent pathed quietly into her mind.

She snorted and spoke out loud.

"As long as this one isn't anything like your Aunt, I think I'll be fine."

Vincent cut his glance to his wife and smiled.

"No. I'm afraid there aren't any orgies going on in this house. But if it would make you feel welcome..." Stephanie asked politely, her lips fighting a grin.

Shari turned to the woman, a smile of her own clearly showing, and paused as if thinking about the offer Queen Stephanie had made.

"Well. Perhaps if I was the only woman and didn't have to share..."

The four men gaped at her comment, shock clear on their faces.

Queen Stephanie laughed out loud, a clear wonderful sound nothing like the melodiously false mirth of Queen Sara that Shari knew she would hear for the rest of her life.

"Please. Come in and be welcome." Queen Stephanie gestured toward the door still blocked by all four of the now disgruntled men. "I'm sure there is much you have to tell and I'd rather have a strong drink with the telling."

Shari smiled, a feeling she was coming for a visit with family.

"Thank you, Queen Stephanie, a drink would be most welcome. Any chance you have some of that *primpate* fruit juice?"

The young Queen smiled, nodding her head.

"Oh definitely. And we mustn't forget the Tine Chocolate Torts to go with it. I hear they were a hit on your wedding night."

Shari turned to the woman, a blush forming. But the Queen just laughed.

"Wait until you hear about *my* wedding night. And since you will eventually, please, call me Stephanie. After all, we're family."

Shari smiled again, her blush fading quickly as she heard Shan Lin and Vincent growl sarcastically to their cousins loud enough for the women to hear.

"We just got here. Can the orgy wait for a few hours? I'd like to catch my breath."

Laughter followed the group as the door closed behind them.

Epilogue

Stephanie stepped through the *Tear* into Aranak for the very first time and went to her knees. Her head filled quickly with millions of voices before she could block them out. It took her a few moments to realize someone held her arm in a reassuring grip.

"The first steps are always a doozy. Are you all right?" the female voice asked Stephanie as the same hand helped her to her feet.

"I'm...fine. Thank...you." Stephanie murmured, managing to gain her feet without stumbling, the hand on her arm steadying her. She looked up and stared into the face of a female Warrior. Looking the woman over carefully, Stephanie found the insignia proclaiming the woman's rank.

"Captain, correct?" Stephanie asked, the cacophony in her head easing enough for her to breathe.

"Yes." The woman smiled gently. "Captain Lawsai of the Queen's Guard. Are you in need of assistance, ma'am?" Stephanie opened her mind and wondered if perhaps she should have rethought leaving her husbands behind.

...going to have to make sure she gets to where she's going. Wish they would listen when told about the side effects.

Stephanie closed the pathlink, and straightening, gave Captain Lawsai a smile of her own.

"Thank you, Captain Lawsai. I think I can take it from here. It's my first time through a *Tear* and I wasn't paying attention when they told me of the side effects." Stephanie smiled, leaning closer to the woman. "I thought Katerina and Phillippe were joking when they told me stepping through a doorway might knock me on my ass. 'Pride goeth before a fall'...huh?" Stephanie laughed at herself.

Captain Lawsai smiled, giving a chuckle of her own.

"If you're feeling better then, I'll leave you here." The soldier paused before confirming, "Unless you care to have an escort take you to your destination...?" Lawsai raised her eyebrows inquiringly.

Stephanie smiled sheepishly.

"Nope. I'll be fine. I'm sure there are things you've got to take care of. After all, this is my first trip back from the Earth Realm and I did tell Katerina I could make the complete roundtrip on my own. Course, Phillippe doubted it, but..." Shrugging helplessly, Stephanie shook her head. "Wait until I tell them a Captain of the Queen's Guard had to help me right myself. I don't think I'll live this down."

* * * * *

Theresa looked slightly down at the woman and knew she would have to follow this woman to her intended destination. Dressed as the woman was in jeans, T-shirt and sneakers, Captain Lawsai knew there was no way she was from Aranak.

"Well, you be careful. The night is young, but there are still roving bands of mercs marching around."

Theresa watched the woman nod an agreement and wander off down the paved road toward Aranak. At a gesture from Theresa two shadows stepped out of the darkness and followed the woman. Speaking softly Theresa gave her orders.

"Make sure she doesn't hurt herself. She probably stumbled through a *Tear* and thought, 'I'll go on an adventure!'. *Freching* tourist." Theresa mumbled the last and listened to the smothered laughter come back through her earmics.

"We'll meet up with you as soon as her destination is confirmed. Try not to be seen, you two." Theresa said sweetly knowing neither Lt. Roberts nor Lt. Char ever had been.

"Captain." A voice came from Theresa's left and she turned in the direction.

"Yes, Dresden?"

"Sir. Dyden found the lair. All we have to do is route it. What are your orders?"

Theresa sighed, knowing she had just cut her resources in half but the job still had to be done.

"Fine, Dresden. Grab Dyden and Froslin and let's get on with it. I want this finished before that woman reaches where ever it is she's going."

* * * * *

Fifteen minutes later Theresa sported the beginnings of a black eye and a short temper.

"Yea, yea. We've heard it all before. You took a swing at me thinking I was your enemy. Blah, blah. Cry me another river. Get up. The *pryt* lance was only set on clash-impact. The jolt should have worn off by now."

Theresa snarled at the man twice her size and prodded him with the *pryt* lance she had used on him. She was damned tempted to zap him once more just for the satisfaction of seeing his body dance through the electricity. Shaking her head and knowing she would not, Theresa grasped the huge man by the neck and lifted him to his feet.

"Captain." Theresa heard through her earmic.

"What?" she growled, and the man in front of her swiveled his head back at her.

"I didn' say nothin'." He slurred.

"Shut up. Go ahead Roberts."

"Sir. We lost her. We followed at a safe distance but...*Hellios!* She slipped us."

Theresa cursed silently knowing this night was a FUBAR from the get go and gave new orders to her off-sight crew.

"Well, Fucked Up Beyond All Recognition or not..." Theresa mumbled to herself before addressing her crew. "Find her. That's all we need. She was headed in the direction of Aranak City Proper, she couldn't have gone far."

"Quit cawlin me a guuurl." The man ahead of her grumbled.

"Shut up. Isn't it enough you got in the first blow? I'm having fun and that's all that matters here. You want another jolt of this?" Theresa asked, poking him once again with her lance. Satisfaction snaked through her at his whimper and she turned her attention back to Roberts.

"Just find the woman and keep me posted. I've got to take Sir Knightly here in for more questioning. Lawsai out."

"Come on, Cap'n. You don't gotta be like that." The man whined, his voice becoming clearer and his words slurring less.

"I've come, Roxsis, but it definitely hasn't been pleasant. You should learn a few more manners when someone knocks on your door. Don't you know the first thing *not* to do is pick a fight with a QG just asking questions?"

The man's mumbled words sounding suspiciously like pain and retribution, and Theresa smiled. Good. At least she had made someone's night a bit more uncomfortable.

"I didn't know you cared so much. It's sweet of you to be worried for my welfare. Sit." She gestured to the ground beside Dyden.

"Keep an eye on him. I need to go see about transpo for him. He's got a lot of info I know he can't wait to impart to me about the attack made on Grenlak this afternoon. Horrdian's my ass."

"Capan', come on. You know I don' know nothin'." Roxsis whined once again.

"You keep singing that tune and Queen Sara is sure going to have fun extracting those tiny pieces from your mind. When I get back I expect you to rat everyone out, including your sainted mother. Got it?"

Even as she asked him the rhetorical question, Theresa walked away. She had every intention of trying to determine if he had been in on the attack on her currently assigned station, but first, she needed to see if he had broken her nose too.

✵ ✵ ✵ ✵ ✵

It was easy to lose the two following her. Their minds weren't as guarded as they would have liked. Stephanie made her way toward the Palace touching minds as she went along. Her intent was to find her mother-in-law's mind and connect with it. It had been easy at first weaving in and out of the woman's mind. Lately it had become more difficult to access it from Earth as her mind slipped further and further into a place Stephanie knew she could not travel.

A stir echoed in her head and she smothered a smile as her husbands cursed viciously. They had just discovered she was gone.

Woman! Dual roars of disapproval lanced through her head. Wincing at the volume of displeasure, Stephanie sent soothing thoughts their way.

Don't think it will help, Stephanie! Where the hell are you? Mitch barked at his wife.

I'm fine. I'll be home soon.

What's with you? Kristain asked calmly even as Stephanie heard the worry in his voice. Knowing there was nothing the two men could do at the moment, Stephanie decided it was time to go.

Look. I can't talk right now. Don't worry; I'll be home soon.

Shutting the path-link quickly but not before hearing Mitch's shouted *No!* Stephanie concentrated once again on finding a path-link to Queen Sara. She knew her husbands would holler, a lot, when she returned, but this trip had been necessary.

And just how are my sons doing? The voice pathed a direct link into Stephanie's head, stopping her in her tracks. *It isn't as if they call their mother to let her know they're alive still.*

Stephanie grimaced at being found first.

As if I haven't known you were here since you entered the Realm.

Stephanie knew it wasn't true or Sara would have made sure Capt. Lawsai took her into custody.

Well, Mother-in-law. Isn't it about time we sat down and had a chat? There was a pause as Stephanie waited for the answer.

So long as you're coming to see me to give up any claim to the throne of Aranak. If so, please come and be welcomed as my marriagedaughter. The last was said with such syrupy love that Stephanie wondered why her teeth did not ache.

Now you know I can't do that, Sara. Why the laws make it impossible. Just as you know there is no chance of changing those laws contrary to what you claimed with Shan Lin and Vincent. A Horrdian invasion. Really dear. That's so tacky and overdone. Wasn't that the excuse you used when you slaughtered your sisters and nieces?

Stephanie finally path-linked with the woman and felt the rage building to a crescendo as Stephanie's reminder of past deeds struck home.

Frechie *Bitch! You know nothing! Guards. Seize her!*

Stephanie stayed where she was wondering if those surrounding Sara thought the woman was seeing imaginary friends.

They'll never find me. I'll be long gone before they ever get here. Your mind has become child's play to enter. Stephanie made the bluff knowing the other woman would take the bait.

Then why did you have to travel so far to find me? The rage was at an all time high in her mother-in-law and Stephanie knew she could only push so far.

Puh-lez. To show you just how close to you I can get without your knowledge. One day, I'll be behind you and you'll never know I'm there until I slit your throat.

The scream of madness pierced through Stephanie's mind before she blocked it out.

There, Stephanie said contented. *That should be enough for now.*

Turning, she made her way back to the *Tear* she had first entered. As she walked away, she gave the woman a final parting shot.

Pack your bags, Sara, I'm coming to claim my throne.

STEPHANIE'S MENAGE

Mari Byrne

Preview

Prologue

"You shame our people by suggesting there is not one single woman in our entire world good enough to be your bride." The Queen's flowing gown twirled as she turned sharply in her pacing. "Why must you go to the mortal world? There are plenty here in Aranak who would give their daughters to you both."

"Mother. We've had this conversation before," Kristain started out calmly. "This family, this Monarchy, needs new blood." He paused and gave her a disgusted look. "Hell, for that matter, this World needs new blood and well you know it. You must see this is the only way."

Without looking away from his mother, Kristain, using the telepathic link every twin on Aranak is born with, asked Mitch to stand beside him.

Mitch lazily straightened from his lounging position and strolled leisurely over to stand at his brother's side.

I don't care if she can hear us or not. Kristain stated, his calmness disintegrating. *We're going, and in this she has no say.*

Brother mine, Mitch answered sarcastically, *you preach to the converted. You need to tell your Queen, not me.*

For reasons beyond Kristain's understanding, their mother couldn't always read her people, let alone her own children, though the reading of all her peoples' minds should have come with her acceptance of the crown.

Mitch watched as his mother came to an abrupt stop, then with a quiet menace about her, turned around looking from one son to the other.

"You have already made your choice and nothing I say will change your mind."

The two brothers stared back impassively.

"So be it. The consequences are yours to bear." With those last words she went to a door, hidden behind her throne and stormed through it, slamming it behind her.

Kristain stared after their retreating mother for a moment, then turned to Mitch.

"Well, that went well. Shall we go then?"

Mitch slapped his brother on the back and turned him toward the door. "And here I thought you were going to be the one to convince her. But now I see the only way we'll ever convince *Queen Sara* of our determination to seek a bride elsewhere is when we present our bride as a *fait accompli*."

Kristain sighed heavily, "I thought perhaps she would be more amenable to the idea if we gave her time." He started toward the door. "Now I see our trip through the portal is the only way she'll take us seriously."

Mitch nodded his head in agreement. "We have to start somewhere and I've always had a good feeling about Earth. We'll find our mate there. I know it."

So, this is Earth? Mitch looked around as he and Kristain made their way toward the buildings ahead of them in the distance.

It wasn't so very different from Aranak.

Kristain turned and Mitch heard his thoughts. *In fact, I think there might be even less difference than we previously thought. I don't think it'll take very long for us to find our bride and return home.*

Mitch turned his gaze away from an intriguing woman who had caught his eye as he scoped the lay of the land and eyed his brother skeptically. *Let us hope so. I don't want to spend more time away from home than we have to. The laws Mother could implement while we're gone stagger my imagination.*

Kristain nodded in agreement. Both men squared their shoulders, and readied themselves for the search to come.

* * * * *

The screams the inhabitants of the castle listened to coming from the Queen's chambers were ignored, just as they had been every other time they were heard. Those who had lengthy memories crossed themselves and thanked their gods it wasn't them offering up delights to the Queen as they scurried to attend to their own duties.

Sometime later, the bloodied figure collapsed against the wall in exhaustion. Blood streamed from him, even as pain throbbed in places he hadn't even known could be hurt. He had to get to Shan Lin and

Vincent. Those twins were of the very few who could get a message to the Princes about the Queen and her plans.

Slowing his labored breathing as best he could, the man used the last of his strength to push himself away from the wall and stumbled onward. The Twin Warriors might be the Princes' last hope.

Almost One Year Later

"Wait! Don't move." The woman continued to hold onto Kristain's arm as she scanned the room for her sister. "I know she was talking to — well, I can't remember their names right now, but it was over there near the buffet table."

She finally turned back to Kristain and looked into his eyes imploringly.

"I'm so sorry. I don't mean to keep you, it's just...well, an acquaintance of ours suggested I ask...ummm—" She paused, and stopped completely to look over his shoulder.

Kristain felt Mitch behind him and knew what had made the woman silent. It happened every time a woman laid eyes on the brothers together.

"Hello." Kristain heard Mitch say and knew he could have gotten away from the woman. She reached out her other hand clasping his brother's in welcome while mumbling a hello.

Mitch let go of her hand and turned to his brother. "Are you going to introduce me?"

Kristain smiled. "It seems our reputation has preceded us. This is Jan Armand, and at present, she is looking for her sister. Jan has informed me her sister, Stephanie, has asked her about finding two interested partners for a *ménage à trois.*"

Kristain watched as his brother's eyebrows rose and his face took on an intrigued look. In truth, Kristain had sent a call for his brother to come and meet the woman. Now all they needed was to find the actual interested party.

He sidestepped, slightly blocking Jan's view of Mitch, and willed her to focus on him.

It took a few moments, but she finally turned her gaze back to him.

"Do you want to see if you can find her now, or would you rather we planned to meet her some other time?" It took her a few more moments of staring, but she finally shook her head in a negative response.

"No." She looked between the brothers, then once again over her shoulder and started to speak when she turned back to them with a smile on her face. The look was one of a quiet happiness, a look a mother would give a child, or—

Kristain and Mitch turned to look at the same time.

"There she is. There's my sister." Mitch and Kristain both heard the love in Jan's voice as she pointed to where a woman stood with two other men. The three seemed to be in an animated conversation.

Kristain and Mitch felt each other's response and knew they had found their mate.

With their minds linked and their cocks swelled, they felt everything inside which made them who and what they were shout out that they must run, not walk, to claim her.

Kristain both heard and felt the feral growl that escaped his brother and matched it with one of his own. It was all he could do not to go over to the males who surrounded her and stake a very public claim.

Unfortunately, they were on Earth, and the claim he and his brother would have liked to make involved stripping her naked and ramming their cocks into her so deep and so hard they would lose themselves in her essence.

Easy, brother mine, Mitch said as he reached an arm out and grasped Kristain lightly. *I also feel the pull, but we need to be very sure this time.*

Kristain watched as one of the male's face lit up when Stephanie spoke to him. He began to gesture down his own body as if trying to make shapes appear out of thin air. Kristain had to stop himself from striding forward and smashing a fist in the man's face when he reached his hands out to Stephanie and began to draw lines from the shoulders of her dress to her waist.

Out of the corner of his eye, and in the recess of his mind where his brother's presence resided, Kristain both felt and watched as Mitch took one, then another step forward, as if he also had the idea of getting physical with the man.

Have a care brother. Kristain spoke to Mitch in the others mind. *Do not frighten her before she has even had the opportunity to meet us.*

Kristain turned to look into his brother's eyes. *When we finally meet, she will be ours.*

Damn! Mitch thought. She was finally within their grasp and all he could do was stand here and watch as she laughed at something another man said! If it had been up to him, they would have gone to her, explained who they were, and scooped her up with a shouted exclamation she belonged to them, taken her from the room and ravished her in the nearest spot which afforded some privacy!

The thought of what he and Kristain were soon going to do with her had his cock throbbing in time to the beating pulse in his heart.

He wanted badly to stay and find some reason to go to her, but hesitated at the words his brother had spoken in his mind. They didn't want to frighten her off, and if she got one glance at the hard-on he was sporting, she might just run screaming from him!

Mitch gave his brother a nod and mental thanks.

Kristain nodded his head and turned back to Jan.

"She is all you have said. If you would like, we can meet her now and bind—excuse me, I mean find out if she is willing to accept us."

Jan shook her head once, then again, as her gaze found Kristain's once again and she seemed to come to a decision.

"No, I don't think so. She asked me to set it up, and from what I've heard, the two of you…well let's just say I've heard nothing but wonderful things about your characters."

The brothers smiled in unison, and Jan had to lock her knees to keep from falling from the combination the two men made. If she could bottle whatever it was that made these two men shout moresexmoresexmoresex, she would be a rich woman!

Steeling herself against the lust she felt, she turned once again and looked at Stephanie. That was all it took, her mind focused. She was positive these two men were exactly what her sweet, yet daring sister needed.

Her gaze went to Mitch and she turned her own Million-Dollars-Plus-Contract smile on him.

"So long as you two know this—I will eviscerate either of you if you hurt her in any way. Nothing and no one will stop me."

The men quit smiling for a moment, and a serious look came over their faces. Jan watched as each of them put a hand to their hearts, gave a slight bow, then each reached out and took one of her hands.

The brothers spoke in tandem, and their words were formal sounding.

"By the honor you have bestowed on us, may you own our lives and souls should we fail in our promise given to you this day."

Taken aback slightly, yet in no way put off by their words, Jan gave a regal nod of her head.

"Just see that you don't." With that, both men grinned, and Jan smiled in return...

About the author:

I have been writing for quite a while now and love finding out what goes on in the minds of my characters. I am the daughter of a third generation military family. I grew up all over the world and am happily married to a loving husband who gifted me with two adorable children I had the pleasure of birthing. All three enjoy dragging me away from my characters and showing me the world "outside". (I still think camping should involve "Room Service"!) I am also a voracious reader who devours books and chocolate in between family, writing, and work.

Mari welcomes mail from readers. You can write to her c/o Ellora's Cave Publishing at 1337 Commerce Drive, Suite 13, Stow OH 44224.

Also by Mari Byrne:

Death Reborn
Stephanie's Menage

Why an electronic book?

We live in the Information Age—an exciting time in the history of human civilization in which technology rules supreme and continues to progress in leaps and bounds every minute of every hour of every day. For a multitude of reasons, more and more avid literary fans are opting to purchase e-books instead of paperbacks. The question to those not yet initiated to the world of electronic reading is simply: *why?*

1. *Price.* An electronic title at Ellora's Cave Publishing runs anywhere from 40-75% less than the cover price of the <u>exact same title</u> in paperback format. Why? Cold mathematics. It is less expensive to publish an e-book than it is to publish a paperback, so the savings are passed along to the consumer.

2. *Space.* Running out of room to house your paperback books? That is one worry you will never have with electronic novels. For a low one-time cost, you can purchase a handheld computer designed specifically for e-reading purposes. Many e-readers are larger than the average handheld, giving you plenty of screen room. Better yet, hundreds of titles can be stored within your new library—a single microchip. (Please note that Ellora's Cave does not endorse any specific brands. You can check our website at www.ellorascave.com for customer

recommendations we make available to new consumers.)

3. *Mobility.* Because your new library now consists of only a microchip, your entire cache of books can be taken with you wherever you go.

4. *Personal preferences are accounted for.* Are the words you are currently reading too small? Too large? Too...**ANNOYING**? Paperback books cannot be modified according to personal preferences, but e-books can.

5. *Innovation.* The way you read a book is not the only advancement the Information Age has gifted the literary community with. There is also the factor of what you can read. Ellora's Cave Publishing will be introducing a new line of interactive titles that are available in e-book format only.

6. *Instant gratification.* Is it the middle of the night and all the bookstores are closed? Are you tired of waiting days — sometimes weeks — for online and offline bookstores to ship the novels you bought? Ellora's Cave Publishing sells instantaneous downloads 24 hours a day, 7 days a week, 365 days a year. Our e-book delivery system is 100% automated, meaning your order is filled as soon as you pay for it.

Those are a few of the top reasons why electronic novels are displacing paperbacks for many an avid reader. As always, Ellora's Cave Publishing welcomes your questions and comments. We invite you to email us at service@ellorascave.com or write to us directly at: 1337 Commerce Drive, Suite 13, Stow OH 44224.

Printed in the United States
26171LVS00004BA/67-264